City of Dreams

Harriet Steel

Published in 2014 by CreateSpace
Copyright © Harriet Steel

A CIP catalogue record for this title is available from the British Library.

Acknowledgements

My thanks are due to my editor, John Hudspith, for doing so much to improve this novel, and also, to Jane Dixon Smith for her lovely cover design. As always, my husband, Roger, has given me his unfailing support and he has my deepest gratitude.

Historical Note

The Franco-Prussian War, during which the latter part of this story takes place, is far less studied than the world wars that came after it, but it was of considerable importance. It marked the resurgence of the German Empire as a military power under Prussian domination. The Commune that briefly governed Paris after the siege was also influential. Karl Marx watched its actions from his exile in London with great interest. In the history of it that he wrote soon afterwards, he only made one criticism. It was that the Communards had not gone far enough in destroying capitalism.

Readers familiar with French history of the period may notice that I have made a slight alteration to the date of the Paris Exhibition of 1867. This was necessary for the purpose of the story and I hope they will excuse it.

'Dear old Paris!' little Bilham echoed.

'Everything, everyone shows,' Miss Barrace went on.

'But for what they really are?' Strether asked.

Henry James - The Ambassadors

Chapter 1

St Petersburg,
Autumn 1864.

Mother and I were sewing in the parlour. All day, grey clouds had hidden the sun and even though it was only just past four o'clock, one of the maids had already drawn the plum velvet curtains. The tick of the mantle clock measured out the afternoon and the logs in the grate had crumbled to shards of red and grey. I sighed and jabbed the needle into my embroidery to make another stitch.

Mother looked up from her work. 'Where is Katya? The fire's nearly out. I shall have to scold her yet again.' She reached for the bell pull but before she had time to grasp the tassel, we heard voices in the hall. I recognised Papa's deep tones at once, but the man to whom he was talking didn't sound familiar. His voice was cultured and he spoke Russian, but with an accent I couldn't place.

Mother frowned. 'I'm sure your father didn't mention he would be bringing anyone home today.'

The door opened and Papa walked in. In company he normally stood out as an imposing figure, yet in comparison with the man who followed him into the room, he looked almost uncouth. Our visitor was much younger than Papa, but his air of confidence impressed me instantly. His dark jacket and cream trousers were of a fashionable cut and his beard and moustache trimmed in the Parisian style.

'My dear, we have a visitor,' Papa announced jovially. 'This is Monsieur Daubigny. Daubigny, may I introduce my wife, Caterina Arkadyevna, and my daughter, Anna.'

Hastily, Mother put her sewing aside. Monsieur Daubigny bent low over her hand and kissed it.

'Enchanté, Madame, Emile Daubigny at your service,' he murmured.

I watched the little scene with amusement. Mother seemed flustered and her face had gone quite pink. I had to resist the urge to giggle.

Daubigny released her hand and turned to me. 'Mademoiselle, it is a great pleasure to meet you.'

It would have been improper for him to kiss the hand of an unmarried girl such as I but his smile was enough. All at once, I understood why Mother's composure had been shaken. A tingling sensation went from the top of my head to the tips of my toes.

'Monsieur Daubigny has come from Paris to buy sables and arctic fox,' Papa continued. 'I'm sure we shall do excellent business together. Russian furs are the best in the world, aren't they, my friend?' He clapped Daubigny on the back.

'Indeed they are and I hear your husband's are particularly fine, Madame.'

'You're very kind, Monsieur, and you are most welcome in our home,' Mother gave him a warm smile and patted the seat of the chair beside her. 'Please, sit down while I call for refreshments. Anna! Go and find Katya. I don't know why she's not answering the bell today. Will you take some tea, Monsieur Daubigny?'

I caught the twinkle in Papa's eyes as she rattled on without giving Monsieur Daubigny time to reply.

'Is this your first visit to St Petersburg, Monsieur? I do hope you won't be disappointed. I fear the weather is very poor at this time of year and the days are short.'

Daubigny smiled. 'Indeed, it is my first visit, and I hope it won't be the last. I'm sure I won't be disappointed. I can understand why your city is called the Venice of the North. It is very beautiful – and full of such charming ladies.'

Mother blushed with pleasure. 'But surely in Paris, the ladies are much more fashionable than here in Russia?' she enquired, a note of wistfulness creeping into her voice.

'If you came to Paris, Madame, you would put them all in the shade.'

'You're very naughty to tease me so.'

Daubigny smiled. 'I stand by every word.'

'Merci, Monsieur. Now, we must take tea.'

Papa cleared his throat. 'Caterina my dear, I think tea can wait. I hope there will be time later for you to ask Monsieur Daubigny questions to your heart's content, but for now, I must take him away. Come Daubigny, we'll go to my study where we can discuss our business without boring the ladies.'

When the door closed behind them, Mother let out a sigh. 'What a handsome man, and such delightful manners. I've always wanted to see Paris - the fashions, the operas, the parties. I'm sure St Petersburg has nothing to compare. Oh, I do hope your father won't take too long. There's so much I want to ask Monsieur Daubigny.'

She smoothed her hair and frowned. 'What is it, child? Why do you look at me so?'

'It's nothing. Shall I ask Katya to bring the tea now?'

'Oh, I suppose you may as well.'

I stood up and went to the door. As I did so, part of me was relieved Emile Daubigny was not in the room to watch me for I was full of confused emotions. I wished my dress was not so plain, nor my hair so simply dressed. I wished I was not seventeen years old and barely out of the schoolroom. I wished I was beautiful.

An hour later, he took his leave, despite Mother's efforts to persuade him to stay to dinner. 'You're very kind,' he smiled, 'but I already have an arrangement for this evening. I doubt that it will be as delightful as the company of your family, but I must keep my promise.'

'Then you must come tomorrow,' Mother said firmly.

Emile kissed her hand. 'I shall be honoured to accept.'

He turned to me. 'Adieu, Mademoiselle, until tomorrow.'

Angry with myself, I felt the heat rise in my cheeks. I must seem a child to him.

'Certainly, Monsieur,' I replied, instantly wishing I had not sounded so prim.

As soon as Emile had left, Mother gave vent to her agitation. 'I must see Cook immediately,' she exclaimed. 'I should have had more time to prepare, Sergei. Why didn't you tell me sooner Monsieur Daubigny was coming? A Frenchman, and from Paris too! He will think us very dull and our food so plain.'

Papa shrugged. 'I didn't know myself until this morning, my dear. In any case, you were the one who insisted on asking him to dine with us. I should be just as happy to take him to my club.'

Mother's chestnut curls bobbed. 'The very idea! Would you have him think we are not hospitable?'

Papa stroked his beard. He was used to Mother's outbursts and always met them with his customary equanimity.

'Surely a day is long enough to get ready?'

'What would a man know? You have no idea how much there will be to do.'

'It's just a family dinner, my love. Why do we need to worry about a lot of formality?'

'And let him go away thinking we have no idea of how a visitor should be entertained?'

Papa sighed and retired once more to his study, muttering under his breath.

*

Torn between her delight at the prospect of such a fascinating guest and her anxiety that her hospitality would not be sophisticated enough for him, Mother spent the rest of the evening changing her mind about which dishes Cook should prepare for the following night and fretting over what Emile would think of us.

'Give him good hearty Russian food,' said Papa at last, his voice betraying a hint of exasperation. 'Borscht, roast goose and those excellent mushrooms baked in cream. I do like those.'

'Perhaps he would prefer spiced beef and pickles,' Mother mused.

She saw Papa's expression darken.

'Very well, Sergei, if that is what you would like. I only hope it will please everyone,' she added pointedly.

Early the next morning, Cook herself was despatched to market to buy the ingredients for dinner. This was unusual. Normally one of the older kitchen maids was entrusted with the job. Cook complained that too much rushing about made her feet ache and she shouldn't have to go, but on this occasion, Mother insisted.

She instructed Katya and the under-housemaid to bring all the best silver and crystal to the scullery. Out from their tissue wrappings came glasses for wine and water, silver mounted decanters, antique cutlery, slender candlesticks and delicate filigree baskets lined with deep blue glass for flowers or fruit. Mother inspected each piece, clicking her tongue with disapproval at any smudge of tarnish on the silver or the touch of bloom on a glass.

'I want everything polished until I can see my face in it,' she snapped, pouncing on Cook as she returned grumbling from market. Behind her straggled our two footmen, laden down with baskets of meat, vegetables and fruit. As the day went on, the house filled with delicious aromas of roasting and baking.

Mother and I went upstairs early to dress for dinner. I was to wear the white satin dress that my parents had given me the previous winter on the occasion of my first ball. I'd thought it very elegant then, but now I wasn't sure. I hoped Emile might think I looked pretty. Mother lent me her nicest pendant, the one with an oval sapphire set in a ring of tiny diamonds and her maid helped me to arrange my dark hair becomingly.

'You look charming, Anna,' Mother said as she surveyed the finished effect. 'Now don't forget, if Monsieur Daubigny talks to you, you must let him lead the conversation. Art, music and books are all suitable topics that he might choose but if he does talk of books, don't let him think you've read very many. Men don't like a woman to be too clever.'

Mother had never really approved of Papa's habit of letting me have the run of his library. I see now that I must have been a trial to her. In her eyes, I should have been content to spend my time as my elder sister, Sonja, had done, acquiring the accomplishments considered suitable for a young lady - playing the piano, singing, embroidering and drawing, and most important of all, learning the rudiments of running a household of my own. Instead, I snatched every chance of losing myself in the thrilling romances of Dumas and Sir Walter Scott. They were my gateway to a world I longed to inhabit.

Three years older than me, Sonja had already married well and given birth to a lusty baby boy. Little Nicolai was adorable and I was very fond of Sonja's husband, Petrov, but I wanted something more exciting than the dutiful life of a Russian wife and mother.

I studied my reflection in the glass. I did not have Sonja's womanly figure, being slim and considerably taller than her, but the dress made me look satisfyingly grown up and the sapphire pendant emphasised the blue of my eyes. Perhaps Emile would not think me such a child after all.

He arrived, looking very handsome in smart evening dress. Sonja and Petrov joined us and Mother had also invited her sister, my Aunt Tatiana, with her husband, Vassily. There was always a bit of rivalry between my mother and my aunt. I suspect Mother secretly relished the chance to show off such a glamorous visitor.

Dinner was announced and we went to the dining room. The table was covered with Mother's best white damask cloth and candlelight glowed softly on the newly polished silver and glass. Emile sat between Mother and Aunt Tatiana. I was placed between Petrov and Uncle Vassily.

We all bowed our heads while Papa said grace then Petrov held out my chair for me and I sat down. As I did so, I stole a look across the table from under my eyelashes and a shiver ran down my spine. Emile was smiling at me.

Rich, crimson borscht garnished with ribbons of sour cream followed soft, warm blinis smothered in tasty morsels of smoked fish and black, pungent caviar. Next, Cook herself brought in the roast goose, and deftly, Papa carved thick slices of the succulent meat and crisp skin. The maids handed round dishes of buttery vegetables and Papa's best burgundy swirled in our glasses.

Mother began to relax. 'You must tell me all about Paris, Monsieur Daubigny,' she said. 'Have you ever seen Emperor Napoleon and the Empress Eugénie?'

I was worried Emile might think I was ignorant so I was relieved that I remembered what I had learnt in the schoolroom: Emperor Napoleon was by all accounts a well-intentioned man, very different from his uncle, the notorious Napoleon Bonaparte who had terrorised Europe for so many years.

'Indeed,' Emile was saying, 'I have had the honour of attending an Imperial Ball at the Tuileries Palace on more than one occasion.'

Mother looked impressed. 'Oh, how wonderful! Is the Empress as beautiful as they say?'

'Yes, she is beautiful in the Spanish style but here in Russia I have found many ladies who are just as much to be admired.' He smiled and raised his glass to Mother, Aunt Tatiana, Sonja and me in turn, and I could swear I heard us all catch our breath.

As dinner went on, the conversation was more entertaining than usual. Emile told many amusing anecdotes about life in Paris, but he also endeared himself to my parents and my uncle and aunt by taking a great interest in their affairs. We spoke in French out of deference to our visitor, but after a while Emile suggested that we continue our talk in Russian.

'I would appreciate the chance to practice the language,' he assured us. Perhaps the real reason was that he had noticed Mother and Aunt Tatiana were having some difficulty understanding the conversation in French.

Mother looked splendid in her midnight-blue velvet, with gold bracelets on her plump white arms. She smiled with delight when Emile complimented her on her dress and praised the food wholeheartedly.

As usual, Uncle Vassily was far too busy enjoying his dinner to say much to me beyond the usual pleasantries. Petrov and I talked awhile about Nicolai, and Petrov's other favourite topic – his horses - but then the conversation flagged. I heard Emile and Papa discussing the relative merits of sable and mink then suddenly Emile broke off and looked over at me. 'And you, Mademoiselle Anna? Which fur is your favourite?'

I felt my cheeks warming. 'I'm not sure, Monsieur.'

'In Russia, girls do not wear expensive furs until they are married,' Aunt Tatiana said in a dismissive voice.

Emile's dark eyes crinkled in a smile. 'I'm sure that when she does, Mademoiselle Anna will be a vision of loveliness whichever she chooses.'

Aunt Tatiana sniffed and stabbed her fork into her goose. I tried to look composed and pretend I was used to accepting compliments, but the hint of mischief in Emile's expression was unsettling. I doubt whether my efforts to appear sophisticated were very successful.

When the meal ended, Mother, Aunt Tatiana, Sonja and I left the men to their brandy and cigars. I waited in the drawing room, impatient for Emile's return.

'I do hope Vassily won't drink too much brandy,' Aunt Tatiana fretted. 'It's so bad for his gout. He had a terrible attack last winter and was like a bear with a sore head for weeks.' Mother made a sympathetic noise and sipped her tea. Another roar of laughter came from the dining room. The men were taking much longer than usual, and clearly, the conversation was very amusing.

'How are you managing with your new cook?' Mother asked.

Aunt Tatiana pursed her lips. 'She prepared soup last night and the dumplings were like cannonballs. I had to reprimand her severely this morning. You know how delicate my stomach is. I spent the night in agonies of indigestion.'

Covertly, Mother and I exchanged smiles. Aunt Tatiana's stomach was a favourite topic of hers, but it never seemed to prevent her from eating copiously.

Recollecting herself, Mother patted her sister's hand. 'I'm sorry to hear that. It's hard to find good servants nowadays. We're so lucky with Cook even if she is grumpy sometimes, but I really think I shall have to let the upstairs maid go. Only the other day I left my cream kid gloves on my dressing table and when I came to put them on, they were horribly marked with dust.'

I was in despair. For how much longer did I have to endure this mundane chatter? With Emile so close, I could barely sit still. My hands trembled as I finished my tea and set down the cup. It clattered against the teaspoon and Aunt Tatiana looked up sharply. 'Be more careful Anna. This is your mother's best porcelain.'

I was saved the necessity of a reply by the sound of chairs scraping back in the other room. Mother put the tips of her fingers on the samovar. 'Oh dear, I hope the tea is not too cold.'

Aunt Tatiana arranged her features into a smile as Papa strode through the door, laughing and talking over his shoulder to Emile and Uncle Vassily. He sank into his favourite chair by the fireplace and my uncle sat down between Mother and Aunt Tatiana.

To my delight, Emile came over to sit beside me. 'How charming you look tonight, Mademoiselle,' he said in French. 'White is perfect for your complexion.' Suddenly the dress was my favourite of all the dresses I had ever owned.

Emile talked easily, drawing me out and asking my opinions. He seemed to know about so many things; I wished I had listened more attentively to my tutors. It was only when we talked of books that I gained any confidence that I could hold my own.

'I see you are a great reader, Mademoiselle,' he said after a while.

I almost clapped my hand to my mouth with dismay. I had grown so relaxed in his company that I had completely forgotten Mother's advice; but then to my relief, I realised he was smiling with approval.

I saw Mother glance at us from time to time, only half listening to Aunt Tatiana rattling on. I must admit, Mother's poor understanding of any language but Russian was fortuitous. She might have considered that some of the novels Emile and I discussed were unsuitable for a young lady who was not supposed to be 'too clever'.

Papa looked to be deep in conversation with Uncle Vassily but I did catch a few meaningful looks passing between him and Mother. Soon, however, I almost forgot anyone else was in the room. My delightful conversation with Emile continued uninterrupted and the rest of the evening flew. By the time the carriages arrived and our guests took their leave, I was in love.

After that evening, Emile visited often. On some occasions he joined us for dinner, at other times he simply sat with Mother and me in the afternoons. I think Mother was as dazzled by him as I was. She obviously adored his compliments and became positively flirtatious in his company. Even though she found it difficult, she tried hard to converse with him in French.

She often encouraged me to play the piano and sing when he visited. 'People always say your voice is so pretty,' she said one afternoon, 'and those Russian folksongs you learnt last summer are delightful.'

Sonja who was spending the day with us gave me a wicked smile. 'Those folksongs are very lively. Perhaps you should sing something more romantic, Anna.'

I blushed and Mother wagged her finger at Sonja. 'Anna is too young to be thinking of that kind of thing. I only mean it is polite to entertain Emile when he is kind enough to visit us.'

Sonja shrugged. 'I was not much older when Petrov and I married.'

In any case, I was only too happy to play now. It gave me an excuse to be close to Emile as he turned the pages for me. I felt a delicious thrill at having him so near. Resting on the music stand, his hands looked strong but elegant, with long, tapering fingers and smooth, immaculate nails. His skin gave off a faint smell of almonds.

Up until then, I had met no men outside the family apart from my parents' friends and their sons. None of them had Emile's suave manner and witty turn of conversation. Once, when I played for him and Mother's attention was distracted by her needlework, he reached out and touched my cheek, brushing a stray curl from my face. I shivered with pleasure at his touch.

Papa began to tease me. 'I think even your Mother should be satisfied with your diligence in practising the piano now, Anna,' he chuckled. 'I hear that French music is the most fashionable nowadays.'

One afternoon a few weeks later, Papa came into the parlour early with a serious expression on his face. He sat down and cleared his throat. Mother looked at him questioningly. 'What is it, dear?'

'Emile has just been to see me. He asked for my permission to marry Anna.'

Mother dropped her embroidery. 'Oh, my goodness!'

I sat there frozen. For weeks I had dreamed of this happening, but hardly dared to hope the dream would come true. *Madame Daubigny:* the words spun in my head until I was dizzy with joy.

Dimly, I realised Papa was speaking to me. 'I don't need to give him an answer straight away, Anna. You're still very young. It might be better to take more time to get to know each other. Paris is a long way from home.'

'But I thought you liked Emile,' I blurted out. 'Don't you want us to be married?'

Papa took my hand. 'Of course we like him. He seems an excellent match and I won't deny that such a connection can only be good for business, but the most important thing is that you should be happy.'

'Papa could suggest a long engagement,' Mother interposed. 'After all, he and I did not marry for over a year.'

I found my voice, 'Oh but I want to marry Emile now - I want it more than anything in the world. I couldn't bear to wait for a whole year.'

Anxiously, Papa and Mother looked at each other and then at me. 'We shall miss you,' Mother said sadly.

'And I you, but I love Emile. I want to be his wife.'

Papa bent his head for a few moments. When he looked up I saw a tear in his eye. 'If you are sure

Emile will make you happy, I won't stand in your way.'

I hugged him, feeling as if my heart might burst. Gently, he disentangled himself and held me at arm's length, studying my face. 'You're certain? No doubts?'

I smiled and leant forward to kiss his cheek. 'Not one.'

'Very well, I shall send a message to tell Emile he may speak to you alone.'

*

It was November and soon, the heavy snows would come. Emile had already sent a large consignment of furs to France by sea from St Petersburg, but by now, ships were coming into port for the winter. Even if we found one that would sail, the voyage would be rough and possibly dangerous. The roads would be no better, for the autumn rains had already brought thick mud and treacherous conditions. We would have to travel by train.

Emile did not want to delay his return to Paris any longer. He suggested kindly, but firmly, that the wedding ceremony should take place with all possible speed.

Mother wept. She had wanted a grand wedding for me and there would be no time now to make complicated preparations.

'My dear,' Papa reasoned with her, 'Emile's business is in Paris. He can't neglect it for much longer. It's better for them to travel straight away. The journey will be more hazardous with every week that passes. Surely you would prefer Anna to have a quiet wedding and a safe journey?'

Mother's brow furrowed. 'Of course I would, but I had so hoped—'

I put my arms around her. 'I'm sure you'll organise a lovely wedding. You are so good at these things.'

'I suppose it is better to arrange the ceremony before Advent,' Mother mused. 'I don't know how I would manage if we had to observe the fast.'

I hugged her again. 'How clever of you to think of that.'

Her face brightened. 'We must start to plan your trousseau straight away.'

The days flew by as the house was invaded by a small army of dressmakers, milliners and shoemakers. Mother commanded them like a general, marshalling her conscripts of muslins, silks and velvets into battalions of bonnets, frocks and gloves.

A few days before the wedding, I was upstairs looking at some samples of fabric the dressmaker had delivered that morning when I heard a rustle of skirts. I looked up to find that Aunt Tatiana had come into the room.

'Good morning, Anna, you're busy I see.'

I held a piece of fuchsia silk up to my cheek. 'Do you think this would suit me?'

She took it from me and turned it to and fro so that it caught the light. 'I could have worn this colour once,' she said, half to herself. She gave me a sour smile. 'Well, you've got your own way. I must say I was surprised your father agreed, but then you've always had him wrapped around your little finger, haven't you?'

I was speechless with astonishment as she continued. 'Good looks and charm aren't everything you know. You have only known the man a short time. I hope you won't live to regret your haste.'

Anger welled up in me, mingled with surprise as a suspicion crossed my mind. Could it be that my aunt, who always seemed so sure of herself, was jealous of my good fortune? Determined not to let her see she had upset me, I smiled coolly. 'I'm sure I won't.'

She gave one of her snorts of annoyance as Mother bustled into the room, far too preoccupied to notice the frosty atmosphere.

'Well, I must be going,' Aunt said stiffly. 'You look tired, Caterina. Such a lot of work for you.' She paused. 'And so little time to do it.'

Unaware of the jibe, Mother smiled. 'Must you go so soon, Tatiana?'

Yes, I muttered inwardly, *she must*.

On a bright, cold morning, two weeks before my eighteenth birthday, I went to church to be married. Before I left the house, I studied my reflection in the cheval-glass in my bedroom. My full-skirted cream dress was cut low at the neck and edged with delicate lace. It looked luminous in the shafts of light cast into the room by the low winter sun. My heart sang: Emile, Paris and a new life were almost mine.

The perfume of lilies and incense wafted towards me as I walked down the aisle on Papa's arm. Here and there, the shadowy stone walls glowed with gilded icons and high up in the gallery, the choir sang as sweetly as angels. Emile waited for me at the ornate brass rail separating the richly draped altar from the rest of the church. I took my place beside him.

The old priest, with his forked grey beard and gorgeous robes, pronounced the words of our betrothal then blessed the rings. Emile's hands were steady and warm as he slipped one of them on my finger but mine trembled as I put the other on his. The priest made a sign of blessing over our heads then took two lighted candles from the servers. He gave one to each of us to hold while he intoned the prayers for our good and happy life together.

From beneath the Brussels lace veil Mother had worn at her own wedding, I stole a sideways glance at Emile. In the flicker of light and shade cast by the flame of his candle, he looked eerily remote. Somewhere in the depths of the church, a door banged and I shivered. Aunt Tatiana's words echoed in my head and suddenly, I was afraid. What if she was right? Did I really know Emile?

He turned his head a little and our eyes met. His were warm and kind. My courage returned. How foolish of me to fear that anything could go wrong. We loved each other. Aunt Tatiana was just a jealous old woman.

The wedding feast was a merry affair. I sat beside Emile glowing with pride when the servants addressed me as Madame Daubigny. When everyone had eaten their fill, a sharp rap on the table silenced the buzz of conversation and Papa rose to his feet.

'Caterina has made me promise not to give a long speech,' he began.

'Hear, hear,' Uncle Vassily roared, his face flushed with good food and wine. Aunt Tatiana shot him a disapproving look.

'So I shall simply ask you all to charge your glasses and raise them in a toast to Anna and Emile: our beloved daughter and our fine new son-in-law.'

The room resounded with the clink of glasses and loud good wishes. Papa smiled. 'Keep her safe for me, Emile.'

Emile rose from his seat. 'I shall guard her with my life, sir.' He smiled down at me fondly. 'I'm a very lucky man.'

Mother and Sonja came upstairs to help me prepare for the journey. The dressmaker had made a dark green skirt of fine merino wool, caught up behind over a bustle. It was to be worn with a tight-fitting jacket of the same material, edged with black braid.

Mother had laid out enough warm underclothes and petticoats to clothe half of St Petersburg. 'Must I put them all on?' I asked dismayed.

'You'll thank me when it is freezing tonight.'

Sonja, who had drunk a little too much wine, giggled. 'Poor Emile,' she whispered. 'He'll have so many buttons to undo.'

Mother flushed. 'That's quite enough, Sonja.'

'Sorry, Mother.'

When Mother left the room to find my hat, Sonja stood on tiptoe and murmured in my ear. 'Don't worry, Anna, you'll soon learn how to please a husband.'

I thought of Emile's kiss and the taste of his lips on mine. How I wished for time to ask her more but Mother was already in the doorway holding the little green hat with its jaunty black feather. She set it on my head. 'There,' she said as she adjusted the angle and stepped back. 'Perfect.'

'You look lovely, Anna,' Sonja beamed.

Downstairs, our family, friends and servants waited to say goodbye. Most of them had known me since I was born. A lump came into my throat as they showered me with their blessings. Through the open door, I saw the carriage waiting outside, the horses' breath rising in clouds into the freezing air and the coachman stamping his feet to keep warm.

Emile tucked my hand into the crook of his arm. I took a deep breath then stepped outside. A flurry of snowflakes stung my face and my feet slithered on the crusted snow that was already freezing in the night air.

I looked back at the cosy hallway. A sea of faces shone in the lamplight. There was Papa, wiping his eyes; Mother with her handkerchief clasped in a ball to her mouth; Sonja and Petrov waving frantically and Uncle Vassily blowing me a kiss.

In a whirl of too many emotions - hope, apprehension, joy and sadness, I hesitated.

'Just one last goodbye.'

'Enough farewells, Anna: the train won't wait for us.'

The sudden sharp note in Emile's voice startled me. I gave him an anxious glance.

'Come, let me help you into the carriage,' he said more gently.

When I was comfortably settled, he followed me in. A gust of wind slammed the door shut.

We were alone.

Chapter 2

Papa's coachman drove us through the dark streets of St Petersburg to the Warsaw Station. It was cold and I was glad of the warmth of the sable cape that had been my parents' wedding gift.

At the entrance, several other carriages already disgorged travellers and luggage. Two porters, dressed in smart navy uniforms with gold buttons and epaulettes, rushed forward. Swiftly unloading our trunks, they began to hoist them onto a large wooden trolley.

Carts laden with mountains of bags and boxes rumbled over the cobbles, porters shouted at the crowds to make way and the hoots and hisses of the locomotives drifted from the station hall. Our coachman struggled to keep the horses still as, alarmed by the commotion going on around them, they jerked up their heads and rolled their eyes.

Emile tossed a handful of coins to one of the porters. 'The Paris train!' he shouted above the noise. 'First class - be careful with our baggage and you might get some more.'

The porter nodded and he and his companion began to push and pull the trolley towards the great stone archway that led to the concourse. As Emile took my arm to lead me in, I saw that the younger of the two men was ogling me. He gave me a cheeky grin when he realised I had noticed him. I assumed the haughtiest expression I could and flashed the gold ring on my finger in his direction.

The Paris train was already at the platform. My excitement mounted as we made our way to our compartment. Porters struggled to stow heavy trunks in the baggage cars and people crammed into the second and third class carriages, but we swept past them all. The attendant who waited for us bowed obsequiously.

'Make sure our luggage is safely on board and then bring us vodka,' Emile commanded him. 'My wife and I are cold.' The man hurried away.

Our compartment consisted of two rooms: a bedroom and a small sitting room. They were very luxurious, panelled with dark mahogany and lit with gleaming brass gas jets that cast a warm glow. The bedroom was too small for any furniture except a bed, but in the sitting room there were chairs upholstered in red plush and a round table covered with a white lace cloth.

Emile took off his greatcoat and threw it over a chair. He unpinned my hat and removed it for me, then unfastened the clasp at the neck of my cape and lifted the fur gently from my shoulders. 'The outfit is extremely becoming.'

He smiled and bent down to kiss me, but at a soft tap on the door, he let me go. 'Enter,' he called out.

The attendant came in with a decanter of vodka and two glasses on a silver tray. He put the tray down on the table. 'Will there be anything more, sir?' he asked.

'Yes. We won't be going to the dining car tonight. You may serve supper here.'

The man bowed obediently and left.

Emile took my hands in his. 'Are you happy?'

I rested my head on his shoulder and his arms slid around my waist. 'I think I'm the happiest girl in Russia.'

He laughed and bent down to kiss the top of my head. I closed my eyes. How could life ever be more perfect?

I heard the guard's whistle and the sound of carriage doors slamming shut. A few moments later, there was a loud burst of hooting from the locomotive and the train jolted forward. As we left the station, it picked up speed and we were soon travelling through the outskirts of the city.

The attendant arrived with our supper but I had no appetite. The warm compartment and the vodka had made me drowsy. Emile, however, drank some wine and ate a leg of chicken, tearing the meat off with his teeth as he talked.

After a while, he must have noticed how quiet I was. Gently, he touched my cheek. 'You're exhausted, Anna. We should go to bed.'

In the tiny bedroom, he knelt at my feet and slowly unbuttoned my boots, removing them in turn. His hands slid beneath my voluminous petticoats and up my thighs until they reached my stocking tops. I held my breath, dizzy with nerves, while he unclasped the lacy garters and rolled down the silky material. His lips brushed my knee then he looked up into my face and I saw the mischief in his eyes.

'Anna, I know this is winter, but you have so many clothes on, it might take me until spring to remove them and I don't think I can wait that long.'

Laughter welled up in my throat and I began to feel bolder. Our fingers intertwined as we untied ribbons, eased open laces and undid buttons. A languid sensation of warmth suffused me. I reached up and helped him to unpin my hair. Its dark waves tumbled over my bare shoulders; he twined a strand around his fingers and kissed it then laid me on the bed. He dimmed the gas jet, took off his own clothes and lay down beside me. I felt the heat of his skin as he caressed my breasts. 'You're very beautiful, Anna,' he murmured planting feather-light kisses down to my belly. He reached the cleft between my thighs and his fingers found a deep place where the sensation was so intense that I stiffened, suddenly afraid. 'Don't be frightened, my love,' he whispered. 'Let me teach you. I promise I would never hurt you.'

His lips traced a new path over my skin until they reached one of my breasts. A fierce, exquisite sensation, even stronger than the first one, went through me as he licked and sucked at my nipple. I had the strange feeling that there was a taut string running from it to the place below, where he still caressed me. He guided my hand down and folded my fingers around something thick and hard. I wasn't sure what to do but I wanted to give him the same pleasure he gave me, so I started to make little stroking motions. He was silent for a moment then he let out a groan that seemed to come from deep in the pit of his stomach.

I stopped, fearful that I had displeased him. 'What is it?' I asked. 'Did I do something wrong?'

He laughed softly. 'My beautiful little witch. No, you did something I like very much.' He straddled me and I felt the hard shaft enter me a little way. At first there was a pain so sharp that I would have cried out if his lips had not sealed mine. He raised his head, 'Hush,' he whispered, 'the pain will be gone soon.' He was right and, as it ebbed, he entered a little further and a little further until he filled me completely.

The marrow in my bones seemed to catch fire, melting my loins. The world disappeared: nothing existed except the two of us. Some instinct made me tilt myself up to meet him. He thrust deeper until I cried out again, but this time not with fear or pain, then my body stepped off a high place and floated in the clouds.

He thrust once more then shuddered in my arms. His body slumped and his head rested on my breast. A film of sweat slicked my skin. Beads of perspiration glinted on his forehead along the line where his dark hair sprang back. A stray thought flitted through my mind. Was this what Sonja had meant? Did Petrov give her this bliss? An image of them doing what Emile and I had just done rose up, and an involuntary giggle escaped me.

Emile lifted his head and scowled. 'What is it? No woman's ever laughed at me before.'

'I'm sorry,' I gasped. 'It's nothing.'

He pounced. 'Tell me, or I'll tickle you until you beg for mercy.'

I squirmed and tried to wriggle away but I couldn't escape. 'Stop, stop, I'll tell you.'

He propped himself up on one elbow. 'Sonja and old Petrov, eh?' he chuckled once I'd explained. 'I bet he hasn't got it in him.' He bent down and gave me a lingering kiss. 'Are you happy, my darling?'

'Yes, I've never been so happy.'

'Good.'

He smoothed my hair and grinned then jumped off the bed. 'Come, you need to wash.'

The washing water the steward had brought was still warm. Emile dipped the sponge and wiped it between my legs then dipped again. With a stab of shock, I saw the water turn crimson.

'Don't be afraid,' he said, 'this happens to all women but fortunately, it only happens once.' He handed me a towel and cautiously, I dried myself.

'We should sleep now,' he said, taking me back to bed.

'You're sure I didn't disappoint you?' I asked anxiously.

He put his arms around me and laughed. 'My darling, you were marvellous. I knew you'd be a wonderful pupil.'

*

Our journey took more than a week. At first, as we travelled through Poland, the countryside was flat and monotonous. It was impossible to distinguish the point on the horizon where monochrome land became leaden, winter sky. However, across the border in Prussia, the scenery was more interesting. There were hills topped with ancient castles, rivers, valleys, villages and farms.

One morning, we woke early to find that the train had halted. Emile pulled up the blind and looked out. The countryside was blanketed with snow.

He pulled on his greatcoat and fur hat. 'I'll go down and see what's happening,' he said.

A few minutes later, I heard a tap on the window and he was outside. I wrapped my robe around me and opened the sash. Snowflakes eddied into the warm compartment.

'There's been a drift across the line. A gang of men are up there digging. We could be here for hours.' He stretched up to caress my wrist. 'We shall just have to spend the day in bed.'

I reached down to brush the snow from his dark hair. 'Then hurry up and come back inside.'

He laughed. 'Didn't I say you would be a wonderful pupil?'

*

I was so excited at the prospect of seeing Paris. Emile teased that I was more in love with the city than with him.

'Well,' I said, rather nettled, 'I've never even been out of Russia before. I expect there's nowhere in the world you haven't been.'

He ticked off on his fingers: 'Greenland, the North Pole, the South Pole . . .'

I giggled and he hugged me to him hard. At that moment, I didn't mind where we went as long as I was with him.

'I promise you,' Emile said, 'I am as excited about showing you Paris as you are to see her. Emperor Napoleon is a brilliant man. Paris was still a medieval city when he came to power. The changes he has made in barely twenty years are remarkable. He's shrewd as well. He knows Parisians are like children; they need novelties and amusements to keep them out of mischief. He's given them a city they can be proud of, one the rest of the world envies, and they love him for it. It has been good for business too. A lot of people have become very rich.'

'Are we rich?'

'Oh, immensely,' he laughed, kissing my neck. 'You shall have everything you desire.'

I leant happily against his shoulder. 'I already do.'

Chapter 3

We reached Paris late one afternoon, just as the gas lamps were being lit. I marvelled at the wide boulevards, the elegant houses.

'That's the Tuileries Palace and next to it is the Louvre,' Emile said, pointing out a vast array of magnificent buildings. 'There used to be slum districts all around them, reeking, narrow alleys, full of wretched hovels. They've all been torn down now.'

'Where did the people go to?'

'Who knows,' he shrugged. 'The Belleville district perhaps.'

'I hope someone cared for them,' I ventured.

'There's no point wasting your pity on people like that,' he said abruptly. 'They're the dregs of Paris – the mob that interprets any kindness from its betters as weakness: weakness that brings out the mob's vicious and depraved instincts.'

His verdict seemed very cruel, but I fell silent, not wanting to displease him by arguing.

The streets seethed with pedestrians and carriages; sparkling Christmas lights festooned the trees. We passed a huge building whose brightly lit windows displayed smart clothes.

'That's Printemps, one of the grands magasins,' Emile said. 'You can buy everything you could possibly want under one roof. I shall probably forbid you to go there,' he added with mock solemnity.

Emile had told me that our apartment was on one of the new boulevards close to the river. I could hardly wait to see it. We were greeted by the concierge who made a great fuss of us and welcomed me warmly. Emile gave instructions to the coachman to bring our luggage and then led me upstairs. When we reached the second floor, he told me to close my eyes. I felt myself being swept off the ground as he carried me over the threshold.

'Open your eyes,' he commanded as he set me down.

I did so and fell in love with the place immediately. It was spacious and airy. In the drawing room, the chairs and chaises longues were upholstered in blue and cream striped silk. A gilded rococo mirror hung over the mantelpiece and a pretty jardinière overflowing with flowers stood under the window. The blue and gold tones of a Persian carpet gleamed against the polished wood floor.

'Well, do you like it?'

'Oh,' I breathed, 'I love it. It's even better than I imagined.'

'Come on, I'll show you the rest.'

I followed him into a small dining room in the centre of which stood a fine mahogany table surrounded by balloon backed chairs. Their seats were covered with scarlet damask that matched the elaborately draped curtains.

Our bedroom contained a huge bed, resplendent with ivory silk curtains and lace edged pillows. The bathroom had a marble floor and panels of marble on the walls. Hot and cold water gushed from large brass taps and did not need to be fetched up by a maid.

In the days that followed, I need not have worried that I had forgotten most of Mother's instructions on the correct way to run a household, for the maids were all directed by the housekeeper, Madame Duval. She was a formidable woman who oozed charm when Emile was present, but when she and I were alone, her manner was quite frosty. She made it clear, without actually saying so, that she preferred me not to interfere in her duties. In the back of my mind, I heard Mother and Aunt Tatiana sermonising.

'Servants must always be closely supervised.'

'They will cheat you if you give them the slightest chance.'

'You must always make sure they know their place.'

But young and inexperienced as I was and, in truth, a little afraid of Madame Duval, I did not want to challenge her authority. In any case, what good would it have done me to find fault? Emile never complained and the household ran like clockwork without any effort on my part.

In the first few weeks, I would have been happy just to be with Emile and enjoy our new home but from the very beginning, we were swept up in an endless round of pleasure. Even if Emile was out on business or at his club, I was rarely left alone for long. There were always visitors.

The fashionable women who descended on me were like flocks of peacocks with iridescent plumage and sharp, knowing eyes. I suspected they were only really interested in seeing this foreigner who had snared Emile. They were all so chic and witty, talking a lot about people whom I didn't know and never asking me about my own life. Some of the visits left me feeling very lonely, but I cheered up as soon as Emile came home.

The hairdresser came twice a week to dress my hair in the latest styles and Emile insisted I ask my visitors to recommend dressmakers. The clothes I had brought with me looked considerably less stylish in Paris than they had in Russia. Full skirts were no longer fashionable and everyone wore dresses modelled on the new sleek lines designed by the English couturier, Monsieur Worth.

Emile was very generous and bought me whatever I wanted. Each evening, I put on one of my elegant new ensembles and we went out. We enjoyed magnificent dinners at fashionable restaurants and attended plays, concerts and operas. Emile seemed to know so many people. He was greeted wherever we went.

Spring came and Paris looked lovelier than ever. Fresh colour splashed the city. The plane trees shading the boulevards sprouted pistachio leaves and the flower stalls were gay with daffodils and scarlet tulips.

On one memorable evening, we attended a costume ball where the guests had been asked to dress in the theme of four continents. As a memento of home, I had brought with me my sarafan, the traditional loose, flowing dress worn by Russian women. Mine was of fine, black wool, decorated with bands of scarlet and gold embroidery. That evening I wore it in the proper fashion over a linen shirt with a little round hat encircled with pearls. A gold necklace and a plaited girdle of red silk around my waist completed the outfit.

'You look splendid,' Emile beamed when he saw me. 'Now we must hurry. It could take a long time to get in. I hear more than three thousand people have been invited.'

I gasped. 'So many?'

He chuckled. 'This is Paris, my love. People do things in style.'

The mansion where the ball was held was so crowded that it was almost impossible to move. In the ballroom, the thousands of candles glittering in the chandeliers and the press of people made the heat overwhelming. Wishing I had chosen a cooler outfit, I clutched my glass of champagne close to me. I did not want it to be knocked out of my hand and spilled down my precious dress.

'Look,' Emile shouted over the hubbub. 'Something is causing a stir.'

The sound of trumpets cut through the roar of conversation and stilled it to an expectant hush. Every head turned in the direction of the huge crystal and gold doors at the entrance to the ballroom.

Through them came an extraordinary procession. At its head, drawn by a slow-footed camel, rumbled a wheeled cage containing four live crocodiles. A woman standing close by shrieked and promptly fainted. Her friends pulled her back to safety as a gilded palanquin, borne on the shoulders of twelve Africans, swayed through the doors. When they passed us, I saw how their muscles strained under their blue-black skins. Aloft, a beautiful woman dressed in a golden robe reclined on a pile of exotic pelts. Four black attendants, wearing only leopard skin breeches and cloaks, fanned her with ostrich plumes, the gold bracelets on their ebony arms catching the light as they worked.

'Our hostess, Madame de Galliment,' Emile whispered. 'They say she is the most expensive woman in Paris. Her husband is a brute, but a rich one.'

People began to clap and cheer. The woman inclined her head gracefully to acknowledge their applause. Slowly the procession reached the far end of the room and descended the sweeping ramp that led to the gardens. The crowd followed.

In the gardens, a large area had been luxuriously canopied and palms and other exotic trees and plants arranged to create the illusion of a jungle clearing. To one side, backed by a beautiful tree covered in large, trumpet-shaped white flowers, a waterfall cascaded over a bed of artfully arranged rocks. The colour of the water changed at intervals from red to green and back again.

'Oh,' I gasped, lost in admiration, 'how wonderful.'

Emile let out a low whistle. 'It must have cost a fortune.'

A man nearby overheard us and remarked, 'I'm told de Galliment will be four million francs the poorer after tonight. Clever the effect with the water, eh? I understand it's all done with this new electricity.'

The bearers had by now set the palanquin down in front of the waterfall.

'It will take our host and hostess hours to receive all these guests,' our new friend observed. He smiled at me. 'Fortunately, I hear the crocodiles are already on their way back to the zoo. We don't want any more ladies fainting, do we?'

I felt Emile's hand in the small of my back, pushing me forward.

'Where are we going?' I asked anxiously.

'To pay our respects, of course.'

Surrounded by all this sophisticated opulence, I felt like a provincial newcomer all over again. 'Emile, please; I can't.'

'Don't be ridiculous. Of course you can.'

He gave me another push and slowly, we moved through the eager crowds jostling to reach our hostess. A tough-looking man whom I took to be her husband stood beside her. He was so heavily built that I feared he might at any moment burst through the seams of his glossy black evening clothes.

Emile put his lips close to my ear. 'I'm glad de Galliment has refrained from treating us all to the sight of him clad in lion skins and feathers,' he murmured. I could not help laughing at the picture that rose in my mind and a little of my nervousness evaporated.

Close to, I caught the sensuous perfumes of musk and frankincense that hung around Madame de Galliment. Her beauty really was dazzling.

Emile bowed low and kissed her hand before introducing me. With practised charm, she greeted us as if we were some of her dearest friends. She and Emile exchanged a few remarks before her eyes slid to her next admirers.

We moved on to Monsieur de Galliment. He smiled broadly, showing sharp, white teeth. When he took my hand to kiss it, I felt as if I was being embraced by a bear.

'There,' Emile said as we walked away. 'Easy, wasn't it? If we're lucky, they might remember us another time. It's confidence that matters in this city. If you have that, you can achieve anything.'

'I'm sorry I was so foolish,' I said guiltily.

He shrugged. 'Let's forget it.'

I found his offhand manner hurtful, but I said nothing.

*

A week later, we were dining at the celebrated restaurant Le Petit Moulin when I noticed an elderly man with fleshy features, sallow skin and coarse, springy black hair sitting at a table nearby. He was talking animatedly to his companions, who hung on his every word. Apparently, he was oblivious to the fact that many of the other people in the room were looking at him too.

Emile leant across the table. 'You know who he is, don't you?'

I shook my head and at that moment, the man broke off from his conversation and looked up. With a wide smile, he raised his glass in our direction. I coloured with embarrassment but Emile toasted him in return.

'You seem to have made a conquest of the celebrated Monsieur Dumas,' he laughed as Dumas returned to his conversation. 'Perhaps he will find a role for you when he writes the next of those books of his that you so admire.'

In the midst of my confusion, I felt a frisson of excitement. A few months ago, I should never have believed I might find myself sitting a few feet away from the author of *The Black Tulip* and *The Three Musketeers*.

A few days after that, we went to the Louvre and Emile led me through a series of grand rooms until we stopped in front of Winterhalter's new portrait of the Emperor. It showed a haughty, aristocratic man with dark hair and an impeccably waxed, tapered moustache. His powerful physique was emphasised by the magnificently braided and decorated uniform of the commander of the armies of France, the black coat and tight white breeches set off by a scarlet sash, a gold collar and the insignia of the Legion d'Honneur. A sumptuous ermine cloak, slung from his broad shoulders, cascaded to the ground.

'A fine work, wouldn't you agree?' Emile asked. 'It flatters him, of course, but then if it didn't, I doubt the painter would work in Paris again. I—'

'Good afternoon, Daubigny.'

Emile turned and bowed to the tall, distinguished-looking man who had spoken. An elegant woman leant on his arm; very beautiful and of above average height with a slender figure, she wore a gown of white satin and her blonde hair was plaited in the form of a diadem. A black velvet cloak hung loosely from her shoulders. The deep décolleté it left bare looked as if it had been carved from the purest marble.

Emile drew me forward.

'My dear Count! Countess Castiglione! What a pleasure to see you. May I present my wife, Anna? Anna, this is Count Marly and the Countess Castiglione.'

The Countess gave me a cool smile.

Count Marly bowed and surveyed me. 'Enchanté, Madame. I didn't know my friend Daubigny had a wife.'

Emile answered before I could reply. 'We married a few months ago in St Petersburg. Anna is Russian.'

'Ah, most interesting. So, what do you think of the Emperor, Madame Daubigny?' He gestured to the painting.

'He looks like a god, Monsieur.'

The Count laughed and turned to his companion.

'An answer of which he would approve, don't you think?'

The cool smile again.

We talked for a few more moments then the Count bid us adieu, but before the couple walked away, he bent his head towards Emile and said something in rapid French that I was not fluent enough to follow.

Emile tucked my hand into his arm and led me on to the next painting. I sensed something was wrong. 'What did he say to you?' I asked.

For a few moments, he didn't reply. I wondered if he had even heard me, then he appeared to rally. 'Nothing you need trouble yourself with,' he said in a voice that closed off any more questions. 'Let us enjoy the rest of the exhibition.'

'The Countess didn't seem very friendly.'

He laughed. 'She's well known for that and she doesn't like to be outshone, my love. She hates anyone to be more beautiful than her.'

I flushed with pleasure. I loved it when Emile complimented me.

'After all,' he added, 'her face is her fortune.'

'What do you mean?'

'I mean, my lovely innocent, that she grants her favours to the highest bidder. She was the Emperor's mistress until he tired of her. Marly is his replacement. He's a very rich man but not such a catch, of course. Still, I'm told that when the Emperor dropped her, she was consoled by some very generous gifts.' He lowered his voice, 'The Emperor is no fool though. I've heard the secret police searched her house to make sure she kept nothing that she might use against him later.'

'Would she do something so disloyal?'

'I'm sure she would. People will do anything for money, my love.'

*

The following night, we attended the premiere of *La Belle Hélène*, the new opera by the German composer, Offenbach, who had taken Paris by storm. The Emperor was to be in attendance.

When he and the Empress arrived, the whole audience rose and clapped as the couple took their seats in the Royal Box. Emile gave me his opera glasses and I looked through them eagerly. I was disappointed to see that the Emperor was not as tall and imposing as his portrait had promised and he had a very large nose.

The Empress, on the other hand, was just as beautiful as I had heard, her glossy ebony hair drawn back from a pure, oval face and her large, dark-blue eyes fringed with long, thick lashes. A low-cut gown of rose silk revealed her exquisite shoulders; her slender neck was ornamented with a double row of lustrous pearls.

I gave the opera glasses back to Emile and he scanned the audience. Sat quietly beside him, I drank in the scene: the flashing jewels, the silks and satins, the heady odours of patchouli and musk.

The woman who sat on my other side looked at me with an amused expression. 'The Empress is lovely, isn't she? Have you never seen her before?'

'No, I have only been in Paris for a short time.'

'Ah yes, I can tell by your accent.'

She inclined her head and whispered behind her fan. 'They say that the Emperor only married her because she refused to let him have her any other way. Her resistance intrigued him. Finally, he was so mad for her he could think of nothing else. She played a very clever game. Her family were nobodies with more titles than cash.'

She glanced up at one of the boxes opposite us. 'Do you see that woman?'

I followed her eyes and saw a pretty, petite woman, dressed in white and dripping with emeralds, flirting and laughing uproariously with the men on either side of her.

'That's Marguerite Bellanger. She was the Emperor's mistress until her appetites began to wear even him out. They say he collapsed one morning after a particularly energetic night and the Empress sent her packing. Oh, and how amusing! In the next box is her successor - Valentine Haussmann. You've heard of her father, of course? Baron Haussmann? He masterminded the Emperor's plans for rebuilding Paris.'

She pointed out another woman wearing a zebra striped silk with black feathers in her golden hair.

'The Countess de Mercy-Argenteau. I have it on good authority the Emperor has set his sights on her now,' she looked back at me and laughed. 'Why, I do believe you're shocked.'

'But the Empress must be so unhappy,' I began.

The woman spread her ring-laden hands in a gesture of dismissal. 'I hear she is not fond of the pleasures of the boudoir, but the Emperor has the appetites of a true Bonaparte.'

She fell silent as, to a flurry of applause, the conductor arrived. He raised his baton and the overture began, but I was too distracted to enjoy the music. My neighbour's remarks had left me strangely upset and confused. The suggestion that there was something cynical and vulgar behind the glittering Imperial façade had broken the spell created by my romantic notions.

One of the regular letters from Mother and Papa came a few days later. As usual, Mother's part was full of family news and I smiled at her description of the antics of little Nicolai. When Papa took over, he mentioned that he had recently shipped a consignment of furs to Emile.

That is the last one, he wrote. *I hope you will make certain that he gives you any you would like before it is too late. There was some superb white mink that would make a beautiful jacket for evening wear.*

Although Papa's tone throughout the letter was jovial, I worried a little about his news. I had assumed he and Emile would continue to do business together.

Emile and I were driving in the Bois de Boulogne one day when I decided to broach the subject. I tried to do so tactfully but to my dismay, Emile's response was an angry one.

'Of course there is no trouble with your papa,' he snapped. 'He understands business as well as I do and knows my reasons. We made a killing but the Paris market is saturated. It's time to move on.'

'I'm sorry . . . I didn't mean . . .'

'You didn't mean what? Women know nothing of business. It would be best if you kept your foolish opinions to yourself.'

Alarmed, I recoiled as if he had slapped me. His eyes glittered and his lips were tightly compressed. I hardly recognised my suave lover.

Then as suddenly as it had come, his mood vanished. All smiles again, he patted my hand.

'Forgive me, my love, I'm boring you. No more business talk. Now, where would you like to dine tonight?'

*

Increasingly, Emile spent time away and I was lonely, longing for his return. The ladies' inspection visits had dwindled. Madame Duval continued to be cold and remote and if I tried to talk to the maids, they scuttled shyly from the room.

Sometimes I felt very homesick. In a way I never thought I should, I missed the quiet afternoons at my old home in St Petersburg. Sonja had written to say she was expecting another baby. No doubt she and Mother would spend many happy hours chatting and sewing layettes as we had done before little Nicolai's arrival. I pictured Papa coming home each evening, smelling of the warehouse and amiably brushing away Mother's objections as he sat with his feet warming on the fender and talked over the day's events. I thought of how beautiful the city had always looked after the first snowfall. I remembered the simple pleasures of summer excursions to picnic in the countryside.

The first anniversary of our marriage came and went. Emile had just returned from one of his absences when we were invited to the Russian ambassador's Christmas Ball. I was looking forward to meeting people from my homeland, but Emile seemed distracted. When he did speak, he was impatient and abrupt. I tried to find out what was troubling him but it was no use; he simply brushed all my questions aside.

That evening, I dressed for the ball with extra care, choosing his favourite dress and the pearl necklace he had given me for my birthday. I hoped the occasion would dispel Emile's bad mood. He usually enjoyed parties.

As we drove up the Champs Elysées and the ambassador's mansion came into sight, I gasped with admiration. It had a fairytale beauty, its tall windows golden with light against the dazzling white of the walls. Thousands of lanterns festooned the trees, throwing the lofty portico and its classical columns into sharp relief.

In the candlelit ballroom, the air was heavy with perfume and the buzz of conversation; I still found it thrilling to see such a brilliant spectacle. Emile and I moved through the crowd, greeting our acquaintances, but to my disappointment I still felt he was tense. His usual easy manner was absent and he seemed nervous, as if he was an actor playing a part he had not properly rehearsed.

Suddenly I saw Count Marly. Emile steered me towards him and greeted him warmly. The Count made a stiff bow.

'I'm very glad to see you, Monsieur,' Emile began. 'I've called at your house three times but your servants said you were not at home.'

To my surprise, the Count's expression was cold and his tone of voice even more glacial. 'You must excuse me. I doubt that we have anything to say to each other.'

As Emile coloured and fumbled for words, the Count turned to me. 'Merry Christmas, Madame Daubigny. I hope you enjoy the ball.'

Alarmed, I stuttered my thanks, but he was already walking away. Emile's face was a mask of fury. I hardly recognised this stranger as my suave, urbane husband. 'How dare that man insult me,' he hissed.

'Emile,' I implored, 'what's the matter? You must tell me.'

'I was a fool to trust him.'

People around us were beginning to stare. Emile grabbed my arm. 'Come,' he said angrily, 'we're going home.'

'Please tell me what has happened,' I pleaded as we drove away.

'I don't want to talk about it.'

'Emile, I'm your wife. Can't you trust me?'

'There's nothing you can do.'

The carriage rolled to a halt in front of our apartment building, 'Wait there,' he called to the driver as he helped me down and led me to the door.

'Surely you won't go out again tonight?' I asked anxiously.

'I must. I need to talk to someone.'

I clung to his arm. 'Emile, please stay here.'

He shook his head. 'Don't wait up for me,' he said and jumped back into the carriage. Bewildered, I watched it rumble away.

I passed a miserable, restless night in our cold bed. In the morning, Emile had still not returned. I tried to eat breakfast but the food stuck in my throat.

When there was no word from him all that day and the next, I became frantic with anxiety. Terrible visions filled my mind. I should never have let him go.

Early the following morning, Madame Duval came to me.

'You have a visitor, Madame.'

'I can't see anyone, Madame Duval. Please tell them I am not in.'

To my surprise, I saw something in her eyes that might have been pity. 'I believe you have no choice.'

My heartbeat quickened. 'Who is it? Has something happened to my husband?'

'It is not for me to say. I only know that the gentleman insists on speaking with you.'

The blood drained from my heart. 'Ask him to come in,' I said, struggling to steady my voice.

A few moments later, a man dressed in a shabby black frock coat and breeches entered the room. He removed his top hat to reveal thinning, grey hair.

The end of his long, pointed nose looked red and swollen.

'Thank you for receiving me, Madame Daubigny,' he said in a thick voice.

My spirits lifted. He looked too down-at-heel to be a doctor or official coming to give me bad news about Emile. Perhaps he was some poor man Emile had offered to help.

'How can I help you, Monsieur?'

'I want to know where I can find your husband, Madame.'

'I am afraid I have no idea where he is, Monsieur. I've had no word from him for several days. In fact I feared you had come to give me bad news.'

The man pulled out a large handkerchief and blew his nose vigorously.

'I regret that I have,' he said, returning the crumpled square of linen to his pocket. 'But not in the way I imagine you expected.'

I looked at him in confusion. 'I don't understand.'

'Your husband is bankrupt, Madame Daubigny. I've come to give you notice that his possessions are to be sold by auction to pay his creditors.'

He held out an official-looking document. 'Monsieur Daubigny owes a great deal of money to Count Marly and the Count will not wait any longer to be repaid.'

I was too shocked to speak.

The man cleared his throat and carried on in a flat tone, as if he had parroted the words a thousand times. 'I am sorry, Madame, but I must ask you to leave immediately. You may not take anything of value with you. You have the right to inspect the order of the court in my possession if you so wish.'

His words tore my world apart. I must leave immediately? Where on earth would I go?

My voice came back to me in a rush. 'Surely you can wait until my husband comes home? I know that he will be able to explain everything.'

He shook his head sadly. 'That is what they all say.'

I couldn't believe this was happening to me. Could it really be that the beautiful apartment, the elegant furniture and fine carriages, were no longer ours? No, it couldn't be true: impossible that all the underpinnings of our delightful life were to be ripped away like this, leaving nothing. Emile would come back and everything would be all right.

The man shifted his weight from one foot to the other. 'Again I am sorry, but I must carry out my instructions. Perhaps you have family? Are they in Paris?'

'No.' I bit my lip hard. I didn't want to cry in front of this stranger.

'Then you have friends in the city?'

It dawned on me that I had no real friends in Paris. Everyone I had met was connected with Emile. The elegant ladies who had made the inspection visits would certainly have no time for me now. There was no one to whom I could turn for help. I felt as though I was shrinking inside; for the first time in my life, I was totally alone.

'So I have to go straight away?' I asked miserably.

He nodded and I saw a flash of relief in his eyes. Afterwards I wondered whether I should have challenged him: cried, screamed, refused to leave, but by then it was too late.

'Yes. The law forbids you to remove anything of value, but you may take a few clothes.' He lowered his voice. 'I ought to watch you pack them but in the circumstances, I'll leave you alone for a few minutes.'

Like a sleepwalker, I went into the bedroom, but there I knew I must force myself to think. I didn't have long. I pulled a suitcase out from the wardrobe, snatched up my sable cape and some clothes and stuffed them into it. My purse contained a little money and there was also the pearl necklace and brooch that Emile had given me.

'I must ask you to hurry, Madame,' the man called out.

I snapped the case shut and prayed he would not ask to look inside. In the drawing room, he was already listing the pieces of furniture and ornaments Emile and I had bought together, no doubt calculating how much they were worth.

He looked at me solemnly. 'Goodbye, I wish you luck.'

'The servants,' I faltered, 'what am I to tell them?'

'I imagine they won't be surprised. There's no need for you to be concerned with them. I will deal with all that. Possibly the Count will retain them for his next tenant.'

'The Count?'

'Of course, Madame, he's the owner of this building and many more besides.'

He folded his arms and stood looking at me silently. There was nothing more to say.

As I left the apartment there was no sign of Madame Duval or any of the other servants. I crossed the passage that led to their quarters and heard a door slam.

The concierge came out of her apartment as I reached the bottom of the stairs to the front door. I didn't want to speak to her but there was no use pretending nothing was wrong. She probably already knew what was happening.

'There are much cheaper places, you know,' she said quite kindly. 'Maybe up behind the Gare du Nord?'

'I'll find somewhere for a few days,' I replied with as much dignity as I could muster. 'I'll send you the address. When my husband returns perhaps you would be so kind as to tell him where to find me and this silly mistake will be put right.'

She gave me a wintry smile. 'Of course, Madame - of course.'

Chapter 4

In my agitation, it never occurred to me to ask the concierge for directions. I doubt that I would have remembered them anyway. My vision blurred with tears, I walked aimlessly, not caring which way I went until I found myself by the river at the Pont de la Cité. I watched the turbid, brown water race through its metal arches. For a brief moment, its offer of swift oblivion tempted me, but then the thought of that dark water closing over my head, rushing into my mouth, terrified me. I turned away and set off northwards.

Beyond the elegant boulevards, the streets were shabby, flanked by narrow ditches choked with evil smelling rubbish. No trees grew. People dressed in faded blue or putty grey came and went from drab tenement blocks and shops. Many of those had bars on their windows to protect the pitifully sparse offerings of goods they contained.

Once, exhausted and bewildered, I stopped to rest by a public drinking fountain. At first, no one spared me a glance but then a man in tattered clothes with his feet bound up in old rags reeled towards me and pushed his face into mine. His breath smelt of stale wine. Frightened, I twisted out of his grasp and hurried on again.

I turned into a side street and found a cart blocking my way. A rough-looking man was trying to back a horse into the shafts but it skittered from side to side on the slippery cobbles. Rather than go back, I squeezed past the animal; I felt the heat coming off its sweat-darkened flanks and smelt its fear.

'Get out of the way, you stupid cow,' the man shouted. 'Do you want to get yourself killed?'

I stumbled on with his curses ringing in my ears. No one had ever spoken to me in such a way before.

Further along the street, a woman wiped down tables outside a café.

'Excuse me,' I called out. She looked at me curiously. 'The Gare du Nord, which way is it?'

She pointed a finger and went back to wiping her tables.

Hours seemed to have passed by the time the grimy bulk of the Gare du Nord loomed before me. Wearily, I enquired at one or two small hotels nearby but the owners looked at my clothes and named a price which seemed alarmingly high. At last, as darkness fell, I came to a narrow street paved with dirty, uneven cobbles; halfway down it, just beyond a small café, stood a green door. Above, a lantern with cracked, yellowish glass illuminated a section of the wall where a clumsily painted sign read: 'Hôtel Beau Séjour.'

With little hope, I pushed open the door. The tiny lobby smelt of boiled onions and damp. From behind the desk, a slatternly woman eyed me suspiciously.

'Do you have a room?' I asked.

'A single's five francs for the week.'

'May I see it please?'

She shrugged. 'If you wish.'

She waddled out from behind the desk and led the way up the stairs.

'Is that all the luggage you have?'

'Yes. I doubt that I'll be staying long.'

'Payment's a week in advance.'

She was out of breath by the time we reached the top floor. As she stood aside to let me into the room, I caught the sour smell of sweat.

It was a narrow, chilly room, with an iron bedstead covered by a stained mattress. A small table stood in front of the window; on it was a mirror with cracked glass. A battered wooden chest and a chair with a frayed rush seat completed the furniture. I crossed to the window and looked out. Rooftops blocked out most of the light. The sky above them was a thin smudge of charcoal.

The woman coughed. 'It's a good room. You'll be hard put to find anything as nice for the money. Bedding's extra. If you want to buy food, there's the café next door and the cook shop round the corner. There's a washroom and privy on the ground floor,' she added, 'but you can pay for service.'

I looked at her uncomprehendingly.

'I have a girl working for me,' she said irritably. 'If you want service, she'll bring up hot water and empty your wash bowl and chamber pot in the mornings.'

I paid for the week in advance with service and the bedding.

After she had left, I sat down on the lumpy mattress. It would not be for long, I told myself. Soon Emile would come to find me.

The stairs creaked under someone's feet and there was a knock on the door. When I opened it, the woman thrust a bundle of shabby bedding into my arms and left without another word.

I made up the bed as best as I could and then undressed to my shift. The air in the room smelt horribly stale. I went to the window and, in spite of the cold, threw it open wide.

A drunken man lurched down the street. He reached the corner of the alleyway opposite and doubled up clutching the wall. In the dim light of the lantern, I saw a stream of yellow vomit splatter the cobbles.

A wave of nausea overcame me. I grabbed the threadbare curtains and wrenched them shut then tottered back to the bed and lay down gingerly under the thin quilt. Through the open window, I heard babies crying and people quarrelling. A clattering and scraping of plates and pans rose from the kitchen of the café.

A gust of icy air lifted the curtains making me shiver, but I didn't want to get out of bed again to close the window for fear of what sights might meet my eyes. I longed for sleep, but even though I was exhausted, it was a long time before it came. The sounds from the street were still audible and the old building groaned with the creaks of its occupants moving around it. Strange scuffling noises rustled in the walls and I shuddered at the thought of the rats and mice that might be close by.

So many lives must be packed into the shabby buildings around me. Suddenly I remembered the wooden doll I had played with as a child. She was one of those brightly painted Russian dolls that split into two revealing a smaller doll inside. That doll contains another doll and so on, until you reach the tiniest of all, no bigger than an acorn.

I thought of that last doll with her tiny painted features, so small as to be barely discernable and the tears I had held back since the morning streamed down my cheeks. I was alone in a world of strangers. What was going to happen to me?

*

I must have cried myself to sleep for the next thing I knew, the gap where the curtains did not quite meet had changed from black to grey. In the distance I heard a clock strike six. A dull rumble of trains, pierced by the whistles and hoots of engines came from the direction of the station.

I got up from the bed, wrapped myself in the quilt and walked barefoot to the window. In the wan daylight, the street looked even more depressing than it had done the night before. Nobody was out, but a wedge of lemon light spilled from the door of the café onto the dingy cobbles. The faint aroma of bread and coffee drifted upwards and made my stomach knot with hunger.

I looked at my face in the broken mirror. My eyes were puffy but I had no water to bathe them. I took out the pins I had left in my hair the previous night and used my fingers to smooth the strands back from my face then refastened it at the nape of my neck.

My dress lay creased on the floor, the skirt stained with the mud splashed up by carts and carriages the day before. I opened the case and took out one of the other ones I had brought with me - a cornflower blue silk, trimmed with cream lace. In the gloomy room, it looked as incongruous as a lily on a dung heap.

When I had dressed, I walked to the café. My eyes took a moment to become accustomed to the gloomy interior. When they did, I saw walls the colour of the rye beer that the servants drank at home in Russia and a ceiling dyed nicotine yellow by years of smoke.

A middle-aged woman, dressed in rusty black, looked up from setting the crowded tables. Her eyes widened when she saw my dress.

'We're not open yet, but I can bring you some coffee,' she offered. I thanked her and sat down at the table she indicated.

The coffee was good. As I sipped it, I held my hands around the cup to warm them. If the woman was curious about me, she was too polite to show it. She merely smiled when I had finished the cup and fetched me another with some bread. I ate hungrily.

I must have been sitting in the café for half an hour when I noticed that the street had become busy. A constant stream of people, some dressed in overalls, some in office suits, flowed by like a river of grey, black and blue.

The woman came to fetch my cup and plate. 'Where are they all going to?' I asked.

'They come in to work from the suburbs at this time every morning,' she replied. 'Only rich people can afford to live in the centre of the city now. It's not for the likes of us.'

The café started to fill up. Anxious to avoid inquisitive stares, I paid for my breakfast and returned to the Hôtel Beau Séjour.

I passed the next two days as if in a trance, staying in bed and dozing for hours. After all, what was there to get up for? In the dark hours when I was fully awake, I was forced to acknowledge that my parents had been right to advise caution. My experience bore out the fact that I had not known Emile well enough when I made my decision. Had he ever really loved me or did he marry me on a fleeting whim? The way he had left me, with no apparent regret, pointed to that horrible answer to my question. At some times, I tormented myself with the fear that it was my own fault. I had failed him in some way. At others, I wished bitterly I could fall out of love with him as readily as he seemed to have fallen out of love with me.

Each morning, the girl knocked timidly at the door, bringing my washing water and carrying away my bowl and chamber pot to be emptied She looked little more than nine or ten, her reddish hair hanging lank and unwashed around a hollow, pale face dusted with freckles.

On the third day, weak with hunger, I realised I had eaten nothing since that breakfast at the café. It was lunchtime and the place was busy when I returned there. I was embarrassed by the curious stares of the other customers – men with sly grins who undressed me with their eyes and women who whispered and giggled to each other as they looked in my direction. After a few mouthfuls of food, I fled back to my room and the next morning, I asked the girl if she would fetch my meals for me.

She seemed glad to have the chance to make a bit more money and readily agreed, but I had very little appetite for the food she brought. The smell of the over-ripe cheeses repelled me and the cold meat was dry and stringy. I thought of the delicious pirozhki stuffed with fresh vegetables and meat that Cook used to make at home. How I craved their comforting savoury taste.

'Please Madame,' the girl said awkwardly one morning. 'Madame Magnier says she wants paying for next week.'

Her words hit me like a hammer blow. Had a whole week really passed with no news of Emile?

When I took the money down to the desk, Madame Magnier took it without a word. She counted the coins carefully and tested one with her teeth. Apparently satisfied, she unlocked a small drawer with the key she wore on a long chain around her neck, placed the money inside and turned the key once more.

'I won't stand for late payment again. Don't forget that,' she grunted.

Stung by her rudeness, I returned to my room.

I sat at the table and studied my reflection in the mirror. It was hardly surprising that Madame Magnier mistrusted me. My hair was unkempt, my cheeks hollow and my eyes bloodshot from crying. The wretchedness of my situation overwhelmed me and I buried my face in my hands and gave way to tears once more.

Yet suddenly, a ray of hope stopped me. I jumped up from the chair. What a fool I had been not to return to the apartment. I had never told the concierge where I was. Even now, Emile might be searching for me.

I tidied myself up as best as I could and found out which omnibus I needed to take to reach the centre of the city. It seemed strange to be among crowds of fashionable people again, disorientating and unnerving. By the time I reached the apartment, my head throbbed.

The concierge looked surprised. 'I thought we'd seen the last of you,' she remarked. Her dismissive words stung but I tried to smile.

'Has there been any word from my husband?'

She shrugged. 'He's not been seen around here.' She looked at my downcast face. 'I suppose you may as well tell me where you're living. I'll give him the address if he comes back.'

I wrote the address on the scrap of paper she found for me. She glanced at it briefly but did not comment.

I returned to the hotel and counted out my remaining money. Fearfully, I realised I had barely enough to last more than a few weeks. I laid my clothes out on the bed. Perhaps I might manage without some of them. They were so dirty, but if I could clean them, maybe they would be worth selling.

Of course, I had no idea how to find somewhere to launder them. At home the servants had done all that kind of thing and in Paris, Madame Duval saw to it. I did not want to ask Madame Magnier for advice and give her an opportunity to be rude to me again, but the owner of the café seemed a kind woman. I decided to ask her what I should do.

She smiled at me when I walked in. 'It's good to see you up and about again. I was sorry when the girl said you were ill.'

'May I ask your advice, Madame?'

'Of course.'

'I need to wash my clothes and I don't know where to go.'

She looked surprised. 'Why, you go to the wash house, child, where else?'

Feeling foolish, I listened while she explained how to get there.

The next morning, I bundled up my clothes and set off. The place was not far away, an ugly building with a flat, tin roof on which stood three enormous metal tanks. To one side of the tanks, a narrow brick chimney belched smoke into the sky.

I carried my bundle of clothes through the wide doorway. In front of me, a tired-looking woman sat in a small booth. Behind her, a few shelves contained cakes of soap and a variety of jars and packets. Incuriously, she looked up from the ledger in which she was writing.

'Two centimes an hour and hot water's a centime a bucket. You pay the boy for that when he comes round.' She gave me a ticket with a number on it.

'Do you need soap?' I nodded and paid for a small cake of it.

The washing shed was an immense room, its tin roof supported by a massive iron framework of beams and pillars. Hot steam hung in the air, greyish-white like skimmed milk; condensation dripped down the walls. The air smelt of foul water and fatty soap, sharpened with a whiff of bleach.

All at once, my stomach heaved. The shed became a blur and I had to hold onto the doorjamb to stop myself from falling until the sensation passed. When my vision cleared, I saw that on either side of a central walkway, women stood in front of tubs and washing boards, beating and scrubbing at their clothes. Their sleeves were rolled up above their elbows and their skirts caught up between their legs to stop them trailing in the puddles on the floor. Some of them had thrown modesty to the wind and pulled down the necklines of their dresses to cool their necks. Even so, they perspired freely.

Loud snorting and clanging noises came from a huge engine standing next to two large copper tanks on one side of the room. The women all shouted at the tops of their voices to make themselves heard over the din. I guessed from the clouds of steam rising from the tanks that the engine was for heating the water. What with the noise, the heat and the oppressive smells, the scene seemed like a vision of Hell itself.

I saw a free tub a little way down the left hand side of the room and picked my way over to it, skirting around the puddles. Near the tub was a tap with a bucket underneath. I filled the bucket and tipped the water into the tub; it was cold and I looked around for the boy with the hot water.

A brawny woman on my left, with arms like skittles, tugged at my sleeve. 'What are you after?' she asked.

'I want some hot water.'

She shook her head. 'Hot water costs money. Start with cold, dearie. Give everything a good beat and a scrub and it'll do the trick. You can use a bucket of hot water later when you need to rinse.'

I thanked her and put in another bucket of cold water, then dropped the clothes into the tub.

'That's it,' she said. 'Now you've got them wet, put them on the washboard one at a time and scrub them and beat them.' A wistful look crossed her face. 'Such pretty things you've got. They'll come up lovely. Where's your brush and beater?'

'I forgot them,' I lied, not wanting to seem too ignorant.

'I'd lend you mine, but I've got a lot to do.' She collared a boy loitering nearby, swishing his boots in one of the puddles. 'Here, get the lady a brush and beater she can borrow and look sharp about it.'

'Thank you,' I stammered as the boy skulked off. 'You're very kind.'

'It's nothing. That idle good-for-nothing needs to be kept busy. My name's Madame Roche, by the way.'

'Anna Daubigny.'

'You're new round here, aren't you?'

'Yes, I am.'

The boy arrived with the beater and scrubbing brush and I set to work.

Madame Roche nodded approvingly. 'Not bad for those dainty white arms of yours.'

She chattered on as I soaped and scrubbed. Each time I dipped a garment back in the water, the scum of grey suds on the surface grew thicker and more rancid. My arms ached by the time I had finished.

'You tip your dirty water into that drain over there.' Madame Roche pointed to a gully running with water slicked with soapy grease. 'Here, I'll help you, these tubs are heavy.'

She told another boy to bring hot water for me and I began to rinse the clothes. When that was done, Madame Roche offered to help me wring them out and I accepted her offer gladly. Her kindness was very welcome and I soon found myself answering her questions as if we were old friends. I realised how much I had needed someone to confide in.

'It's a disgrace,' she tutted. 'But you aren't the first girl in the world to have man trouble and you won't be the last.'

'Emile will come back one day, I know he will, but I can't pay for many more weeks at the hotel where I'm staying, and then there's food to buy. I don't know how to manage by myself any longer, I—' Tears overwhelmed me.

Madame Roche put her sturdy arm around my heaving shoulders. 'Bless you,' she laughed. 'With all these pretty things you've got? Haven't you ever heard of the pawn shop? That way you get your money, but if your man ever does come back, you can have your things again. If you like, I'll come with you and make sure you don't get swindled.'

Just then, a commotion broke out on the other side of the room. A tall, angular girl was shrieking at a younger one who looked terrified. The tall girl had her by the hair and was aiming vicious kicks at her shins. All around, women had stopped work to watch, their faces greedy for excitement.

Madame Roche straightened up from her tub and peered across the room through the steam. 'That's little Marie she's hurting,' she exclaimed.

She marched over to the group and grabbed the tall girl by the arm, spinning her round. The girl let out an even louder volley of curses but she let her victim go.

'Now then!' Madame Roche glowered. 'What have you got to say for yourself?'

'She's been making those sheep's eyes of hers at my Jacques, the little cow.'

'It's not true,' the girl called Marie sobbed, rubbing her bruised shins.

Madame Roche poked her finger in the tall girl's chest. 'If he prefers Marie to a skinny piece of misery like you, who'd blame him?' she snapped. 'Now leave her alone, or you'll have me to deal with.'

The girl opened her mouth then closed it. Contenting herself with shaking her fist at Marie, she picked up her bundle of laundry and stalked off.

Madame Roche put her arm around Marie. 'Let's finish this washing and then you can come home with me for a bit. Don't upset yourself. She's a bad lot that one and no better than she should be. I've no time for her sort.'

'I have to be at work soon,' Marie said anxiously.

Madame Roche collared one of the gawping onlookers. 'Here, Francine, go to Madame Caron's and tell her Marie's had an accident and she'll be late in. If there's any trouble, tell her I sent you.'

I helped to rinse and wring out the rest of Marie's clothes then Madame Roche and I collected our own. 'We won't bother with the dryers,' she said. 'I've got space to hang up this lot at home.'

We paid on the way out for our time and I walked home with the two of them.

The block where Madame Roche lived was a few streets from the hotel. It was just as shabby but the central courtyard looked clean, as if it had been swept recently. Marie climbed the steep stairs first and I followed Madame Roche as she puffed and panted in Marie's wake.

In the cramped apartment, Madame Roche pushed a table out of the way and opened a cupboard. She produced a length of thick cord and went out to the balcony to string a line from one side of it to the other.

'There you are. Peg up as much as you can and we'll put the rest on the clothes horse. Everything will be dry by tomorrow and I'll bring it round when I come to take you to see uncle.'

'Uncle?'

'The pawnbroker, of course - what an innocent you are!'

Marie was still shaken from her encounter and Madame Roche insisted we all sit and have a glass of wine. It was the roughest wine I had ever tasted and I had to make an effort to swallow it without making a face. The conversation, however, was easy and pleasant. After so many days alone, it lifted my spirits. Madame Roche brought out the remains of a loaf and some cheese which we shared.

Marie seemed a quiet girl but as Madame Roche did most of the talking, it would have been hard for her to say much in any case. I noticed she watched me with great interest and smiled shyly when I caught her eye. The sweetness of the smile brightened her hazel eyes and suffused her face with charm.

'I should go now,' she said when the simple meal was over. 'I'm very grateful to you, Madame, but I don't want to make Madame Caron angry.'

Madame Roche put one of her large, work-roughened hands on Marie's cheek and looked at her intently. 'Promise me if you have any more trouble, you'll come to me straight away?'

'I promise.'

'Off with you then.'

'I must go too,' I said. 'Thank you so much for your kindness.'

'It was nothing. I'll see you in the morning.'

My heart lighter than it had been for many days, I walked back to the hotel.

Chapter 5

When I woke the following day, my stomach felt bloated and there was a nagging pain behind my eyes. I hoped the wine I had drunk the previous evening had not made me ill.

The sun was already up. I needed to dress before Madame Roche arrived, but when I tried to stand, a rush of nausea seized me and my legs almost gave way. I stumbled to the table where a bowl of water stood, cold and scummy from my wash last night, and retched into it violently. My throat burned and the taste of vomit filled my mouth. I sat down on the bed again, my head between my knees.

When the dizziness passed, I picked up the pitcher that stood beside the soiled bowl. Shakily, I poured the last few inches of clean water it contained into my only cup and sipped it slowly, then I found a piece of rag and covered the bowl. Not long afterwards, the girl arrived on her daily errand. She wrinkled her nose at the foul smell but didn't say anything, just picked up the bowl and pitcher and carried them outside, before coming back to take the chamber pot. She returned after a while with everything cleaned and fresh water in the pitcher. I gave her an extra sou by way of a thank you. With a quick movement she tucked it into the toe of her shoe.

Washed and dressed, I felt much better. Soon, I heard heavy footsteps on the stairs and there was a knock at the door. I opened it to find Madame Roche standing there, her cheeks flushed from the climb.

'All ready?' she asked, then looked at me more closely. 'My, but you look peaky today. Are you ill?'

'No,' I lied. I didn't want to offend her hospitality of the previous evening. 'I'm perfectly well. It's so kind of you to help me, Madame.'

She looked around the room, taking in the sparse furniture and dingy walls.

'How much is old Ma Magnier charging you for this?'

'It's a disgrace,' she muttered when I told her. 'She's a greedy old bag. Well, let's have a look at what you have for the pawnbroker.'

Her eyes widened when she saw the sable cape. 'Whew! That must've cost a packet.' Her work-roughened hands lingered on the soft, glossy fur. 'Just wait until I tell Roche. If you'll take my advice, you'll pawn this first - it's too good to risk keeping it here. If old Ma Magnier found out, I wouldn't trust her to keep her hands off.'

The bell above the door jangled as we entered the pawnbroker's dim and dusty shop. A flicker of excitement disturbed the impassive face of the man behind the counter when he saw what we had brought him.

'How did you come by it?' he asked sharply. 'I don't take stolen goods. You should know that by now, Madame.'

Madame Roche snorted. 'And you should know better than to accuse me of bringing you them. This belongs to Madame Daubigny here - fair and square - and she can pawn it if she likes.'

He studied me for a few moments. 'Very well,' he shrugged. 'I'll take your word for it.'

While Madame Roche haggled with him, my eyes strayed around the shop to the rails of shabby dresses and threadbare overcoats. Dark wooden shelves lined the walls, piled high with worn crockery, battered saucepans and gaudy bric-a-brac. A small glass-fronted cabinet held the treasures of the collection: three cheap-looking bracelets, two necklaces, some lace collars and a small brass clock. Behind the counter, a door led into another room. Just inside it, I could see a lumpy mattress with stained blue and white ticking propped against the wall.

At the sight of so many sad testimonies to hardship, melancholy flooded over me – and a nagging fear for my own future. I could not wait to leave this dismal place and it seemed an age before Madame Roche agreed a price.

'Women,' the pawnbroker grumbled as he counted the greasy coins into my palm and handed over the pawn ticket. 'Do you want to ruin me? I'll make no money on this. Lucky for you I have a soft heart.'

Madame Roche gave a derisive snort. 'Don't expect my sympathy. You make plenty more than you deserve.'

Outside the shop, she chuckled. 'Not a bad morning's work. Did you see his face? I'll wager he's never had anything so fine in his shop before.'

'I must repay you for your kindness.'

'Gracious no, you keep your money for yourself, my girl. It never goes as far as you think it will.'

'Please, let me do something.'

'Well, a cup of coffee would be welcome.'

I protested but she would accept nothing more.

'How's your friend Marie?' I asked as we sat in a nearby café.

'Her legs are bruised but she says they don't hurt too much. Marie's like a daughter to me. I'll make that girl sorry she was born if she touches her again.'

We talked on for a while until Madame Roche said suddenly, 'I've been thinking we might be able to help each other out. If you'd like to pay me a bit, you could come and eat with Roche and me in the evenings. It would be much cheaper for you.'

'That would be wonderful, Madame.'

'Good, that's settled then.'

*

Of course, the food at the Roches' apartment was not what I was used to. They ate plain dishes like baked tripe with onions, or stews made with cheap cuts of meat and half-spoiled vegetables bought late in the day from the market, but I was so grateful for their kindness and good humour that I would have eaten almost anything.

Marie was often there, and slowly, I found out more about her. She was only a year older than me but both her parents were dead. She had worked for Madame Caron, the dressmaker in the rue de la Chapelle, for several years.

'Lovely neat work she does,' Madame Roche said proudly. 'They think very highly of her there.'

I laughed ruefully. 'Mother always said my sewing was the worst in the world.'

Marie smiled. 'I could help you improve if you want.'

'I'd like that. Most of my stockings have holes in them and I tore the skirt of my dress on a nail yesterday. It would be good to mend them properly.'

She beamed. 'Then I'll show you how.'

*

I didn't want to mention it to anyone, but the sickness I had suffered on the morning of my first visit to the pawnbroker still troubled me. I told myself it must be due to the poor food I ate, but I couldn't ignore the fact that my clothes were becoming too tight.

I remembered Sonja's dresses being altered when she was expecting Nicolai; how the seams had been endlessly unpicked and stitched up again so that you could see the old marks of the needle on the exposed fabric. When my courses continued not to come, I unwillingly faced the truth: I was pregnant. Confused and anxious, I tried to keep the news to myself, but Madame Roche's sharp eyes missed nothing.

'Don't you worry,' she said kindly. 'I know someone who helps girls out of that sort of trouble, and she doesn't ask any questions.'

The suggestion horrified me. 'Oh no, I couldn't,' I stammered quickly. 'Emile will be back soon—' I looked at Madame Roche's expression. 'It will be all right, I know it,' I said lamely.

'Then you must do as you think best.'

In truth, I was far more afraid than I dared to admit, even to myself. Since my visit to the pawnbroker with Madame Roche, I had had to go back again. Soon I would have nothing left to offer him. I would not have enough money to support myself, let alone a baby, and still there was no news of Emile.

On my next visit to the concierge at our old apartment, several letters from my parents awaited me. I read them and the temptation to go home was very strong. Perhaps Papa would even come and fetch me himself. Then Aunt Tatiana's face rose before my eyes, simpering with a triumphant smile. The prospect of the humiliation I would endure if I returned to St Petersburg was more than I could bear.

I spent money I could ill afford on pen and paper, and, closing my ears to my conscience, wrote a reply to my parents. I told them that I was the luckiest woman in the world. Emile's new business

ventures were a great success and our life was full
of exciting entertainments and delightful friends.

*

At the wash house a few days later, I noticed a girl
with lank, brown hair and tired eyes scrubbing at a
pile of foul-smelling rags. At her feet, a toddler
played with a scrap of discarded paper on the wet
floor, but he soon lost interest and crawled towards
the gulley. His pudgy hands dabbled in the scummy
water then he sucked his fingers and started to cry.
The girl scooped him up and delivered an angry
swipe to his bare bottom.

'Stupid kid!' she snapped. 'You'll be puking all
night if you drink that.'

The toddler's face turned puce and he let out an
almighty bellow. He flailed about with his stubby
arms and legs like an octopus trapped in a net.

The girl dumped him down and shot me a
defiant look. 'What are you staring at? You don't
know the half of it, and anyway, it's none of your
bloody business what I do with my own kid.'

That night, I lay in bed turning my problems over
and over in my mind and trying to decide what I
should do. I kept coming back to the words of that
girl in the wash house: *my own kid.* My hand slid
over my belly. The baby had not moved yet, but it
was there: our baby - mine and Emile's. We had
never spoken of having a family of our own but
surely when he came back, he would be overjoyed
at the news? I pushed away the memory of the

toddler in the wash house. For our child, everything would be different. Of course it would.

I drifted into sleep and dreamt I heard Emile's voice. It seemed to come from far away, as soft as the rustle of autumn leaves. I could just make out the words. He was telling me to wait for him. In the morning, I made up my mind. However difficult it might be, I wouldn't go home to Russia. I would stay in Paris.

But the enormous sense of relief I felt once I had reached my decision was soon overshadowed by anxiety. In order to stay in Paris, I needed to find a way of earning money, for I had nothing left for the pawnbroker.

'I'll ask at the dressmakers and see if Madame Caron has any work,' Marie offered.

'They wouldn't keep me for long. I told you Mother always said my sewing was the worst in the world.'

'Well then, perhaps we could see if there's something at Monsieur Tissot's laundry.'

'And spend twelve hours a day in that heat and noise? No, I can't face that.'

It was Madame Roche again who came to my rescue. She took in ironing from the wealthier neighbourhoods and always had more work than she could manage. She could not afford to pay me very much, but offered to give me my meals on top. If I was careful, I should be able to get by.

I soon learnt how to heat the heavy irons on the stove so that they were hot enough to smooth out wrinkles and creases to Madame Roche's exacting standards, but not so hot they would scorch the clothes. I did my best to work hard and the tasks were not uncongenial. I found a kind of satisfaction in transforming the crumpled linen of a dress-shirt into smooth perfection so that its starched pleats were sharp as knives; in deftly guiding the polonaise, the small rounded iron used for delicate work, through the billows of lace and chiffon on a dress or a cap. Only occasionally did I think of my own dresses and my sable cape, still languishing in the pawn shop. In a few months' time, it would be too late ever to recover them, but it was no use repining.

*

I moved to cheaper lodgings where I could just manage to pay the rent. If my thoughts strayed to my comfortable childhood and my luxurious life with Emile, I pulled them back sharply. I was determined not to feel sorry for myself and above all, never to give up hope.

It did not take me long to appreciate that even though they had little enough, Madame Roche and her husband were better off than some of their neighbours. There was a door at the bottom of the staircase that led to their apartment and one day, it was open. A foul stench came from inside what looked like a large cupboard, but there was someone asleep there, huddled under a heap of rough grey blankets. Beside the shrouded figure lay a tin plate and cup.

'Poor old man,' Madame Roche said when I asked her about it. 'He's soft in the head. You needn't be afraid of him though, he wouldn't harm a fly. People give him a bit of food when they can or he begs in the streets. At least he has somewhere dry at night. More than many can say.'

'Has he no family?'

'I don't think so, but he won't speak much. Once he told Roche he had fought for Napoleon and been wounded at Waterloo. The concierge turns a blind eye. If the landlord knew he was there, the bloodsucker would probably charge him rent.'

In spite of the Roches' kindness, I doubted I would ever get used to the harsh life I had been forced to lead. More than anything, I hated the callow attentions of the men. Their salacious leers and crude suggestions made an ordeal out of a simple walk down the street. The bolder girls threw back insults and laughed at them; I didn't have the courage for that. I would fix my eyes on the pavement and hurry past as fast as my legs could carry me.

Madame Roche often warned me to be on my guard, especially after dark. Her conversation was peppered with tales of girls who had – as she put it – been taken advantage of down a dark alleyway. Wryly, I thought of the now-perceptible thickening of my waist. It was rather late to worry now.

Increasingly I found myself drawn to Marie for her kindness and generosity. I never heard her complain about the hardship of her life but the plight of others often brought tears to her eyes and she would help them whenever she could. Used to fending for herself, she knew how to be careful with her money. Often when Madame Roche asked me to go to the market, Marie came too and helped me find the best bargains. She also showed me how to spy out the stallholders' tricks and make sure I wasn't cheated.

'If you give them a chance,' she said, 'they'll give you spoiled food from the back, stuff they want to sell quickly. The butchers are the worst. Everyone hates them.'

She clicked her tongue in mock reproof when she visited me one evening and found me mending my stockings. 'Time for one of those lessons I promised you. The stitches should be smaller and you must smooth the material as you sew. It's just as well you didn't want to try for a job with Madame Caron.'

I put down my needle and looked at my work glumly. 'And I thought I had improved a little.'

Marie laughed. 'Never mind. Let me do it for you.'

When she had finished, she eyed the straining seams of the bodice of my dress.

'I could alter your dress for you too if you want.'

I nodded gratefully.

'You'll need to take it off.'

Obediently, I stood up and raised my arms to let her pull the dress over my head. We sat side by side on the bed as she worked, her nimble fingers moving swiftly among the folds of cloth.

'You're so clever at sewing, Marie,' I remarked.

She smiled. 'When Mother and I came to Paris, she went to work for Madame Caron and there was no one to look after me at home, so I went with her and watched how everything was done.'

'You've never told me what happened to your father.'

A cloud passed over her face.

'I'm sorry,' I said hastily. 'I didn't mean to pry.'

'No, it's all right. I don't mind telling you. He was a carpenter. When I was five years old, he had a bad accident. It was while we were still living in the country.'

She shook her head sadly. 'I still remember that awful day when they came to fetch Mother. She told me to stay at home, but I followed her to the building where Father worked. A heavy wooden beam had fallen and trapped him underneath it. He just lay there groaning, his face all grey. Mother was shaking and crying. She slapped me for being disobedient when she saw me. She'd never raised her hand to me before and I cried and cried. Some of my father's workmates carried him home on a trestle and I helped Mother to nurse him. For weeks, the pain was so bad it hurt him too much to eat. He got so thin I was afraid he'd die. The doctor used to come to the house to see him and talk to Mother. He always looked very solemn and pulled at his long white beard a lot. Mother cried even more after he'd gone.'

'Did your father get better?'

'In the end he did, but he was different, not kind like he used to be. He never played with me anymore and was always shouting. Sometimes he had work, but more often he'd stay at home and Mother had to wait on him all the time. He often sent me out to buy him wine and if he didn't think I'd been quick enough, he'd hit me. Mother tried to stand up for me but he started to hit her too. Once she fell down and he kicked her, over and over again. I was terrified he'd kill her.'

'Wasn't there anyone who would help you?'

She shrugged. 'Everyone in the village knew, but no one wanted to interfere. Father wasn't the only man to use the flat of his hand when he'd had too much to drink. One day, Mother bundled up our things while he was out and told me we were going away, and that's how we came to Paris.'

'I expect you miss your mother.'

'Yes, I do. I wish she was still here with me.' She shook out the dress. 'There, it's done. Try it on before I neaten the seams.'

'Oh, that's much better,' I said, feeling how the bodice sat comfortably over my breasts and waist once more. Marie knelt on the floor and scrutinised her work with an expert eye, then pinned a small tuck where the material puckered a little. I felt the light pressure of her hand slip down the seam and come to rest at my waist. She looked up at me, her dark eyes unfathomable.

'It would be nice to have someone of my own,' she said softly. 'Someone special.'

I smiled. 'Perhaps you'll be lucky and find a good man to marry.'

She looked away without answering.

'Madame Roche says that Guy Jussac, the baker, likes you - he seems a kind man,' I ventured.

'I don't want to go to bed with an old man every night.'

'Oh Marie, he's only a few years older than us.'

Abruptly, she stood up and went over to the window, turning her back on me.

'I don't want him,' she snapped. 'I don't want any of them.'

'Marie, I'm sorry. I didn't mean any harm.'

She turned to face me, but against the light from the window, her expression was unreadable. 'Let's forget it,' she said flatly. 'I'm sorry too.'

*

When we met a few days later, Marie seemed to have forgotten the incident, chatting happily and suggesting we visit a local market together. I was glad we were still friends and accepted readily.

We wandered among the stalls, looking at the displays of trinkets and ornaments that I would once have dismissed out of hand. On one stall, I noticed a little brooch made of artificial violets. The stallholder held it out to us; against her liver-spotted hands the flowers looked fresh and pretty.

'Only two sous,' she said.

'One,' Marie replied, holding out a coin. The woman shook her head. 'It's a bargain at two.'

'One,' Marie repeated firmly.

The woman scowled, then with a shrug she took the coin and slipped it in the pocket of her apron. Marie undid the brooch's clasp and pinned it to my bodice. For a moment, a poignant memory of Emile's strong, elegant hands, fastening a brooch in just the same way, sent a wave of emotion through me. I might have been looking at Marie, but my mind was really elsewhere.

Dimly, I heard her say something; I dragged myself back to the present.

'I can't pay you back today,' I said, 'but I will as soon as Madame Roche gives me my wages for the week.'

'I don't want you to pay me back.'

I frowned. 'You shouldn't spend your money on me. You need it for yourself.'

'I want to, just to thank you for being so kind.'

On an impulse, I leant forward and kissed her cheek. 'It's you that's kind,' I said.

She flushed and we walked on. After a few moments, she tucked her hand under my arm.

*

In the wash house a few days later, I was filling my bucket at the tap when a girl passed and slipped on the wet floor. She jolted my arm and some water splashed the skirt of my dress.

'I'm sorry,' she said righting herself. She looked at me more closely. 'I know you, don't I? You're the girl who works with Madame Roche.'

I nodded.

She put her bundle of laundry down by the tub next to mine and began to undo it.

'I'm Cécile.'

'Anna.'

'Pleased to meet you, Anna. She's a good sort isn't she, Madame Roche? I bet she pays better than the old skinflint I work for. He'd starve his own grandmother.'

I smiled. 'Yes, she's very kind.'

'I've seen a dress I want in the window at Printemps,' Cécile confided – I remembered the brightly lit windows of the huge store Emile and I had passed on that first evening in Paris – 'but it'll take months to save up on the wages my boss gives me.'

She gave a wistful sigh. 'You should see the dress, it's beautiful. Blue taffeta with narrow sleeves trimmed with black lace. It's in the new fashion, like posh ladies wear, very close-fitting and sleek instead of a great full skirt over a hoop. I could never have afforded one of those anyway, too expensive with all that material.'

She rattled on as we worked until another girl came over to us. Her dress was much more stylish than anyone else's. I recognised her as the one who had attacked Marie that first day at the wash house.

'You look nice, Amélie,' Cécile said, looking at the dress with unconcealed envy. 'By the way, this is Anna.'

Amélie looked me up and down. 'I've heard a lot about you.'

I wondered what the gossips were saying but I wasn't going to give her the satisfaction of asking.

She turned to Cécile. 'So, what have you been up to? Bought that dress yet?'

Cécile made a face. 'No, not yet, I just hope it doesn't go before I've saved up.'

Amélie grinned and nudged her in the ribs. 'A few weeks and the Great Exhibition will be open.'

She turned to me. 'You should go too, Anna. It's a real chance.'

'I don't think I have the money for that sort of thing.'

She laughed. 'You don't go to spend money, idiot. You go to make it.'

'What do you mean?'

'There'll be men visiting Paris in droves. They spend their days amusing themselves and looking at the exhibition, then some of them will be ready for a different kind of entertainment, if you know what I mean.'

She chuckled. 'Jeanne over there told me that when the last one was on, she made a small fortune. She even got enough to put some in the savings bank. I'll bet you'd make more in a night than most girls earn in a month, Anna.' She looked me up and down. 'You're very pretty and you're not showing all that much yet. Anyway, a lot of men don't mind.'

Cécile frowned. 'What about the police? If they catch you, they make you register with them.'

'You just have to watch out for them, don't you?'

'I wouldn't want to end up in one of their inspection chairs,' Cécile shuddered. 'Indecent I call it. Some dirty old man calling himself a doctor, poking and prodding you and looking in places he shouldn't.'

'They all poke and prod you, love.' Amélie laughed. 'The only difference is - some of them pay.' She glanced at me. 'There's no need to look so high and mighty. Lots of girls do it. You'll get sick of living on a pittance sooner or later, like the rest of us do. Just don't come anywhere near my patch.'

She smiled but her tone held a hint of menace.

I tried to keep the anger out of my voice but I was shaking. 'My husband will be back before the baby's born.'

'And my husband's the Emperor of Japan.'

'Oh stop it, Amélie,' Cécile broke in. 'Leave her alone.'

With a shrug, Amélie flounced off.

Cécile squeezed my arm. 'Don't mind that bitch. If you do go to the exhibition though, try to look cheerful and smile at the men. They're more generous if you flatter them.'

When I didn't answer, she sighed. 'Oh well, please yourself, I was only trying to help. Of course if you want to change your mind, there's plenty of time. The exhibition will go on for months. You never know, you might be glad of the extra money after the baby comes.'

Chapter 6

June came and Paris sweltered. In Madame Roche's apartment, the stove had to be kept burning for the irons and the heat was almost unbearable.

With every day that passed, I felt heavier and more lethargic. While Monsieur Roche was out at work, Madame Roche allowed me to take off my dress and stockings and work in my petticoat, but even then, sweat bathed every inch of me and my damp hair clung to my forehead.

'Madame Meutrier next door says she'll lend you clothes for the baby,' Madame Roche remarked as we worked one day. 'They've been handed down through all of hers, but they might come in handy. I said you'd go and see her later on.'

I didn't relish the thought of Madame Meutrier's stained, threadbare things but I thanked Madame Roche and said I would go.

'Nine kids she's got. She'll be glad when she's past it. She took up with that no-good husband of hers when she was fourteen. Look where it's got her. It's a pity he doesn't put his energy into working instead of knocking her up all the time.'

I couldn't help thinking how scandalised Mother and Aunt Tatiana would be by such a remark. I finished folding a shirt and reached for another; it was of fine cream linen, intricately tucked and pleated, with ruffles on the cuffs. I dipped it in the bowl of starch on the floor beside me then set it aside and began to press a nightcap while I waited for the starch to set. But I worked on the nightcap too slowly. By the time I finished it, the shirt was past ironing. I dipped it again.

Madame Roche made an irritable noise. I expect she was as hot and out of sorts as I was. 'Starch costs money. You should know better by now.'

'Sorry,' I sighed, raising a limp arm to push my hair out of my eyes.

'Oh, never mind. Here, help me fold this sheet while you wait.'

I took two corners of the heavy sheet and began to fold it with her, but suddenly, the room swam. The sheet fell to the ground as I staggered against the ironing table, sending one of the hot irons crashing to the floor.

Madame Roche was beside me in a flash. Her strong arms lifted me up and she half dragged me to the chair by the window. She flung it open as wide as it would go.

'There, you'll be better in a trice with some air.'

My stomach felt as if it was full of hot coals. I gripped the sides of the chair and the sharp ends of the rushes under the seat bit into my palms. My heart thudded.

'What's happening to me?'

'Let's get you on the bed,' Madame Roche said. She sounded anxious.

A surge of pain consumed me. 'Not yet,' I gasped, fighting for breath.

When the pain subsided, supported by Madame Roche, I stumbled towards the bed, but before we could reach it, another wave forced me to stop. The respite that followed allowed me a few more shuffling steps but by the time I lay down, my jaw ached from clenching it. Through a wall of fog, I heard voices and running footsteps. Someone shook me violently and I opened my eyes to see Madame Roche's face looming over me.

'I've sent for Madame Binoche.'

I recognised the name of the local midwife.

'But it's too soon.'

'Lie quiet now.'

I struggled to sit up but it was too hard and I gave up the attempt. Over Madame Roche's shoulder, I saw one of our neighbours, flushed and panting for breath.

'Is she coming?' Madame Roche demanded.

'Yes, she wasn't far away.'

'Thank the Lord!'

There were heavy footsteps on the stairs and a stout, grey-haired woman bustled into the room. She inspected me with a detached air. 'How many months?'

'Nearly eight, I think,' I whispered miserably.

She took off her shawl and turned to Madame Roche. 'Bring me hot water and soap. I must wash before I take a look.'

Madame Roche brought the soap and water and Madame Binoche dipped her hands and soaped them briskly. When she had rinsed and dried them, she came to the bed. I was in too much pain to feel humiliated by the matter-of-fact way she pulled my legs apart and squinted between them, but I flinched as her plump, mottled fingers pushed inside me.

'You'll have to stay still,' she grumbled. 'I can't examine you properly if you don't.'

I gritted my teeth and tried not to cry out.

'It'll be a while,' she said, withdrawing her fingers after what seemed an eternity. 'Keep her warm, Madame Roche, and don't let her push yet. She'll need all her strength for later. I'll try and come back in an hour or two.'

After Madame Binoche had gone, Marie arrived. Her face was pale. She stroked my hand and began to cry.

'Now,' Madame Roche said firmly, 'none of that. Go to the café and fetch some brandy.'

When Marie returned, she held a glass to my lips. I sipped the fiery liquid and my throat burned. 'No more,' I spluttered, trying to push the glass away.

'You'll finish it,' Madame Roche said firmly. 'And be glad you did.'

I did as she said and soon, my eyelids drooped. I lost track of time and knew nothing except the pains, each one worse than the last, but dulled by the brandy as Madame Roche had known they would be.

Eventually, Madame Binoche returned. When she bent to examine me once more, I smelt absinthe.

'It's time,' she grunted. 'When the next one comes, you must push.'

I did as she said, but it was no good; my strength was ebbing fast.

Madame Binoche frowned and murmured something to Madame Roche. I gripped her hand as another contraction knocked the breath out of me.

'What did she say?' I gasped when it had it receded.

'She says the baby must come out. It can't wait any longer.'

Madame Binoche took something from her bag. It felt cold and hard as she pushed it between my legs. The pain had been bad before but now it was excruciating. I screamed.

'Hold her down,' ordered Madame Binoche.

I struggled as Madame Roche's powerful arms gripped me but she didn't let go. Just as I thought I could bear no more, Madame Binoche gave a shout of triumph. 'It's coming! Once more - push!'

I summoned the last of my strength and pushed. A moment later, an extraordinary sensation of release swept over me. Madame Roche stroked my forehead. Her cheeks glistened.

'Well done, Anna.'

I was too exhausted to speak, but I was so happy. It was over. I had survived. Then in the midst of my relief, fear crept in. Why didn't the baby cry? Surely all babies cried?

'The baby?' I croaked. 'Is it all right?'

'Poor little thing,' Madame Binoche muttered. The sadness in her voice made the back of my neck prickle. A chill came over me.

'What's wrong? Tell me!'

'It was a girl, but she came too soon. There's nothing I can do.'

A flood of emotion assailed me. 'Please,' I begged. 'Let me hold her.'

Madame Roche wrapped the wrinkled scrap of blood-smeared skin and bone that was my daughter in a shawl and held her out to me. I took her in my arms and rocked her gently. Under her fuzz of dark hair, every feature of her tiny face was perfect, but her skin was tinged blue-grey with bruising and the onset of death.

'Give her to me now, Anna,' Madame Roche said softly.

I didn't resist as she lifted the baby from my arms, but felt as if she'd ripped out my heart.

*

I burned then I was ice-cold. Whispering voices came and went in the fog that enveloped me. Sometimes I had a raging thirst that faded as someone dripped water into my mouth. Hours might have passed, or days, when I woke to feel something heavy press me down. Terrified it would suffocate me I thrashed out blindly, but when I opened my eyes I realised it was nothing more than the blankets piled on the bed.

Madame Roche hurried to my side. 'Anna, thank goodness. You're awake. You frightened us.'

All at once, my memory came back and my tears brimmed.

Madame Roche put her arms around me. 'There, there, you must be brave.'

I gulped and nodded.

'How long is it since . . .?'

'Nearly a week. You had a fever.'

'I've caused you so much trouble.'

'It was nothing. Marie sat with you when I couldn't.'

'My lodgings! They'll be angry I haven't paid. They'll throw me out.'

Madame Roche shook her head. 'Roche went to get your things and settled what you owed. Marie wants you to stay with her. You mustn't be alone yet. I would have you with us but there's only one room and with Roche it wouldn't be proper.'

*

Marie came the next day and took me to her lodgings. She lived on the top floor of her building and the climb up three flights of steep stairs exhausted me. Her room was at the back of the house, rather gloomy and bleak. Madame Roche, who had come with us to help, stayed for a while but I was too tired to talk and Marie seemed quiet. Soon Madame Roche stood up.

'Well, Roche'll be needing his dinner. Will you come over in an hour or two and fetch a plate for Anna, Marie?'

The thought of food made me gag.

'I couldn't eat,' I said hastily.

Madame Roche quelled me with a look. 'Nonsense, you need to build up your strength.'

Later that evening, Marie watched anxiously as I pushed the stew around the plate with my spoon.

'Please try, Anna.'

'I'm sorry, I can't. You eat it.'

She took the plate reluctantly but soon polished off the remains of the meal.

I fought to keep my eyes open but my head slumped on my breast. I jerked it back up when Marie patted my shoulder. 'You're worn out,' she said. 'Come, I'll help you to bed.'

'What about you?'

'Oh, I'll be all right. I can sleep on the chair.'

'You'll be so uncomfortable.'

She hesitated. 'We could share the bed - if it won't disturb you, that is.'

'It won't.'

She lay down beside me and her warmth soothed my weary, aching body. All at once, sorrow overwhelmed me once more and I wept.

'Poor Anna,' she said gently. She reached out and cradled me in her arms. 'Try to sleep. I'm here, I won't leave you.'

*

My constitution was strong and in a short time my body began to mend. The heartache was not so easily cured. However difficult it might have been to look after the baby, I would have cherished her for she would have been mine and Emile's.

I dreamt of him every night, his face suffused with delight to find that he was a father. The dreams made it all the harder when I woke and remembered the truth. Little by little, my faith in him returning ebbed.

I went back to live at my old lodgings and also resumed work with Madame Roche. I was often tearful and distracted but she quietly remedied my mistakes and bore my erratic moods without comment.

She normally chatted a lot while she worked, but as we ironed together one Monday afternoon, she was quiet and thoughtful.

'We should all go out to the country on Sunday,' she said suddenly. 'The fresh air will do you good. I'll speak to Roche about it.'

Marie came to eat with us that evening and as we cleared the dishes, Madame Roche talked about her plan. We would take the train from the Gare de l'Est and go to La Grenouillière, a popular bathing pool outside Paris.

'You'll love it there, Anna,' Marie said happily. 'It's so beautiful and the water will be warm at this time of year.'

'But I don't know how to swim!'

'It's easy, I'll show you. I've swum since I was a little girl. At home we used to go down to the river every day in the summer.'

'Marie swims like a fish,' Monsieur Roche chimed in. 'She'll be a good teacher.' He winked, 'Perhaps I'll come in too.'

Madame Roche snorted. 'We're both too old to go in the water now. Anyway, nobody wants to see an old whale like you floundering around. We'll just let the girls enjoy themselves.'

Marie spent hours making bathing costumes for us. For modesty, there were gathered pantaloons under the skirts and she also sewed mob caps so that we would be able to tuck up our hair.

When I arrived early on Sunday morning to go to the station, I found Madame Roche dressed in her best black, with purple ribbons decorating her bonnet.

Monsieur Roche nudged me. 'She's a splendid figure of a woman, eh Anna?'

Madame Roche wagged her finger at him. 'You won't get round me like that. Save your compliments for the girls, you old rogue.'

'They're lovely too of course,' he laughed. Already perspiring in his Sunday-best suit, he looked quite different from his workaday self. I was used to seeing him in his overalls and locksmith's apron.

Under the station canopy, the big black locomotives belched clouds of steam that wreathed and coiled into the soot-blackened roof. We had to shout to make ourselves heard above the rumbling and hissing of the engines. The screech of whistles and the clank of the great turntables used to swing the engines only increased the din.

Monsieur Roche surveyed the scene, a look of intense pride on his face. 'French engineering - it beats anything the rest of the world can do.'

It was already crowded when we arrived at La Grenouillière. The pond was large with a small island in the middle. Many people were swimming and the water looked cool and inviting. Beside a small wooden jetty, a handful of rowing boats bobbed up and down at the ends of their painters. Others were already out on the pond and the chatter and laughter of their occupants drifted over the water to where we stood.

We found a place in the shade of a tree and put down our baskets. Madame Roche spread out a large blue rug for us all to sit on. Nearby, a young woman was feeding her baby. The man with her, red-haired and luxuriantly bearded, played with a toddler who must have been barely a year older than the baby. The boy squealed with excitement as his father swung him up onto his broad shoulders and bounced him around. I looked wistfully at the happy family group, thinking of what might have been.

A little further away, a noisy group of young men and women sat on the grass talking and laughing. The men were dressed like dandies in canary yellow trousers, black frock coats and the absurdly high top hats that had been nicknamed 'stovepipes'. In comparison with theirs, our finery looked shabby. One of the girls had a little grey dog on her lap. It gazed adoringly at her with its black, button eyes and wagged its stumpy tail as she cooed to it. Her looks reminded me of my sister, Sonja.

I still collected the letters from the concierge at my old apartment. Last time I went, Mother had written that Sonja was expecting again. It was rather soon after the birth of Nicolai's baby sister, but Sonja was happy and in good health. I felt so sad to think I would probably never see any of my sister's children now.

'Roche and I will unpack everything,' Madame Roche said. 'Would you girls like to swim now?' She gestured to a large wooden hut. 'The changing rooms are over there - you'll need money for them.'

She handed Marie a few coins. 'When you've had enough, come and sit in the sunshine for a while before we eat.'

'Remember the area on the left of the island is for the men to swim in,' Monsieur Roche grinned. 'Don't let Marie lead you astray, Anna. You must go to the right, and no peeking!'

Madame Roche cuffed his arm. 'What nonsense you talk. Marie's a good girl.'

The woman at the entrance to the hut took our money and told us to bring our clothes to her for safekeeping when we'd changed. She pointed to a stack of towels on a low shelf inside the entrance. 'You can help yourself to one of those when you come back.'

We thanked her and went on through. There were only a few small windows in the changing hut and it took a moment or two for my eyes to become accustomed to the dim light. When they did, I let out an exclamation of dismay. We stood in a large room where all the bathers had to change into their costumes without any privacy. I had never taken my clothes off in front of strangers before.

'What's the matter?' asked Marie.

'I hadn't expected it to be like this.'

'Oh, I see. Don't worry - no one will look at you.'

She was already unfastening her dress but I hesitated.

'Come on, or we'll never get to the water.'

Feeling very awkward, I took off my clothes and put on the bathing costume as fast as I could. Marie helped me to tie the ribbons that fastened it at

105

the back and then turned around for me to do the same for her. She tilted her head forwards and swept her hair out of the way to allow me to reach the topmost ribbon. Where the sun hadn't touched it, the nape of her neck was pale and covered with fine golden down. I tied the last bow and smoothed the ribbon. Marie didn't move for a moment, then she turned and smiled.

We walked out into the sunshine. Suddenly, I was nervous. 'Marie, perhaps I should go back,' I began, but she took me firmly by the hand.

'It's easy, I promise you.'

I let her lead me to the edge of the pond and watched as she slithered into the water with the suppleness of an eel. She held out her arms. 'You can stand here. It's quite shallow. Sit on the bank first and then slide in.'

I sat down and put my feet into the water; it was delightfully cool. Marie took my hands and pulled me in gently. My feet sank into the soft sand on the bottom.

'Hold onto me and we'll go a bit deeper. Don't be afraid. I won't let you go.'

The ground disappeared beneath my feet and I shrieked, swallowing a mouthful of water.

Marie slid her hands under my armpits to hold me up. I spluttered and choked as she towed me back to the shallows.

'You're supposed to keep your mouth shut,' she laughed. 'Now, let's try again, and this time, if your feet leave the ground, kick gently with your legs. But we'll try and stay in the shallow part for now.'

At my next attempt, I managed much better. Marie towed me round in wide circles, smiling her encouragement.

'Now we must teach you how to float, so if you're frightened when you're out of your depth, you can just roll over on your back and you'll be perfectly safe.'

I turned onto my back, but sank almost immediately, taking in more mouthfuls of water.

'You must relax. Perhaps it will be easier if I hold you up.'

This time I was more successful. Marie spread her fingers under the small of my back and the gentle pressure held me afloat. I lay on the surface of the water, its warmth relaxing me. I seemed to be suspended between the pool and the sky in a blissful dream. For the first time in weeks, I felt a sensation of peace.

The splashing of other swimmers around us roused me.

'Do you think you could swim to the island?' Marie asked.

'I think so, but you will hold me if I sink won't you?'

'No, I'll let you drown,' Marie giggled.

We set out into the middle of the pond. Marie swam backwards, holding my hands as I kicked with increasing confidence even though the island had at first looked a very long way away. We had to make a lot of twists and turns to avoid other people. At last we reached the island and I grabbed the bank with relief.

'There, you did it. Aren't you proud of yourself?'

I was too breathless to speak for a few moments and just nodded.

'You're tired,' Marie said. 'We'll rest awhile before we swim back.'

There were willow trees growing on the island. Their trailing branches dipped into the pond like pale-green curtains, concealing little refuges from the sun. We drifted into one of these shady places; I smelt the rich scent of peaty earth.

The reflection of the cascading leaves and the rays of sunshine that penetrated their trailing fronds had turned the water to a haze of green and gold. Where the bank had been worn away by water, the willows' roots stood proud of the earth, twisted into fantastical shapes and crusted with yellow-green moss. I traced a finger along one of the serpentine lines, feeling the hard wood under the mossy covering.

'I'm so glad we came,' I remarked. 'Madame Roche was right. The fresh air is doing me good and this is such a lovely place.'

I heard a rustle of leaves and a girl's face parted the green curtain.

The newcomer giggled. 'Oh Lord,' she called over her shoulder to some unseen companion, 'we're interrupting something.'

Marie scowled at her.

'Sorry,' the girl said. 'It was just a joke.'

'Good riddance,' Marie muttered, as the girl dropped the green curtain and swam away.

'What did she mean?'

Marie shrugged. 'Take no notice.'

After a few more minutes, we went back to the jetty and got out of the pond. We returned to the hut, passing the queue of women and girls waiting to put their wet costumes through a mangle, and took our towels and clothes from the attendant.

The hut was even more crowded than before. The attendant took a quick look and told us that we could use one of the old cabins round the back if we'd prefer it.

The old cabins were hidden in a stand of spindly pine trees. The ground was carpeted with needles that scratched our bare feet. With difficulty, Marie pulled open a cabin door. It had splintered at the bottom and hung awkwardly on rusty hinges.

As I followed Marie into the gloomy little room, something sharp ripped into the sole of my foot. I gave a yelp of pain.

'What is it?' Marie asked anxiously.

'I think I've cut my foot.'

A narrow wooden bench stood against one wall. I sat down and Marie gently lifted up my foot and inspected it.

'It's just a splinter. I think I can get it out. Stay still.'

'Ouch! That really hurts.'

'I'll do it this way then.'

She put her lips to the place and began to suck out the splinter. I held my breath.

'There, all done,' she whispered, looking up at me. She bent over again and kissed my foot then her lips moved up my calf and stopped at the soft hollow behind my knee. It was so long since anyone

109

had touched me there; in spite of my shock, something in me stirred.

She looked at me beseechingly. 'Oh Anna, don't you understand? I can't bear to hide it any longer.'

I recoiled as if someone had thrown cold water over me. Marie looked at my horrified expression and her face crumpled. She snatched up her things and ran out of the hut, banging the door behind her. My thoughts in turmoil, I changed as quickly as I could and went outside. She was nowhere to be seen.

I returned to where the Roches had been sitting. Marie was helping Madame Roche to set out the picnic and Monsieur Roche was stretched out in the shade, contentedly puffing on his pipe.

'Did you enjoy your swim?' he asked. 'Marie is a good teacher, eh?'

I smiled and tried to behave as if nothing was amiss. Marie wouldn't look at me.

'It's time for our picnic,' Madame Roche said. 'You must be hungry after the exercise.' She continued to arrange loaves of bread, a triangle of cheese, apples and some bottles of wine on the rug.

My appetite had gone but I did my best to eat. It was so generous of Madame Roche to provide such a feast and of course she would be bound to want to know what was wrong with me if she saw I was not touching the food. Marie only spoke to Monsieur and Madame Roche and wouldn't meet my eye.

At last, Monsieur Roche announced he was stuffed and couldn't eat another mouthful. He lay back on the grass and was soon snoring under the brim of his tilted hat. Madame Roche chattered on for a while and then fell asleep too.

Marie jumped up.

'Some of the girls from Madame Caron's are here. I'm going to find them.' She was gone before I had time to reply.

I sat in the shade, squirming at the thought of my innocence. One of the books in Papa's library – one he would probably have forbidden me to read if he had known what it contained – had spoken of love between women. I remembered the hugs and kisses, the confidences Marie and I had shared. How had I been so blind? I should have realised that to Marie, they might have meant something more than friendship. I had hurt her and I regretted it bitterly. It would be impossible for us to be easy together again.

The shadows lengthened by the time Marie returned. Madame Roche woke with a start and shook her husband. 'Wake up, you lazy creature! Do I have to pack up everything by myself?'

I was glad of the bustle of our preparations to leave. Madame Roche was too busy to notice that Marie and I avoided each other's eyes and didn't speak.

Along with many other groups, we straggled back to the station, loaded down with our baskets. Refreshed by her sleep, Madame Roche talked all the way to Paris. I helped to take everything back to the Roches' rooms and unpack. I wished I could think of some way of asking Marie to forgive me. She looked so unhappy and my heart bled for her. Soon, she thanked the Roches and left us.

I walked back to my lodgings with a heavy heart.

Chapter 7

I met Cécile again late one afternoon as I was coming back from work.

'Hello, Anna!' she called out cheerfully from the other side of the street and walked over to me. It lifted my despondent spirits to listen to her good-natured, gossipy talk.

'I'm going to see the Great Exhibition tomorrow. Do you want to come with me?'

I hesitated.

'Oh, take no notice of what Amélie was saying. There doesn't have to be anything like that. Do say yes, it'll be a lark. You'll be sorry if you miss all the fun. We could ask your pal Marie along too if you like.'

To my dismay, heat rushed to my cheeks and Cécile looked at me curiously. 'Have you two had a row?'

'No, of course not. I just don't think she'd enjoy it'

Cécile shrugged. 'If you say so.' She squeezed my arm, 'Look, the man at the tabac next to the bakers let me have this. Perhaps it'll change your mind.' She handed me a crumpled newspaper, several days old. It was full of pictures of the exhibition and the people who had visited it.

Cécile pointed excitedly to a picture of a stout, swarthy man dressed in opulent oriental robes and a bejewelled turban. 'Doesn't he look grand? I wonder who he is.'

'It says here he's the Shah of Persia.'

'And this one?'

'The British Queen, Victoria.'

'A queen? But she looks so short and dowdy. What does it say about her?'

'Cécile, can't you read?' I asked and immediately regretted my lack of tact.

She looked away and mumbled, 'I'm not clever like you.'

'It does look great fun,' I said quickly, wanting to smooth over the awkward moment. 'I'd love to come with you, Cécile,'

She beamed. 'Good, that's settled.'

*

When we reached the Champ de Mars the following evening, a wonderful sight met our eyes. The great pavilion housing the main exhibits blazed with light. It was hard to credit that such an enormous building was composed of nothing more than glass and iron. To our disappointment however, when we went up to the ticket desk, we found we didn't have enough money to go in.

'Never mind,' Cécile said. 'We'll still have fun looking around at everything out here.'

Gas lamps and flares illuminated a crowded scene that might have come straight out of *The Tales of the Arabian Nights*. All kinds of buildings that had been specially constructed for the exhibition had sprung up everywhere – a fantastical toy collection of temples, palaces, domes and minarets. There was even a model of the Coliseum in Rome. Banners and flags rippled in the warm breeze and the bewildering number of languages being spoken around us heightened the deliciously exotic atmosphere.

I heard a few words of Russian and saw two men with the broad, flat, Mongolian features I recognised from home. They were leading little steppe ponies loaded with colourful woollen rugs. I smiled and bid them 'good evening' in Russian.

Cécile frowned. 'What was that language you spoke in?'

'Russian - I was born in Russia.'

'Gracious, it does sound odd.' She grabbed my arm. 'Come on, I want to have a look at the bracelets on that stall over there.'

At the stall, she examined the wares carefully and haggled over a pretty, enamelled bracelet, but the stallholder wouldn't budge on his price. In the end, she agreed to pay it.

We moved on to another area. It was clear there was no need for anyone to go hungry for there were dozens of stalls selling food. There were bowls of all kinds of appetising stews; many types of cheeses; pears, apples, grapes and Spanish oranges; dates from Egypt and sugary Turkish sweetmeats crammed with nuts. The variety was endless. I saw a stall where a Russian woman in traditional dress was offering festival biscuits, freshly baked in a charcoal stove. I couldn't resist buying some. It was lovely to speak Russian with her, even if it was only for a few moments. The woman smiled at me and slipped a few extra into the bag.

Munching the warm biscuits, Cécile and I walked on past a stall where girls in crimson skirts and tight black bodices worn over embroidered blouses were selling foaming tankards of beer. The powerful aroma of hops and yeast mingled with the rich smell of the coffee brewed at another stall by an old man in Arab robes.

A loud, wailing sound nearby made both Cécile and me jump.

'What on earth is that?' Cécile shrieked. We turned to see a tall, dark-skinned man standing at the entrance to a silky tent crowned with scarlet plumes. He blew a second blast on his strange-looking trumpet, puffing out his cheeks until they were as round as apples. He wore a tunic and an elaborate, golden headdress that reached down over his shoulders. Around his neck was a heavy gold necklace in the shape of a snake and thick gold bracelets circled his arms.

He let the trumpet fall to his side and his deep voice rose over the hubbub. 'Next show in half an hour!' he boomed. 'Look upon the mysteries of ancient Egypt! See the two thousand year old mummy, brought from the tombs of the pharaohs for your edification!'

He swung round to smile at us. 'How about you, lovely ladies? Do you want to see it? I'll make you a special price.'

Cécile's nose wrinkled. 'No, I'd be sick to my stomach.'

She took my hand and pulled me away. 'I bet it's a trick anyway,' she whispered. 'That was bootblack on his face. I could smell it.'

We moved on to watch a fire-eater breathing out jets of flame in a most alarming way. Beyond him was an aisle decorated to look like an Arab souk. A veiled woman sat cross-legged beside a small fire offering to tell fortunes in a crystal ball. She saw us and beckoned, setting the silver bracelets on her brown forearms flashing in the firelight.

'Keep walking,' Cécile said. 'We're not wasting our money on spooky nonsense.'

We left the souk behind and came to a row of wine shops. Around there, many people were already drunk and I started to feel uncomfortable. A grinning man lurched into me, so close that I could smell his fetid, winey breath. I dodged him and he fell into the arms of a red-haired woman who swore and pushed him away.

It was getting very hot in the crowd. I plucked at Cécile's sleeve. 'Perhaps we should go home?'

'Whatever for?' she asked crossly. 'The night's only just beginning.'

A few steps further on, she grabbed my arm. 'Slow down. They're following us.'

I looked behind. Two men loitered there, watching us.

'Let's walk on quickly,' I whispered.

117

'No, go slowly.'

The men were quite young and both nattily dressed. The tall one had black hair and a neatly clipped beard and moustache. His friend was stocky with corn-coloured hair and mutton-chop whiskers. They tipped their hats to us when they saw we had noticed them and sauntered in our direction.

'Good evening, ladies,' the stocky one said in clumsy French. 'We've just arrived from London. Might we be so bold as to ask for your company?'

Cécile giggled. 'Perhaps for a little while.'

She took the arm he proffered and his friend offered me his. The crowd eddied around us as we introduced ourselves. The stocky man was called Alfred, the tall one George.

It was difficult to stand still in the press of people, so we walked on. Cécile chattered animatedly and teased Alfred about his French accent. He ploughed on, admiring her new bracelet and laughing at remarks he probably only half understood. George was much quieter and beads of perspiration glinted on his forehead. I wondered whether it was the heat of the crowd or whether he felt as uncomfortable as I did.

Alfred turned to him. 'Come on, old chap: talk to the girl,' he said in English. 'You won't get anywhere like that.' He obviously didn't realise I spoke some English and understood, but I couldn't follow George's muttered reply.

'My friend says he's hungry,' Alfred said in French. 'Would you ladies do us the honour of joining us for a bite?'

Before I had time to open my mouth to say no, Cécile had agreed.

We found a restaurant and a waiter showed us to one of the few empty booths. It was partitioned off from the rest of the room by mahogany screens, inset with panels of engraved glass. The gaslight shining on them made them glow like mother-of-pearl.

It was a treat just to sit there. The white table cloth was thick and crisply starched. The cutlery gleamed and the china wasn't chipped. In the middle of the table, a small crystal vase held a single yellow rose. The cosy atmosphere reassured me a little as I savoured the smell of good food wafting from the kitchens.

Alfred made a great play of studying the wine list and ordered two bottles. 'Just for starters, eh,' he said squeezing Cécile's arm. I sipped the glass the waiter poured for me. It tasted deliciously of plums and wood smoke.

The men ordered oysters, followed by beef with asparagus and peas. The oysters slipped down my throat like nectar. Cécile ate hers greedily, tipping her head back as she swallowed each one so that she showed off her slim white neck. I could tell Alfred was fascinated by her. He had drunk a lot of the wine by then and his face was flushed.

They sat closer and closer together as the evening wore on, laughing uproariously at each other's jokes. George watched their antics with amusement. Empty bottles littered the table and he had begun to talk more readily in a halting mixture of French and English.

We finished our meal and went back outside. It had been a long time since I had eaten such rich food or drunk so much wine; my head was swimming. Alfred and Cécile swayed along in front of us, arms around each other's waists.

'Come on, we're going to a show!' Alfred shouted over his shoulder. Cécile wiggled her hips and he laughed and planted a kiss on her neck.

The cabaret we went to was dark and stuffy. We found a table near the back and Alfred ordered more wine. On stage, in the glare of the gaslight, a heavily rouged girl with flame-red hair was dancing the cancan, kicking up her long legs exuberantly in time to the music and swinging her orange and yellow skirts from side to side, showing the black stockings she wore underneath. The music reached a crescendo and on the last crashing chord, she landed on the boards in the splits. The audience roared with approval.

Alfred and Cécile soon lost interest in the show and began kissing enthusiastically. His hands paddled in the neck of her dress and she didn't push them away. The wine and the atmosphere had made George bolder too. He began to stroke my neck. I froze as he pressed his thigh against mine.

Alfred pulled Cécile to her feet. 'There's dancing out in the gardens. Come on, you two, let's go and join in.'

The dance floor was set up in a clearing surrounded by arbours of bushes and trees. The orchestra played a lively waltz.

George took me firmly by the waist and whirled me onto the floor. He pressed his cheek close to mine and his moustache scratched my skin; he hummed tunelessly under his breath.

Suddenly, I noticed that Alfred and Cécile had vanished. The music stopped and George suggested we sit down. However instead of taking me back to our table, he pulled me into the trees, away from the lights of the dance floor. I wished I hadn't drunk so much. My head was too fuddled with wine to protest.

Muffled shrieks and laughter came from the shadows around us. George's wet lips smothered me and alarmed, I tried to get away from him. He stopped trying to kiss me but tightened his grip and clamped his hand over my mouth instead. 'Silly bitch, you can't say no now.'

I struggled but he pushed me against a tree. With his free hand, he fumbled with the opening of his trousers, then grabbed my skirt and yanked it up to my waist. I wasn't strong enough to push him away and I froze in panic.

'Damnation,' George muttered. 'It must be the wine.'

He kept me pinned to the tree while his hand went back to the opening of his trousers. 'Come on, come on,' he groaned.

All at once, my wits returned. His bent head was close to mine. I stretched and sank my teeth into his ear as hard as I could. With a howl, he let me go and before he had time to recover, I ran.

I reached the dance floor, my legs wobbly as jelly and my heart hammering. There was no sign of Cécile. A voice behind me – George's I feared – set me running again, barging through groups of people who turned to look at me in astonishment. It was hardly surprising. I must have been an extraordinary sight with my dishevelled hair and tear-stained face. I didn't stop until a stitch in my side brought me to a halt.

I was in an unlit alley. Heart still pounding, I leant against the wall and listened intently, but no footsteps followed me. After a while, I summoned my courage and walked out to a main road. A few couples wandered along it, laughing and talking. With relief, I heard the rumble of an omnibus and saw a boarding place nearby. I couldn't really spare the money but I hurried to the stop and climbed on.

Back in my lodgings, I stripped off all my clothes and flung a wash rag into the bowl of cold water left over from the morning. I rubbed soap onto it, then scrubbed myself all over until my skin was red raw. As soon as I was able to, I would wash everything I had been wearing.

*

The following afternoon, I saw Cécile in the street. She didn't seem at all perturbed by the sight of me and bounced over with a big smile.

'Why on earth did you run off like that? Alfred was very generous and I expect his friend would've been too if you'd played your cards right. Alfred took me back to the stall where I bought the bracelet and got me the necklace that went with it. And some new shoes as well.'

I didn't reply and her smile turned to a scowl. 'There's no need to look like that. I've not done anyone any harm. You're a bit choosy you know, Anna. Still, they're leaving Paris tomorrow so you needn't worry about seeing them again. Next time we go down, you might find someone you like better.'

I didn't want an argument so I refrained from telling her that for me, there would not be a next time.

*

'It's strange,' Madame Roche remarked as we finished work one evening a few days later. 'Marie hasn't come to visit us all week. Have you seen her?'

I kept my eyes on the shirt I was pressing. 'Not for a while.'

'I'm sure I'd have heard if she was ill, but perhaps you'd go over there to make sure?'

'I still have so much work to do,' I said weakly.

'If you girls've had an argument, not talking won't put it right. You'd better go and sort it out. You can leave the clothes. They can be done tomorrow.'

Apprehensively, I climbed the stairs to Marie's room and knocked on the door.

'Who is it?' Marie called out.

'It's me: Anna.'

I heard a rustle of skirts and then silence. I waited for a few moments, half wanting her to let me in and half dreading it, then, just as I was about to give up, the door opened slowly.

I swallowed hard. 'Madame Roche was worried about you, Marie. She asked me to come and see if you're all right.'

She took a step backwards. 'Will you come in?' she asked in a small voice.

In the gloomy room, the silence lay between us like an ocean. I wished I hadn't come.

Marie crossed to the window and stood with her back to me. Her shoulders shook and I realised she was crying. I went to her and she turned to hide her face against my shoulder. I put my arms around her. She was fragile as a sparrow.

'Let's sit down,' I said. 'We must talk.'

We sat on her narrow bed, for there was nowhere else to sit in the room. Tentatively, I took her hand. Her nails were bitten to the quick.

'I thought that you loved me,' she blurted out.

'Oh Marie, I do.'

'But not in the way I love you.'

Her voice was full of anguish and it racked my heart with pity.

'You said once that I was like a sister to you,' she said. 'I wanted to be more than that and I started to believe you felt the same.'

In spite of myself, I stiffened. Marie pulled away from me and her shoulders sagged. 'I must disgust you,' she said in a low, miserable voice.

'No, never that! Marie, I'd give anything not to have hurt you. I didn't understand how you felt.' Even as I said them, the words sounded inadequate.

'Can we still be friends?' I implored.

Marie looked at me miserably. 'I don't know if I can do that, Anna. I think it would be better not to.'

There seemed to be nothing more that I could say. With a hollow heart, I left her alone in the dismal room.

Chapter 8

On my return to my lodgings one evening, a few weeks after my visit to Marie, I met the landlady bustling out from her room.

'There was a gentleman asking for you earlier,' she said stiffly.

My heart immediately pounded. Emile?

'He said he'd come back later. I hope I don't need to remind you, I don't allow gentlemen in the rooms. This is a respectable house.'

I was too excited to care about her scowling innuendo. Why would a man visit me? It must be Emile. He had surely come back and everything would be explained.

I'd saved some bread and cheese for my supper but had no appetite; my heart was too full. All I could think of was the moment when I would be in Emile's arms again.

Just before nine o'clock, I heard a light footfall on the stairs and the landlady's maid called through the door. 'Please, Madame Daubigny, there's a gentleman for you downstairs.'

My heart raced. I looked in the mirror for a final time, smoothed my hair and pinched my cheeks, then hurried downstairs.

I wish I could say that Emile was waiting for me, ready to sweep me up in his arms and take me away. The truth was that as I reached the bottom step, I stopped abruptly and my greeting froze on my lips.

A small, dapper man, probably in his late fifties, was standing there. He wore dark, conservative clothes and carried a neatly furled black umbrella.

He bowed. 'Good evening, Madame, we have not met before. May I introduce myself? My name is Marcel Noilly. Would you do me the honour of taking a walk with me?'

'It's rather late, Monsieur,' I faltered.

'I assure you, I shall not take up much of your time.' He offered me his arm.

The landlady watched us curiously from the door of her room.

'Very well, Monsieur,' I replied. After all, what harm could there be in a walk?

It was a pleasant evening. As we strolled along, Monsieur Noilly explained he owned some property nearby and had noticed me several times when he came to collect rent from his tenants. I listened politely, wondering where the conversation was leading. Surely he hadn't invited me to walk with him merely to discuss his business affairs?

We passed a café and he suggested that we stop for a drink. The place was noisy, full of people and tobacco smoke. He ordered a glass of wine for me and a cognac for himself. After the waiter brought them, he cleared his throat.

'Forgive me, Madame, if the question is impertinent, but are you alone here in Paris?'

'Why do you ask, Monsieur?'

He looked at my left hand. 'I see you wear a ring, but I have never seen you with your husband.'

A terrible thought flashed into my mind. Perhaps he was one of Count Marly's men. The concierge at our old apartment must have told him where to find me. Panic constricted my throat but I tried to keep my voice steady.

'If you are looking for my husband, Monsieur, I'm afraid I can't help you. I have no idea where he is. I haven't heard from him for nearly a year.'

Monsieur Noilly smoothed his moustache. He doesn't believe me, I thought despairingly. 'I have no money, Monsieur. I beg you to let me alone.'

He leant across the table. I smelt eau de cologne and clean linen.

'I have no wish to harm you, Madame,' he said in a solemn voice. 'On the contrary, I hope to be able to help you. Paris is not always a friendly place. I think that if I were your husband, I would not leave you alone here, but as that is the case, might I suggest something?'

He reached out a plump, well-manicured hand and placed it over mine. Someone more worldly than I would probably have anticipated his proposition. As it was, he had to explain it, which he did with careful delicacy. I learnt he was married, but for many years, he and his wife had not shared a bed.

'Madame,' he concluded, 'no doubt you think my proposal strange, but at my time and station in life, I have very little – how shall I put it - opportunity to console myself, not, at least, in circumstances I find acceptable. It's clear to me from the way you speak and carry yourself that you were not born to the life you lead. I do not wish to offend you. If you refuse my proposal, I shall respect your decision. However, I am confident I can offer you a life that will be more fitting for a lady of your breeding than your present one.'

He fell silent for a moment, apparently deliberating how to phrase his next words, then, 'All I ask in return is that you do not share your favours with other men.'

I was lost for a reply.

Monsieur Noilly smiled gently. 'Your hesitation is understandable, Madame. By all means, take your time to decide. Perhaps I may visit you again in a few days?'

He spoke so courteously, it was impossible to take offence. My horrible experience with the Englishman, George, flashed through my mind, but Monsieur Noilly seemed a kind man. If I turned him down, the prospect of a life of struggling to make ends meet stretched endlessly ahead. I was shocked to hear myself reply, 'Certainly, Monsieur.'

He beamed and squeezed my hand. 'Then I shall come at eleven o'clock on Saturday.'

He walked me home and kissed my hand when we parted. I enjoyed seeing the landlady goggle at the sight of my being treated like a lady, and by a man who was obviously well off and respectable. When Monsieur Noilly had departed, she stopped me before I could run upstairs.

'Don't forget, gentlemen aren't allowed in the rooms,' she said spitefully.

'I'm well aware of that, Madame.'

She went back to her lair, muttering.

I spent most of that night thinking over Monsieur Noilly's proposal and its possible consequences. He was old enough to be my father but he offered a release from drudgery and I was so tired. In my heart, I also knew that accepting him would be tantamount to admitting I had given up hope of Emile's return, but perhaps the time had come to forget the past and try to rebuild my life. Conflicting emotions warred in my heart but slowly, I came to the conclusion I should say yes to Monsieur Noilly.

On the Saturday, he arrived punctually. As we strolled together, I gave him my answer. Smiling, he tucked my hand into the crook of his arm. 'I promise you, my dear, you won't regret it.'

*

Thus, in the eyes of the world, I forfeited my place in the company of respectable women. To describe my fall from grace as a seduction seemed inappropriate. In romantic novels, women lost their good name in a whirl of passion and clandestine intrigue, but from the first, my relationship with Monsieur Noilly was calm and decorous. He was such a gentleman he never made me feel ashamed of what I had become.

Even though I had managed to convince myself that my decision was the right one, at first I had put off telling Madame Roche. Monsieur Roche had no time for the church, but I knew she still went to confession and the church's teaching was that adultery was a sin. I had grown to value her good opinion and I didn't like to think of her disapproving of me. Several days passed before I summoned the courage to speak out.

All morning, we starched and pressed shirts for one of the local tailors. The heat from the stove was oppressive and sweat stuck my shift to my back. Madame Roche huffed and puffed as she lifted a heavy iron and tested it on a piece of old rag.

'About right,' she remarked. 'Joubert gives me plenty of business. We mustn't scorch anything and anger him.'

I took a deep breath. I had rehearsed what I planned to say over and over again in my mind but the words came out in a clumsy rush. Madame Roche banged the iron back onto its stand and stared at me. My heart sank as her brow furrowed. Then a look of sadness replaced the frown.

'It's not for me to tell you what to do,' she said. 'I've always thought you too good for this kind of life, and if you're to escape, you need to do it while you're still young and pretty.'

I'd expected disapproval, coldness even. Her sorrowful expression affected me far more than condemnation would have.

'Thank you for understanding, Madame.'

'Roche and I will miss you.'

'And I'll miss you.'

'Have you told Marie?'

I didn't know what to say. Marie had avoided me since my last visit to her lodgings and, although

I had racked my brains for some way of putting matters right with her, it had all been in vain.

Madame Roche's eyes raked over me. 'Have you quarrelled about some man?'

I shook my head, colouring at the impossibility of an explanation.

She shrugged. 'Well, you must make up your own mind. One thing I won't do is tell her for you.'

*

Monsieur Noilly told me he was preparing somewhere for me to live and it would only be a few more days before the place was ready. I couldn't postpone telling Marie any longer. I walked through the streets to her lodgings, apprehension making my stomach churn. At the door to her room, I reached for the tarnished knocker and rapped once. 'Marie,' I called, 'it's me, Anna. May I come in?'

There was a rustle on the other side of the door.

'Marie?' I repeated. 'Please - can we talk?'

The door opened a crack and she looked out. Her eyes were dull.

'So it's true you're going? That's why you've come, I suppose.'

'Who told you?'

She shrugged. 'There've been rumours.'

'I'm so sorry,' I whispered.

She grasped the door frame. Her knucklebones were white knobs in work-reddened hands. 'I hope you'll be happy, Anna,' she said in a low voice. 'But please go now. I don't want to talk anymore.'

Chapter 9

The pattern of my days changed completely. I had no work to do and unless Monsieur Noilly visited, my idle hours were merely punctuated by the visits of the couturier and the hairdresser he paid for. It wasn't long before time hung heavily on my hands. Sometimes the circumstances of my new life distressed me, but I decided it best not to question the rights and wrongs of it.

The apartment Monsieur Noilly rented for me was in the rue Chateaudun, a street in a newly developed part of the city near the boulevard des Italiens, a little to the south of Montmartre. It was a pleasant, and quite inexpensive, area within hearing distance of the bells of Notre Dame de Lorette.

My comfortable living quarters comprised four rooms: a drawing room, a small dining room, a bedroom and a bathroom. The walls of the drawing room and dining room were hung with heavily embossed wallpaper of a dull brown. The sofas and chairs were upholstered in burgundy plush. In the bedroom, a large, mahogany-framed bed and a massive wardrobe with mirror-fronted doors took up most of the space. Black and white tiles covered the bathroom's floor and walls and its old-fashioned fittings were spotlessly clean. The whole effect was of bourgeois solidity and comfort.

Monsieur Noilly preferred us to spend our time together quietly in the apartment. He was unlike the men I had met when I first came to Paris. *They* had flourished in a glittering social milieu, where business took second place to pleasure, and money to spend on luxuries seemed to flow in endless streams. Although Monsieur Noilly probably had more money than many of them, his aspirations were no greater than to be a respectable member of the bourgeoisie. He was not a man who desired to flaunt his wealth or his mistress.

I was to learn that the punctilious way in which he asked me to become his mistress was typical of him. Even in the bedroom, he was formal and gentlemanly. He visited me several times a week and always brought flowers. Usually he came for a few hours in the afternoon; less frequently he stayed the whole night. The neat way he folded his clothes before climbing into bed made me smile.

I could hardly have expected Monsieur Noilly's lovemaking to thrill me as Emile's had done but he was always considerate. In truth though, I think he was happiest when we sat by the fire together just talking, or when he lay with his head on my breast after he had made love to me.

'Stroke my head, Anna,' he would say. 'It soothes me.'

So I did. His white hair, dwindled to a small crescent at the back of his head, reminded me of a pale new moon. Where it stretched over the hollows and bumps of his skull, his skin was papery and mottled.

I was glad he looked nothing like my father. Papa was a splendid Russian bear of a man. In contrast, Monsieur Noilly was slight in build although a lifetime of good eating had added a substantial paunch to his frame. I refused to let myself think about how different that frame was from Emile's lithe, muscular body.

Monsieur Noilly rarely mentioned his wife, perhaps it was out of delicacy, but he was fond of talking about his youth. 'And when I'm in your company, Anna,' he joked, 'I really believe I have it back again.' He popped the last bite of his second chocolate éclair into his mouth and wiped his lips with his napkin. 'I was born on the 31st of December. My mother used to tease me that I was a naughty boy because I made her miss the fireworks.'

He was the third son of a large family, brought up in a comfortable home in an area of Paris that was prosperous and respectable rather than fashionable. 'France was a great power then,' he said. 'The whole of Europe trembled at the name of Bonaparte, our Emperor's uncle.' He sighed. 'The classics teach us that pride comes before a fall and glory never lasts. When the English defeated us at Waterloo, it was a black day for France. I was too young to know much about it, but they say people wept openly in the streets.'

He eyed the cake stand for a moment then selected a macaroon topped with toasted almonds. He bit off a mouthful and his expression brightened.

'But we rose again from the ashes and look at us now – Paris is the envy of the world.'

He paused while he savoured the little cake then wiped his lips once more. 'Long live the Emperor,' he beamed.

*

The servants Monsieur Noilly engaged to look after me lived in the staff quarters at the rear of the apartment. The youngest, Rose, was a pretty girl with dark brown hair. She looked after my clothes and, when she helped me with my toilette, made up in enthusiasm for what she lacked in skill. Her chatter helped to pass the tedious hours. An older woman, Isabel, cooked and dealt with the tradesmen as well as directing the maid, Jeanne, who cleaned the apartment and served the meals. The heavy work was done by a manservant called Fabrice.

The rue Maubeuge, the main thoroughfare leading up to the Gare du Nord was close at hand. It would have been easy to enliven my solitary days by revisiting my old haunts, but I hesitated to do so. I did want to be sure though that I answered any letters which came from home, so I chose days when I was sure Monsieur Noilly would not visit and continued to go back to the apartment I'd shared with Emile to see the concierge.

'I can't go on saving letters for you forever,' she grumbled on one of my visits. 'Anyway, I've heard Count Marly will be selling the building. I may lose my job and have to leave.'

It seemed unlikely he would want to sell such a profitable investment. She was probably angling for a better tip than usual, but I didn't want to annoy her so I gave her a few francs extra.

On the way back to the rue Chateaudun, however, I decided it was time to tell my parents that Emile and I had moved to the new address. I was confident the news would not raise their suspicions. I would just tell them our lease had come to an end and the landlord did not want to renew it.

A few weeks afterward, a letter arrived from Mother telling me Sonja had been safely delivered of a baby boy. I read Mother's description of the family's joy and suddenly, the contrast between my sister's happy, fecund family life and my own empty one brought tears to my eyes.

A soft sound made me look up. Rose had come into the room with the tea things. She glanced at me sympathetically as she set the tray down on the small table beside my chair.

'Not bad news I hope, Madame?' she enquired.

'No, Rose, it's good news. My sister has had another baby.' My words should have sounded happy but my voice betrayed me.

'Perhaps Monsieur Noilly will take you to visit your family one day?'

'Perhaps.'

She left me and I carried on reading the letter. Mother ended her part by saying Papa too had some good news for me.

Papa's large, flamboyant handwriting covered the next page:

My dearest Anna, I have the opportunity to visit Paris on business and although, as you know, I dislike travelling, the thought of seeing my little girl has convinced me to come. I am looking forward to spending some quiet time with you and, of course, Emile. Please assure him that an old dog like me does not need to be shown the high life! All I want is to see you with my own eyes and hear the voice I have missed so much.
Yours affectionately,
Papa.

My head reeled. I had dreaded my parents finding out my true situation and now it seemed there was little I could do to prevent it. I pictured the scene of Papa's arrival with absolute horror. In my heart I knew it would be cruel to subject him to such a shock at the end of his long journey. I must write to him, even if it meant he cast me off immediately. Yet, whenever I took up my pen, words eluded me. I hated myself for my cowardice.

I felt obliged to tell Monsieur Noilly and his matter-of-fact kindness touched me. 'It is only natural that your father should want to see you, my dear. I think it best, however, if I absent myself. It will avoid embarrassment for all of us.'

Several days later, I was reading in the drawing room when Rose brought in a note. It was from Papa at his hotel. He had arrived in Paris the previous night and wrote that he proposed to visit Emile and me that afternoon. I spent the next few hours in a state of great agitation.

Rose served my lunch but I could not have said what I ate. Just before three, Papa was announced.

He held out his arms for one of his great bear hugs and, feeling sick with apprehension, I went to him.

When he let me go, he looked around him. 'A pleasant neighbourhood, Anna, but I must admit, the apartment is not what I expected. It seems rather old-fashioned compared with the way you described the last one to me.'

'Papa—'

'Will Emile join us later?'

I swallowed hard. 'Papa, I have something important to tell you.'

A broad smile lit up his face. 'Your mother and I hoped you would.'

'It's not that.'

An icy feeling took hold of me. Papa looked puzzled.

'Emile won't be joining us. He's gone.'

'Gone? What on earth do you mean?'

'He's left me, Papa.'

For a moment he was speechless, then he let out a bellow of anger. 'The scoundrel, how could he do this to you?'

I had no answer.

He paced the room, his face crimson. 'How long has it been?'

'More than a year,' I whispered.

Papa could not have looked more shocked if I had struck him.

'More than a year and you never told us?'

'I'm sorry. I didn't want to worry you. I thought he would come back.'

Papa's body sagged. Suddenly he looked like an old man; his breath came in shallow gasps.

Alarmed, I led him to a chair and made him sit down. 'I'll call one of the servants to fetch you something.'

'No, don't call them.' Tears glistened in his eyes. 'How have you lived?'

'Emile left a little money,' my voice faltered, 'and then friends helped me.'

'This apartment?'

'A friend lets me live here.' I couldn't bear to meet Papa's eye.

'A man?'

'Yes,' I whispered.

Papa's face darkened. 'You must come home with me at once. This is no life for my daughter. We'll think of something to tell your mother.'

'No Papa. Please, please, try to forgive me, but I can't. My life is here now.'

'You'll do as I say.'

The sinews on his neck bulged; fists clenched, he lurched from the chair. I recoiled, terrified he would strike me, but then his shoulders slumped and his fists uncurled leaving his hands limp at his sides.

'I have no legal right to compel you: that right belongs to—' Papa's next words were almost inaudible. 'I will not say his name.'

My heart aching, I reached out and touched his sleeve. 'I'll be all right.'

He covered my hand with his and nodded wordlessly.

'Please don't be sad, Papa.'

'Is he good to you, this... this man?'

'Yes.'

'I suppose I should be grateful for that.'

I started to speak but he raised his hand. 'No, I don't want to hear about him. Not now, not ever.'

He left soon afterwards and although I saw him again before he left Paris, we both struggled for things to say. To the end, he did not ask to meet Monsieur Noilly.

When we said goodbye for the last time, he didn't embrace me. It was a bitter blow.

'Tell Mother and Sonja I miss them,' I whispered.

He shook his head. 'Do you, Anna? Do you really care about your family any longer? This will break your mother's heart.'

Tears coursed down my cheeks.

'It's not too late to reconsider.'

I shook my head and turned away. Hollow with misery, I listened to Papa's footsteps, and the sound of the door closing.

*

Monsieur Noilly came the following evening and was very kind. He brought me a huge bunch of white lilac that filled the room with heady sweetness. After Rose had taken the flowers from him to put them in water, he sat down opposite me and took my hands in his. 'Anna, if you want to leave, I understand.'

I shook my head and he smiled and squeezed my hands tightly. Inwardly, I told myself that my decision was right. At least by staying here in Paris, I might preserve a shred of dignity.

Chapter 10

In the months that followed, my letters to my parents were returned unopened. I knew I had only myself to blame.

It was a strange half-life within the confines of the apartment. I turned to books for consolation, but except for a copy of La Fontaine's *Fables*, the books in the apartment were all devotional works. When I asked Monsieur Noilly if I might have something else to pass the time, he agreed readily. 'I know the days are long for you,' he said. 'And I'm afraid I can't be with you as often as I would like. I'll be delighted to find books for you. Which authors would you like to read?'

He was usually so kindly and tolerant that I was surprised at his reaction when I suggested Victor Hugo. The benevolent expression left his face and his tone was peremptory. 'That man's books will never come into a house of mine. Social justice? Sedition and anarchy I call it. The Emperor did well to send him packing. I wish the English joy of him. I shall choose more suitable reading matter for you.'

His irritation reminded me that, if I lost his goodwill, I would have nothing. I did not ask again.

One sultry summer evening at the end of a long and uneventful afternoon, I sat alone in the drawing room. Monsieur Noilly had not visited for several days. It surprised me how much I missed him. I realised I had grown very fond of this quaint, old-fashioned, little man.

On his last visit he had complained at length of his indigestion; perhaps he was really unwell. Guiltily, I remembered feeling bored and thinking how ironic it was that I, who had longed for a more exciting life than Mother's and Sonja's, should be obliged to listen so frequently to his ponderous descriptions of his ill health – a topic of conversation in which Mother would have been a far more interested participant than I could ever be.

The French windows in the drawing room led out to a small balcony surrounded by a wrought-iron balustrade. It offered a pleasant view down the rue Chateaudun and I often sat there on warm evenings. Usually there was very little going on in the quiet street but as the clock of Notre Dame de Lorette struck ten, a small landau drawn by a spirited black horse rumbled over the cobbles and halted in front of the house opposite.

The coachman climbed down from his box and stood at the horse's head holding the reins while a young man in evening dress alighted from the landau and turned to hand his companion down. She looked about my age, smartly dressed in black and white striped silk, cut low to show off her ample cleavage. Around her neck she wore a pink rose pinned on a black velvet ribbon; a spray of black feathers set off her honey-coloured hair.

As they went into the house, the man caught sight of me standing on the balcony and raised his hat. My heart skipped a beat. He had an air about him that reminded me of Emile. The woman turned to see what he was looking at. She shot me a frosty glance and settled a firmer grasp on his arm before they vanished into the house.

I returned to the drawing room and closed the French windows. Monsieur Noilly was very unlikely to come now. I might as well go to bed.

I spent a restless night. In my dreams, Sonja cuddled a small bundle wrapped up in a white, lacy shawl. Mother was beside her. Sonja beckoned to me and drew the shawl aside. I recoiled in horror. Instead of the perfect, miniature features and fresh, blooming skin I had expected, I saw a grinning, monkey-faced monster. Sonja laughed as I ran away.

I awoke so suddenly that for a few moments, I didn't know where I was. Then I saw the familiar pattern of swags and roses on the walls and remembered. My body burned. I pushed off my heavy quilt to let the night air from the open window cool my skin. The memory of the dream mocked me and tears slid down my cheeks. I would never see Sonja's baby. I would never see any of the family I loved again.

*

In the morning, I tried to cheer myself up by taking a walk. I was only a few doors from home when I saw the young woman I had noticed the previous evening. To my surprise, she stopped and gave me a sweet smile.

'Hello, I'm sorry about last night. I'm sure you didn't mean any harm but I don't like my gentlemen to be distracted. After all,' she laughed, 'they are my stock in trade, if you know what I mean.' She offered me her hand. 'My name's Mariette.'

'I'm Anna.'

'Pleased to meet you, Anna. Is he your beau, the old one who comes every week?'

I was taken aback by her directness, but I nodded.

'I don't expect he gives you too much trouble. Often the old ones are the most generous too. I should know - I've tried all sorts. Once I had six of them on the go.'

She giggled, 'I don't mean all at once, of course. I'd have to be like the octopus in the Jardin d'Acclimatation for that! It took some managing though. I had to keep all the dresses they gave me hung in the wardrobe in order, so I'd wear the right one when each of them came to visit. In the end, they found out, but luckily, they thought it was a great joke.'

She let out a peal of laughter. 'They even had a special chest made for me with six drawers. They wanted them labelled with their names but I said they'd have to make do with the days of the week, otherwise it was too hard to remember. So if Monday left behind his gloves, Tuesday his cufflinks and Wednesday his shaving brush, I'd just put them in the right drawer until the next week came round.'

'What about the seventh day?' I ventured, warming to this jolly girl.

'Well, it was my day of rest, but now it's for a *special* friend - a girl has to have a bit of true love in her life, doesn't she?'

'Do you still see them all?'

'No, Wednesday's parents died and he was rich enough to afford me by himself.'

'What happened to the rest?'

She shrugged 'A friend of mine was in the market for a new man, so that dealt with Tuesday. Thursday ruined himself at the card tables and had to leave Paris, and the others – well, they were probably bored with me anyway.' She smiled. 'You're on your own quite often I think?'

Embarrassed, I nodded.

'Come and visit me if you like – as long as the curtains aren't closed, of course.'

*

I began to spend a lot of time in Mariette's company. We soon grew close and I realised how much I had missed having another woman to confide in. She was a strange mixture – half careless and gay, half serious and devout. In spite of her way of life, or perhaps because of it, she went often to pray at Notre Dame de Lorette and she treasured a large collection of gaudy devotional pictures of numerous saints. She had never known her father.

Her mother had died when Mariette was in her teens. To make ends meet, like her mother, Mariette had become what the French called a *fille de joie*.

She loved to visit the shops and particularly adored Bon Marché, the department store that had recently emerged, even more enormous than before, from a vast anthill of toiling workmen in the rue de Sèvres. We didn't always go to the shops though. If the weather was fine, we walked in the Tuileries Gardens, admiring the flowers and the fountains. Brass bands often played there and sometimes we sat and listened to them in the dappled shade under the trees.

Mariette's *special* friend was called Périchon – Péri for short. He managed a rather run-down musical theatre in our area. About ten years older than Mariette, he was good-looking in a raffish kind of way, with a dimpled chin and thick, dark hair liberally slicked back with brilliantine. He seemed genuinely fond of her and I liked him straight away for that. When I got to know him better, we became good friends.

On a visit one day, I found Mariette in her boudoir. Her round, wire-framed spectacles were perched on her upturned nose and she was holding a small piece of some greyish-yellow stuff up to the light, studying it intently.

'Whatever is that?' I asked.

'Don't you know? In France we call them "English overcoats". They're for—' She giggled. 'I don't really need to tell you, do I?'

I blushed. I had never seen one before, let alone used one. Monsieur Noilly always withdrew before the final moment.

'I like to make sure they're safe and sound before I trust them,' she went on. 'Some men don't like them I know, but I insist. Anyway,' she winked, 'they mind less if you put them on for them. It's like dressing a doll, but more fun.'

I smiled, 'Oh, Mariette – that's very naughty.'

She sighed. 'I'd like to have a baby one day, y'know. Perhaps Péri will ask me to marry him and then we could have a big family.'

It was the time of the month when tears came easily and, without warning, they sprang into my eyes. Mariette jumped up and rushed to hug me.

'I'm so sorry, Anna – I didn't think.'

'It's all right,' I swallowed, wiping my eyes. 'I'm being silly.'

'No, you're not.' She patted my hand. 'Come on, let's go and visit Péri now. You've not been to the theatre for weeks. It'll be fun and take your mind off things.'

We went in by the stage door and walked through the maze of dusty corridors. Scenery boards stood propped against the dingy walls; away from the brightness of the footlights, their painted buildings and vistas showed up for the crude daubs they were. The usual pungent smell of sawdust and glue made me wrinkle my nose and sneeze. From unseen rooms, the hum of voices mingled with the music of a tinny piano. A soprano voice warbled the opening bars of an aria. I recognised it was from an operetta of Offenbach's that I had attended with

Emile when I was first in Paris. I bit my lip and hurried after Mariette.

'Come on, Anna,' she called over her shoulder. 'Let's pretend the Emperor's commanded us to perform for him.'

She snatched my hand and suddenly, we were in the wings. On stage, the curtain was up and the auditorium lay before us, shadowy and mysterious in the dim light. Mariette walked up to the front and began to sing a popular, sentimental song.

'Bravo!' a deep voice exclaimed as her last notes died away. Péri stepped out from the shadows. He had a stranger by his side.

'Damn, it's the new owner,' Mariette muttered under her breath. Quickly, she put on her warmest smile.

I studied the man with curiosity. Tall and broad-shouldered, with fair hair and ice-blue eyes, he was impeccably dressed in a dark suit and crisp white shirt. An elegant gold stick pin secured his royal-blue silk cravat.

Péri beamed at Mariette. 'Magnificent! Wouldn't you agree, Monsieur Buhler?'

'Charming,' Buhler murmured in heavily accented French.

I knew Péri well enough to sense he was nervous as he made the introductions. Buhler certainly exuded the air of a man who was used to dominating every situation he found himself in, and didn't care about putting other people at their ease. His expression was unreadable as Péri rattled on about his plans for a new show and the expense it would entail.

All at once, Buhler turned to me. 'And is Madame Daubigny a singer as well as a beauty?'

'I sing very badly, Monsieur,' I replied coolly, annoyed at the way he had interrupted Péri in mid-sentence.

A look of sardonic amusement flickered across Buhler's face. It seemed my tone had not been lost on him.

He turned back to Péri. 'I have another meeting to attend. Send the figures for your show to my assistant. I'll consider them when I have time.'

Péri looked downcast but he nodded. 'Thank you, Monsieur. Shall I see you out?'

'There's no need. I know the way.'

He bowed to Mariette and I. 'It was a pleasure to meet you, Mesdames.'

With a click of his heels, he strode away down the central aisle. The heavy double doors at the far end gave a protesting creak as he pushed them open, and another as they closed behind him.

Silence fell.

'Whew!' Péri muttered. 'You heard how he didn't want to talk about the budget for the next show? He's a hard customer to fathom. I hope he isn't planning to close us down.'

Mariette put her arm through his. 'Why ever would he want to do that?'

'To redevelop the site, my love - property's going up round here. At best he'll probably want to raise the rent. These Prussians are a grasping lot. Ah well, let's go to my office and have a glass of wine. We may as well be merry while we have the chance.'

Chapter 11

Christmas came.

Monsieur Noilly had apologised so many times for the fact he would have to spend it with his family and leave me on my own that I tired of assuring him I didn't mind. In any case, Mariette and Péri had promised to visit me. The autumn had seen a big change in their lives. Mariette had given up her wealthy lover and she and Péri now lived together in an apartment near the theatre. They seemed very happy and I was glad for them.

On Christmas Eve, as the bells of Notre Dame de Lorette struck the hours towards midnight, I sat by the fire with only my thoughts for company. I couldn't help remembering the Christmastime Emile and I had spent together. What an innocent I had been then, never dreaming my comfortable little world might fall apart.

Voices in the hall interrupted my reverie and Mariette came in, followed by Péri. The sight of them cheered me up enormously.

'I'm so happy you came,' I said.

Péri set down a pile of presents. 'Merry Christmas, Anna!'

Mariette hugged me. 'Darling Anna, we couldn't let you be alone tonight.'

She unfastened her cloak and tossed it over a chair. 'Wait until you see what we've brought. Some of it is for Péri and me, and some for you.'

'And I have gifts for you too.'

I fetched the parcels: Péri's favourite Havana cigars and a pair of ivory kid gloves fastened with seed pearl buttons for Mariette – she had admired them in the window of a shop in the rue de Rivoli.

'Oh, how clever of you,' she exclaimed. 'They're gorgeous.'

Péri sniffed appreciatively at the cigars. 'A perfect gift. Thank you, Anna.'

I stroked the silky fur of the muff they had given me. 'And I love this too.'

Péri popped the cork from one of the bottles of champagne he had brought and I fetched glasses. We sat comfortably by the fire, chatting and sipping the straw-coloured wine. It was not as fine as the vintages I remembered from my days with Emile, but it tasted all the better for drinking it with good friends.

'I'm afraid the room looks very bare,' I sighed. 'At home, the house was always decorated with boughs of holly and Christmas candles.'

'It must have looked beautiful,' Mariette smiled.

'It did. We kept all the old customs too. When we were children, Sonja and I used to watch for the first star to come out then we'd rush to tell Papa. It stood for the Star of Bethlehem where Christ was born. Seeing it meant that the Holy Supper could begin.

'The maids would have already set the table with a white cloth - white for the swaddling clothes of Christ - and there would be a bundle of hay to remind us of how poor his family was. A big round loaf of bread symbolised the Bread of Life and a tall white candle in the middle of the table stood for Christ, the Light of the World.'

Mariette made a face. 'I hope you had something nicer to eat than just dry bread.'

'Oh yes,' I laughed. 'It's the tradition in Russia to have twelve dishes, one for each of the twelve Apostles. My favourites were the honey and apricots. Some of them weren't so nice, like the baked cloves of garlic and the plain, unleavened bread. We always had a special porridge called kolya too. It's made of wheat grains, honey and poppy seeds. Papa said that when he was a child, his grandfather always observed the old custom of throwing a ladleful up to the ceiling. If it stuck, the honey harvest would be good that year. Once, Sonja dared me to try, but I must've not thrown it hard enough for the kolya splattered all over the table. Mother was furious.'

Mariette laughed. 'It's funny to think of you being a naughty little girl, Anna.'

'After the meal was over, we'd go to church. We'd be almost bursting with excitement but Mother always said if we weren't good, Dedushka and Baboushka wouldn't bring our presents in the morning, so we sat like mice. On Christmas day, we had a big feast with lots of family and friends coming to the house then we'd play games or dance. Sometimes carol singers came to the door. The first time I saw them wearing the traditional masks of the animals at the manger, I screamed and hid behind Mother. Papa thought it was a great joke and teased me about it for years.'

Mariette looked wistful. 'It must be nice to have happy memories of when you were a child.'

Péri patted her hand. 'We won't dwell on that,' he said quickly. 'We haven't told Anna the good news yet. Anna, we have something else besides Christmas to celebrate.'

'What's that?'

'Karl Buhler has renewed the lease on the theatre,' he beamed. 'We're safe for another year. I was afraid he'd demand a lot more rent but he didn't even mention it. And he's agreed the budget for that new show – well, with just a few cuts.'

'I told Péri not to worry,' Mariette said.

Péri shrugged. 'I know, but I'm still amazed. Everyone you speak to says he's ruthless in business.'

Mariette giggled, a little tipsy with the champagne, 'He asked Péri a lot of questions about you, Anna. I think he likes you. He's a lot richer than Monsieur Noilly, you know.' She studied my expression. 'No? I suppose I don't blame you. He seems rather a cold fish. I wouldn't want him myself' - she glanced at Péri - 'even if I were free.'

'A good thing too, no Frenchwoman should have to do with a Prussian.'

I laughed. 'You sound very stern, Péri.'

He shrugged. 'Buhler may not be so bad, but in general Prussians are not welcome in France.'

'Why not?'

'Because they think they rule the world. Look at how Bismarck extends the reach of the German Confederation—'

Mariette pinched his arm. 'Oh stop it, Péri. Anna and I don't want to talk about politics tonight. It's Christmas.'

'Forgive me, chéri. Let's have some more champagne instead.' He topped up our glasses. 'A toast! To a joyous Christmas and a prosperous New Year! May it be our best ever.'

*

The dark days of winter drew to an end and Paris shimmered in the spring sunshine. Gaily coloured tulips brightened the parks and the shops were full of the latest fashions.

It was a Sunday and Monsieur Noilly was due to visit in the afternoon. I had told Isabel to have tea ready for his arrival at four o'clock – he liked everything to be punctual – but to my surprise, he was late.

'Shall I lay the table yet, Madame?' Jeanne asked.

'I suppose you may as well. Monsieur is sure to be here soon.'

I watched as she set out the silver teapot and its matching milk jug and sugar bowl. Their bulky shapes and heavy ornamentation were so unlike the pretty rococo style that was all the rage now. Monsieur Noilly said they had belonged to his mother, and his grandmother before her. I wondered if those respectable Noilly matrons would have approved of my having them.

Jeanne brought the teacups and a few minutes after she had left the room, the doorbell rang and I heard Monsieur Noilly talking with her in the hall. He sounded tired and Jeanne's voice was full of concern. When he came into the room, I stood up to receive his kiss. His cheek was cold and clammy.

'Are you unwell?' I asked.

'This damned indigestion has troubled me all day, that's all. I'm sorry I kept you waiting.'

Jeanne brought in the hot water and a plate of his favourite éclairs and I started to pour the tea. He drank the first cup while it was still very hot and ate two éclairs. I told him about my last visit to Mariette and made him laugh by recounting one of Péri's anecdotes.

'A little more tea, please, Anna my dear,' he said and passed me his cup. 'Then tell me another of your friend's stories.'

I refilled the cup and handed it to him.

Monsieur Noilly laughed heartily when I reached the end of a story about a particularly pompous actor who had tripped over his own sword.

'Very good, most amusing.'

He reached out to help himself to another éclair but before his hand touched the plate, he stopped with a gasp. A blue tinge spread across his lips.

My heart knocked against my ribs. 'What's wrong? Is it your indigestion again?'

He nodded. 'It will pass in a moment,' he croaked.

'Shall I ask Jeanne to bring a glass of seltzer?'

'No, there's no need.' He took a deep breath. 'See, it's gone already.'

'Would you like a game of bezique?' I asked. It was a game of which he was very fond and I thought it might distract him, but although he agreed, as the game went on, I saw he only gave it half his attention. After a short while, he put down his cards.

'I'm sorry, Anna. I'm too tired for this. Perhaps the meal could be served earlier than usual?'

'Of course.'

We sat in the dining room to eat our rillettes de porc and haricots verts. Monsieur Noilly drank a glass of burgundy but hardly touched a mouthful of food and refused the cheese: his favourite ripe Camembert. I told Jeanne to clear away and bring our coffee to the drawing room.

Now the sun had set, the room had cooled and Fabrice had lit the fire. Monsieur Noilly and I chatted for a while then he stood up. 'I shall have to open a window. It's too hot in here.'

He struggled with one of the heavy sash windows for a few minutes, stopping to mop his brow until his crisp white linen handkerchief was a soggy ball in his hand.

'Let me call Fabrice,' I begged.

'Nonsense, I can do it.'

His face purpled as he tugged at the sash again. It opened a few inches and he gave a grunt of satisfaction. 'There, I told you I could —'

Without warning, he collapsed to the floor with a thud.

157

My hand flew to my mouth and for a moment I couldn't move, then I ran to him and crouched at his side, my mouth dry. I grasped the collar of his jacket and shook him. 'Monsieur Noilly! Can you hear me?' He didn't answer but his eyes were open, filled with terror.

I raced from the room and down the passage to the door leading to the servants' quarters. It was Isabel who answered my hammering, a startled expression on her face.

'Tell Fabrice to run and fetch the doctor,' I cried. 'Monsieur Noilly is very ill.'

'Fabrice!' she called over her shoulder. 'Come quickly!'

He appeared hastily buttoning his footman's jacket. 'I'm sorry, Madame Daubigny,' he said sheepishly. 'I didn't think I'd be needed again tonight.'

'Never mind that. Monsieur Noilly needs a doctor. Hurry!'

I went back to the drawing room with Isabel, Jeanne and Rose following me. Rose let out a gasp of dismay and backed against the wall. Isabel shook her. 'My smelling salts – they're in the top drawer in my room.' She turned to Jeanne. 'You fetch some brandy.'

But the smelling salts were no use, nor the brandy. When Isabel lifted Monsieur Noilly's head and tried to force a little of it between his lips, it just trickled down his chin and pooled on his shirt front. In the way trivialities come to mind in a time of crisis, I thought how distasteful he would have found the mess.

The bell at the front door rang and I sent Rose to answer it. A moment later, Mariette and Péri appeared. 'We met Fabrice in the street,' Mariette said. 'We came as quickly as we could.'

Péri knelt beside Monsieur Noilly and felt for the pulse in his neck. He looked up sadly. 'Anna, I'm so sorry.'

Tears brimmed in my eyes and rolled down my cheeks. 'But he can't be—'

'The doctor will have to confirm it, but I'm afraid he is.'

Péri got to his feet. We all stared mutely at Monsieur Noilly's lifeless body.

'He can't be buried all curled up like that,' Mariette said at last. 'We must straighten his body before it stiffens and the undertakers have to break his bones when they undress and wash him.'

A wave of nausea overcame me and I had to fight it down.

Péri squeezed my hand. 'Let Mariette and me deal with this, Anna.'

With the servants' help, they laid Monsieur Noilly's body out on our bed and Mariette put the palms of his hands together, as if he was in prayer. She stood back.

'When the doctor comes, we'll ask him to tell the family. He'll think of something to say. It won't be the first time he's had to spare a family's feelings I'm sure.'

'You mustn't blame yourself, Anna,' Mariette said after the doctor had gone to make arrangements for Monsieur Noilly's body to be taken away. 'There was nothing you could have done. The doctor himself said so.' Her expression was full of concern, 'You must come and stay with us for as long as you like. You ought not to be alone.'

And so I spent the next few days with Mariette and Péri and I was very glad of it. With their company, it was easier to postpone thinking about the decisions I had to make - if they were not made for me. The doctor had agreed to take on the duty of informing Monsieur Noilly's family so it was unlikely they would find out that Monsieur Noilly's arrangement with me had ever existed, but my respite could not last forever.

'You've been so kind,' I said to Mariette a few days later. 'I don't know what I should have done without you and Péri, but I mustn't impose on you much longer.'

'Nonsense, you must stay as long as you like.'

I blinked back a tear. 'I wish I knew what will happen. The rent - the servants – I haven't even started to think about all that and I must.'

'Something will turn up. Péri found out from the landlady that Monsieur Noilly paid her for the quarter in advance, so you don't have to decide yet.'

She hesitated. 'There is one thing, Anna.'

'What?'

'You have to be prepared.'

'Prepared? For what?'

'The police may come.'

A jolt went through me. 'But why?'

'Sometimes they investigate in this sort of situation,' said Péri, who had just come into the room.

I looked at him blankly.

'They might want to question you. When a man dies like Monsieur Noilly did, sometimes they suspect—'

My blood froze. 'You mean they'll think I killed him?'

'No, nothing like that,' Péri said quickly, 'only you may have to tell them exactly what happened.'

But something in his tone and the looks he exchanged with Mariette made me wonder if that was really all.

'Don't worry,' Mariette said, putting her arm around my shoulders. 'It's only a formality. We just didn't want you to be upset if they do come.'

*

I woke in the night, sweat soaking my nightclothes and images of black-robed judges looming out of the shadows, but in the morning, my courage returned. I would face whatever was to come. I'd done nothing wrong - surely the police would believe me?

That evening I returned to the apartment. Fabrice lit the fires to make the place more cheerful and Isabel prepared a dinner I did not have the heart to eat. It was a small weight off my mind that Fabrice assured me his wages and those of the other servants were paid for several weeks.

The next morning, a policeman called on me as Mariette and Péri had predicted. My throat dry, I rose to greet him but to my relief, he was sympathetic. After a few jottings in his notebook, he left saying there would be no more questions for me to answer. As the door closed on him, I sank down in a chair shaking. In the strange, numb state I found myself in, I had not realised how afraid I had been. Whatever happened now, at least I would not be arrested as a murderess.

A few more days passed then late one morning, Jeanne announced a caller. I squared my shoulders. I was no longer the timid young girl who had crumbled before a bailiff's authority after Emile left me. Whoever this caller was, I would not let them intimidate me. I sat down in a chair with my back to the window.

'Is it a man or a woman?' I asked.

'A man, Madame.'

'Ask him to come up.'

The man who entered the room was slight in build and dressed in black. He carried his top hat in his hand.

'Forgive me for disturbing you at this sad time, Madame. I am a lawyer in the firm of Maille et Delaunay. May I offer my deepest condolences?'

'Thank you,' I answered cautiously.

His deferential tone was unexpected. He did not look like a man who had come to throw me out. But his next words astonished me.

'No doubt financial matters are far from your mind, however I am instructed to inform you that a substantial sum has been deposited at Credit Lyonnais for your use. You may call on it at any time. Should it be insufficient, you need only apply to me and any further expenses will be defrayed. If you wish to remain in this apartment, I shall see to it that the rent and other expenses are paid regularly.'

I was speechless.

'You seem surprised, Madame.'

I recovered my voice. 'Yes, I am. I never expected Monsieur Noilly's family to be so generous.'

'Monsieur Noilly? I'm afraid I don't understand you. My client is Monsieur Buhler.'

A chill crept over me. I did not want to be beholden to this man. How did he even know of my predicament? As soon as the lawyer left, I hurried to the theatre. I found Péri in his office. From his expression it was clear he knew why I had come.

'Anna! I was going to come and see you.'

'Péri, what's going on? How did Buhler get involved in this?'

He hung his head. 'I'm sorry, Anna. I told him. Somehow he heard a rumour that all was not well with Monsieur Noilly. He insisted on my telling him what had happened. I should have spoken to you first, I know, but Buhler's not an easy man to argue with.'

He held out his hand. 'Say you forgive me? He hasn't attached any conditions - he said he wanted merely to help. I don't mean to insult you, Anna, but the sums involved are probably no more than loose change to him. I admit I find it as hard to fathom as you do, but perhaps there is some kindness behind that hard exterior.'

I sighed. 'I forgive you, Péri. But if Buhler expects anything in return, apart from my gratitude and friendship for his generosity, I must decline his help.'

Chapter 12

It was a difficult letter to write and it was only after many attempts that I was satisfied Karl Buhler would understand my feelings. For several weeks however, he did not reply. His silence puzzled me.

Then one day a letter arrived. He requested the pleasure of my company at the opera the following night and, if I was agreeable, he would collect me at eight. It would have been churlish to refuse and I had to admit, I was intrigued.

As Rose dressed my hair, I studied my reflection in the mirror and frowned.

'Is something the matter, Madame?'

'It's so long since I attended the opera, Rose. I fear my dress is probably out of fashion.' I didn't tell her that was not my only cause for apprehension.

'But you look lovely, Madame. You always do.' She put the finishing touches to the spray of feathers in my hair. 'Perfect.'

Karl arrived promptly, looking very distinguished in flawless evening dress. He brought me a bouquet of white roses that gave off a heady scent.

As we took our seats at the opera, the past came flooding back. Wistfully, I remembered all the performances I had attended with Emile. It seemed so long ago that we had been together, but the thought of him still had the power to wring my heart.

With an effort, I made myself concentrate on what Karl was saying. He was very attentive and I discovered that, although my first impression of him had been unfavourable, he was a clever, perceptive man whose company I enjoyed. We dined after the opera and over the next few weeks, I saw a great deal of him.

'So, has he said anything yet?' Mariette demanded one day.

'What do you mean?'

'You know perfectly well what I mean, Anna. Has he asked you to be his mistress?'

'Mariette!'

'Well he's not spending all this money just to find out your opinions on opera, is he?'

I laughed. 'No, I suppose not.'

'And what will you say if he does ask?'

I twisted the ring on my finger. 'I don't know, Mariette. It's all so soon.'

Mariette looked serious. 'If I were you, Anna, I shouldn't take too long over making up your mind. Men love the chase I know, but you can go too far.' She patted my hand. 'I don't think you'll regret it if you say yes. Admit it, he's much nicer than we thought at first. Anyway, all rich men are loveable - as well as handsome and charming – it's a law of nature.'

I had to laugh. 'Oh Mariette, what would I do without you?'

'Take life much too seriously, I expect.'

'It's not as if he's asked me yet. I can't help wondering why he would choose me. There are so many women in Paris, most of them far more sophisticated and beautiful.'

'Don't be so modest, Anna, any man would fall for you.'

Over the next few days, I thought a lot about our conversation. Mariette was probably right about Karl's intentions. What other reason could there be for his generosity? If I turned him down, I could hardly expect that generosity to continue.

As the days went by, I agonised over the problem. More than once, I wished I was more like Mariette with her down-to-earth attitude to life. I had no illusions that I was in love with Karl, but he was an attractive man and it was lovely to be with someone who was so attentive. Perhaps in time, I might grow to care for him.

One evening we were to dine at a fashionable new restaurant, but at the last minute, Karl suggested a change of plan. 'It will be crowded there tonight. I would prefer somewhere quieter, if you have no objection?'

'Of course not.'

We went to the place he chose and were shown to a private room. Karl called for champagne. The waiter brought it and asked if we wished to order our meal. 'Later,' Karl waved him away.

When the man had withdrawn, he raised his glass to me. 'To you, Anna. Or dare I say, to us?'

I held my breath. I already knew what he would say next. A few minutes later, it was settled and I had agreed to be his. We spent the rest of dinner making plans. He wanted me to give up the apartment and come to live in his house on the Champs Elysées as soon as possible. 'It will be a new beginning,' he said, pressing his lips to my hand.

After dinner the carriage took us back to the apartment. He helped me down the steps and walked me to the door. 'Give me two days and I shall have everything ready for you,' he said. 'Then we can be together.'

He touched my cheek and leant forward to kiss me. My heart pounded. What would I say if he asked to come in? All at once, I wasn't sure I was ready. Perhaps this was a mistake after all.

He let me go and I wondered if he had sensed my trepidation, but if he had, he didn't show it. 'Goodnight, my dear Anna,' he said softly. 'Sleep well.'

I couldn't sleep. Everything should have been simple now, but instead, doubts and questions filled my mind. How well did I really know Karl Buhler? How well did I know myself? Monsieur Noilly had been the first step; by taking Karl, I travelled further down the path from which it would be impossible to return. Shame coursed through me. When I married Emile, I had never expected my life to turn out in such a way.

At last, too tired to think, I forced myself to push my anxieties away. Fate had brought me to this life. I must do my best to make a success of it.

The next morning, Mariette divined instantly that something had happened.

'Tell me everything,' she said, seizing my hands. 'He asked you, didn't he? What did you say?'

'I said yes.'

She let out a peal of laughter and whirled me around the room until we were both breathless then she let me go and sank into a chair, kicking up her heels in a froth of petticoats.

'Clever girl!' she gasped. 'Now, tell me the whole story, and don't you dare leave anything out.'

Dizzy, I sat down myself and took a deep breath before starting on my tale. When I finished, she raised her eyebrows.

'Is that all?'

'Yes.'

'He really just left after a kiss? Gracious, he's a cool customer. Usually they can't wait.'

'He said he wants me to come to live with him first. He has a house on the Champs Elysées.'

'I know. It's a huge place. You'll be so grand. I hope you won't forget Péri and me.'

'Of course I won't. I hope we'll always be friends.'

Mariette hugged me. 'Of course we will.'

*

The house on the Champs Elysées was even more magnificent than I had expected. When Karl led me into the vast marble hall, I was speechless for a moment, admiring the graceful curves of the double staircase that swept up to the first floor. The imposing furniture was decorated with tortoiseshell and brass. I recognised the work of Boulle from the fashionable magazines Emile used to buy for me. Pieces like these were both much sought-after and extremely expensive.

Karl took my hand and kissed it. 'I hope you will be happy here, Anna. Come, I want you to see the salon - I use it mainly for receptions. Perhaps in a while, when you have had time to make yourself at home, you will be my hostess?'

The salon was elegantly furnished, its ivory-coloured walls embellished with large panels of sky-blue watered silk set into gilded frames. The huge fireplace was of marble, delicately carved with cupids and intricate garlands of fruit and flowers.

Karl pointed up at the painted ceiling. 'Boucher: in my opinion, no one has ever painted mythological scenes as expressively as he did.'

The spacious dining hall was equally impressive with a huge mahogany table surrounded by twenty-four chairs ornamented with swags of bronze acanthus leaves in the Greek style.

That evening, we dined there alone, candlelight throwing pools of warm gold on the gleaming surface of the great mahogany table; Karl's servants attending so assiduously to our wants that my head ached with tension and the food stuck in my throat.

At last Karl stood up and came round the table to help me from my chair.

'I have one more treasure I'd like to show you,' he smiled. Together we mounted the sweeping staircase to the first floor. Through an open door that led off a wide landing was a sumptuous bedroom – surely the one we would share. My legs turned to water. With difficulty I tried to concentrate on what Karl was saying.

'The carving is exquisite don't you think?' he asked. I realised he indicated the marble statue that was standing in a recess to the left of the open door. It depicted the nymph, Daphne, fleeing from Apollo.

'I can never pass by without wanting to touch it,' he murmured. He took my hand. 'Feel it for yourself.'

His hand guided mine over the smooth roundness of Daphne's arms, the tenderness of flesh melting into wood and leaf where the fingers should have been. In the midst of the transformation that would save her from the rapacious god, her head twisted towards his. Her face was a mask of terror; the veins in her neck bulged with strain. A shudder passed through me.

Karl frowned. 'It does not please you? Then I shall have it removed.'

'No,' I stammered. 'It's beautiful. It's just that it's such a strange story.'

He nodded. 'Does love transform us for happiness or sorrow? A profound question, is it not?' He tilted my chin so that our eyes met. 'What do you think, Anna?'

Words spun in my head but he gave me no time to utter them. With a swift movement, he lifted me in his arms as if I were a doll and carried me into the bedroom.

His lovemaking was violent, urgent, his limbs lithe and muscular. Greedily, his lips explored and caressed every inch of me. My mind seemed to float above us, watching our coupling, but my body answered his in a language of its own. The language Emile had taught me: the language I thought I had forgotten forever. For a moment shame held me back – how could I feel this passion with another man? Then my body triumphed. Karl entered me and, intoxicated with pleasure, I gave myself up to desire.

Chapter 13

By night Karl remained an arousing lover, but afterwards there was emptiness. I was no closer to knowing him than I had been at the beginning of our relationship. Did he even want that? I doubted it. I often wondered why he had chosen me when there must be plenty of women ready to share his bed. Perhaps it had something to do with our both being outsiders in Paris.

He liked to dictate the clothes I wore and the style of my toilette. At first he wanted to replace Rose, who had come with me as my maid, with an older, more experienced woman. It was only when I pleaded that he relented and let her stay. It grieved me that I seemed fated once again to be with a man who would not, or could not, let me into his heart. Yet a voice deep inside me whispered I already had more good fortune than I deserved.

Perhaps it would have helped if we had spent more time alone but we rarely did; Karl's wealth and influence ensured we had countless invitations. No doubt many people envied me the whirl of splendid occasions to which we were bidden, but I was often uncomfortably aware that the warmth of our welcome did not run deep. Péri had been right:

there was little love for Prussians in Paris. They were regarded with mistrust.

When we were not out in society, I spent much of my day alone. Usually, I sat in the small parlour overlooking the gardens at the back of the house. It was far cosier than the grand salon. The walls were hung with rose-pink damask and a richly patterned Persian carpet covered the floor, imparting a warm glow to the room. A chaise longue upholstered in antique gold brocade stood beside the fireplace and the rosewood writing desk was decorated with exquisitely painted porcelain plaques and inlays of mother-of-pearl and ivory. Karl told me the desk was reputed to have been made for Marie Antoinette. Sometimes as I read, or composed replies to invitations and notes of thanks, I thought of her luxurious life and how it had ended in tragedy. The thought made me shiver.

It was on one of those days that I made an intriguing discovery. It was late afternoon and the sun was low in the sky. I had paused to remember the details of the evening upon which I wanted to compliment our hostess when I noticed a faint line running through one of the inlays. I ran my finger along it and felt a crack. I frowned, hoping that I had done nothing to cause the damage. Then I saw there was a similar line running parallel to the first one then turning at the bottom to join it. I put my fingernail into the crack and eased out a shallow drawer, just large enough to contain a tiny keepsake, a lock of hair perhaps or a ring. Was I about to find something that had belonged to the ill-fated Marie Antoinette? No, on closer inspection, the drawer was empty of anything so romantic. It contained nothing but dust.

I mentioned my discovery to Rose, as she helped me to dress for dinner that evening. I knew her fondness for romance and we amused ourselves with speculating on the secrets the drawer might once have concealed.

*

Months passed and any deepening of my relationship with Karl still eluded me. The only time I felt close to him was in the darkness of our bedroom, and that intimacy vanished with the morning light. He made it clear he didn't want me to have a child so it was fortunate I had Mariette to advise me on ways of avoiding pregnancy. When my courses came each month, I always felt a huge sense of relief. I was terrified of what Karl would make me do if an accident occurred. I knew the laughter of children would have no place in his immaculate, beautiful house.

Mariette brushed my anxieties aside in her usual brisk fashion.

'Your problem is that you hanker for love, Anna,' she said. 'Karl's no different from lots of men.' She rolled her eyes. 'Well, a bit worse perhaps, being a Prussian. He has boxes in his life and you fit into the one labelled 'mistress'. You will just have to accept that he has nothing more to give.'

She gestured to the room. 'Isn't all this enough?'

'I know it should be, but . . .'

'I understand, really I do. Being a mistress isn't always a bed of roses. But don't despair; you'll find your special someone one day. Look how I had to wait.'

She smiled. 'Péri and I will soon cheer you up. Come out with us like you used to. If Péri doesn't have to be at the theatre, we go somewhere most evenings.'

'I'd love to but I'm not sure whether Karl would approve of me going anywhere without him.'

Mariette snapped her fingers. 'Why does he need to know? He often goes away on business, doesn't he? Anyway, there'd be no harm in it.'

I smiled. 'Thank you, Mariette. I'll think about it.'

*

Karl had asked the celebrated artist, Edouard Blanchard to paint my portrait.

Edouard was in his sixties, a burly, broad-shouldered man with a leonine head of grey hair and a beard the colours of pepper and salt. His big, humorous personality endeared him to me from the moment we met. He loved to talk and had a fund of amusing anecdotes.

He lived alone in a large house in the place Vendôme. It was one of the smartest addresses in Paris and a fine house, but it had a slightly cheerless air. It lacked the touches that would have given it the warmth of a home.

Edouard spent most of his time in his studio and didn't seem to notice. A creature of habit, he always wore the same favourite suit when he was painting. It was made of English herringbone tweed, clearly expensive but now very battered and rumpled. Thanks to the suit, no matter how cold the north facing studio became, he never noticed, but I often shivered when I went for my sittings.

The costume Karl had chosen for me to wear in the portrait was an ivory tulle dress with full sleeves, caught up at the elbows by wide bows of lilac silk. I wore a broad sash of the lilac silk around my waist.

'Stop fidgeting, can't you,' Edouard grumbled, after I had been sitting still for what seemed like hours. It was December and the room was chilly.

'I can't help it. I'm cold and I ache all over.' I frowned at him in mock annoyance. 'It's your fault for being too mean to burn a decent fire.'

Edouard looked at the grate where the coals had almost burnt out. 'I'm no good at keeping the servants in order. They forget all about me when I'm working. It needs a woman's touch. Do you think Karl would spare you?'

I smiled. 'I'll ask him.'

There was a knock at the door. 'Monsieur Blanchard?'

Edouard gave an irritable sigh. 'That wretch Planchet should know by now not to disturb me when I'm working.' He clicked his tongue. 'I suppose I must see what he wants. 'Come in, Planchet! This had better be important.'

Planchet's rubicund face appeared around the door.

'Forgive me, Monsieur. A young gentleman is asking for you: a Monsieur Paul Vallon.'

Edouard frowned.

'Shall I show him up, Monsieur?'

'Ah, Mon Dieu, the young man I met with at the École des Beaux Arts last week. Did I tell him to come today?'

'I don't know, Monsieur.'

I laughed. 'I think you must have done as he's here. Anyway, I shall be happy to meet him, especially if it means a chance to move and warm up a little.'

'Oh, very well.'

Edouard picked up a woollen robe and tossed it to me. 'Wrap yourself in this. Send him up, Planchet, and bring us some wine - the fifty-eight burgundy. Two bottles.'

'Yes, Monsieur.'

'And more coals. Madame Daubigny's not impressed by our fire.'

Planchet departed, grumbling audibly.

'He's getting old, Planchet,' Edouard sighed. 'This Vallon had some of his paintings in the finalists' show at the École. One of the professors there is an old friend and invites me each year. I like to see what the younger generation are getting up to. Vallon's work is very promising. We had an interesting talk.'

Unfamiliar footsteps sounded in the passage, then a knock.

'Come in,' Edouard shouted.

A young man entered the room. Slight in build, he wore shabby, black trousers and a loose grey jacket. The outfit was topped off, rather eccentrically for winter, by a panama hat. It gave him a bohemian air.

With an affable smile, Edouard went forward and clapped him on the shoulder. 'Monsieur Vallon! A pleasure to see you.'

Paul Vallon looked relieved. 'I was afraid I - that is we - might be interrupting your work. I hope you have no objection to my bringing my brother-in-law with me, Monsieur? May I present Antoine Clérmont?'

Vallon's companion followed him hesitantly.

Edouard nodded. 'Of course, of course, you're both very welcome.' He turned to me. 'Madame Daubigny is in your debt. I am obliged to allow her to rest for a while.'

The young men bowed to me. Antoine Clérmont was the taller of the two, broad-shouldered with dark hair that fell in waves to his collar. Pensive eyes, the colour of charcoal, softened a face with sharp cheekbones and a blunt chin. Like his friend Vallon's, his clothes had seen better days.

'You'll take a glass of wine with us?' Edouard asked.

'That's very kind of you, Monsieur. If you're quite sure we aren't disturbing you.'

'Never fear, I'll let you know when it's time for you to leave.'

Snuggled into the robe, I stood up and winced at the prickling in my legs as the blood ran back into them.

Paul Vallon studied the half-finished portrait on the easel.

'Well, Monsieur Vallon, what do you think?' Edouard asked. 'I know you young men have your own ideas about what art is, but does Madame Daubigny live and breathe convincingly enough for you?'

'She does, Monsieur; I only wish I had the skill to do something as fine. The painting will be a marvel. Will you show it at the Salon?'

Edouard laughed. 'You're too modest, my friend. As for the Salon, that will be up to the Académie's judging panel.'

'I'm sure they wouldn't dare refuse you, Monsieur.'

'Perhaps, perhaps – but in any case, it's a private commission. It will be for the owner to decide whether it's submitted, but I hope he agrees. I really believe it's one of the best things I've done in a long time.'

The door creaked and Planchet shuffled in with the wine.

'Put it down over there, Planchet. We'll serve ourselves.'

Edouard swept aside some of the tubes of paint, brushes and other paraphernalia cluttering the table. Planchet set down the tray then puffed out of the room.

'Help yourselves, gentlemen. Anna, will you take a glass? It's a good vintage, I promise you. Even Karl would approve.'

'I'm sure he would. Thank you.'

Edouard poured my wine then he and Vallon started to look at the rest of the paintings standing on easels around the room. Soon they were deep in conversation.

Antoine smiled at me. 'I'm sorry we interrupted your sitting, Madame.'

'Not at all, Edouard spoke the truth. I've longed for a rest for the past hour.'

'It must be very tedious having to sit still for so long,' he ventured.

'Yes, especially when Edouard is too preoccupied for conversation.'

He smiled. 'But it is a beautiful likeness.'

'Edouard could make anyone look beautiful,' I replied, then wished I hadn't. The remark sounded as if I was fishing for compliments. 'Are you also an artist, Monsieur?' I asked quickly.

'No, I'm a writer. At least that's how I hope to earn my living eventually. I haven't had much published yet, just a few poems. One of them was in *The Literary Review* this week. But I'm working on a novel – a love story. Otherwise I teach literature to the sons of wealthy families to make ends meet.'

'Do you enjoy that?'

He shrugged. 'When they're not complete blockheads.'

The others were still engrossed in the paintings so we sat down on the sofa by the window and talked. Flakes of snow fell from a leaden sky, dusting the pavements and the bare trees. The studio cat jumped up and rubbed her head against my arm. I stroked her glossy black fur and she purred with pleasure then rolled on her back and batted her paws at a piece of loose thread hanging from one of my sleeves.

'What's her name?' Antoine asked.

'Juno.'

He reached out and scratched her behind one ear. She mewled crossly and tried to nip him. He snatched back his hand, his fingertips grazing my wrist as he did so. It might have been an accident, but it sent a tingling sensation through me. Heat rose to my cheeks and I avoided his eyes, muttering something about the cat being old and not used to strangers.

'I've neglected you, Anna.' Edouard was beside us. 'Let me refill your glass. And yours, Monsieur Clérmont?'

'Thank you, the wine is truly excellent. We aren't used to anything as fine, are we, Paul?'

The men continued to talk for a little longer then Edouard drained his glass and put it down. 'Well, Anna and I must get back to work. The light will fail soon.'

Antoine stood up. 'Thank you for your company, Madame Daubigny,' he said. 'I hope I haven't talked too much and bored you.' There was a note of awkwardness in his voice.

'Not at all.' I wished I didn't sound so prim.

Edouard rubbed his palms together in the way he always did when he was anxious to get back to work.

'Excellent. Well, Planchet will see you out. Come again if you like.'

The door closed behind the two young men and I took up my pose once more.

'A talented young man that Paul Vallon,' Edouard remarked, 'and an ambitious one. He seemed very eager to make a good impression.'

He chuckled, 'I think his friend found something more interesting to admire than my paintings.'

Chapter 14

Christmas came round again and frost rimed the trees. The confectioners' windows were full of chocolate Bûches de Noël and rainbow pyramids of candied fruit. Shoppers thronged the streets and Paris sparkled.

For several weeks, the gaieties of the season occupied all my time, but I could not get Antoine Clérmont out of my mind. The sensation I had felt at the touch of his hand kept coming back to me.

Strangely, in spite of the fact he was still my husband, I no longer missed Emile. I decided that what I had felt for him must simply have been a girlish infatuation, fuelled by my dream of Paris. All the same, after he had wounded me so cruelly, I thought my heart would be frozen forever and Karl had done nothing to dispel that belief. Yet in Antoine, I glimpsed someone who might, in different circumstances, have become a friend as well as a lover.

On impulse, I sent Rose out to buy a copy of *The Literary Review* and I read his poem. It was very moving and revealed so much about him that interested me. Soon though, I chided myself for my foolishness. Our meeting had been pure chance and our paths would probably never cross again. The thought made me sad, but it was for the best.

Edouard put the finishing touches to my portrait and at his urging Karl agreed to submit it to the Académie des Beaux Arts. The selections had already been made for the Spring Salon but it was accepted for exhibition at the summer one.

On the opening night, Karl invited a large party to join us and to dine afterwards. Of course Edouard was among them.

'Our painting is a great success, wouldn't you agree, Anna,' he remarked gesturing to the crowd gathered around it.

'It was you who did all the work.'

'Ah, but you did all the sitting still,' he teased.

Just then, I noticed Antoine Clérmont. Many months had passed since we first met; he had probably forgotten me, but at the sight of him, my stomach did a somersault.

Edouard peered over his half-moon spectacles. 'Why, Monsieur Clérmont,' he called out. 'What a pleasure. Come and talk to us.'

'The pleasure's all mine, Monsieur Blanchard. I wasn't sure if you would remember me.'

'I never forget a face. After all, I spend a great deal of my time painting them.'

Antoine bowed. 'Good evening, Madame Daubigny.'

I murmured something, relieved he had not tried to kiss my hand. It wouldn't stop shaking.

Edouard seemed unaware of my agitation. I prayed he wouldn't leave me, but after a short discussion of the portrait's merits, he glanced across the room. 'Ah, I've just seen someone I must catch before he goes. Will you entertain Anna for me, Monsieur?'

'I'd be delighted.'

I felt dizzy and I'm sure my flaming cheeks did not go unnoticed. Alone with Antoine, several moments passed before I managed to compose myself sufficiently to carry on a conversation and ask about his novel – the first thing that came to mind.

A smile lit his face. 'You remembered I was writing one.'

'Yes.'

'I've finished it, but finding a publisher for a novel is even harder than writing it. I doubt I'll be able to give up any of my pupils just yet.' He shrugged. 'Sometimes, I wonder if I'm chasing a dream. Perhaps I should give up.'

'Don't do that.'

'You think I should persevere?'

'I'm sure of it. I expect every writer loses heart sometimes.'

Over his shoulder, I noticed Jules Fauchon coming towards us. In his usual fashion, he was eccentrically garbed in a black velvet smoking-jacket, green shoes and canary yellow trousers. Fauchon was an eminent journalist and literary critic. His favourable review of a novel or play almost guaranteed success. A frequent guest at the literary soirées Karl liked us to host, he was also a great friend of Edouard's.

'Good evening, Madame Daubigny,' he smiled. 'I congratulate you. The portrait is thoroughly charming.'

'Thank you, Monsieur. You must tell Edouard. He'll be happy to hear that you approve.'

Suddenly I wanted more than anything to help Antoine.

'May I introduce Antoine Clérmont?' I asked.

Fauchon bowed. 'Monsieur Clérmont. A pleasure to meet you.'

'Antoine is a writer whose work I greatly admire. I wish you would look at his new novel.'

I saw Fauchon's eyes register the weariness of a man who is endlessly asked for favours but I was determined to persist. With gentle prompting from me, Antoine gave a good account of his work. When he had finished, Fauchon smiled.

'Love is always a popular subject for a novel. It's strange - everyone speaks of it, as if it was the most important thing in the world - but do you know, I don't think I have ever experienced it. Sometimes, I suspect if they were honest, many people would admit the same.'

Antoine looked downcast.

Fauchon laughed and clapped him on the shoulder.

'You mustn't mind an old cynic like me. I like the sound of your work. Come and visit me at my office. Perhaps I can help you in some way. I'm always interested in finding new writers.' He kissed my hand. 'Au revoir, Madame, I fear I have to leave for another engagement, but I look forward to our next meeting.'

Antoine let out a long breath as Jules Fauchon walked away.

'I don't know what to say. You wave your wand and hey presto, I have the sympathetic ear of one of Paris' most influential critics.' A mischievous twinkle came into his eyes. 'It was very generous of you to praise my work, particularly when I doubt you've read it.'

'Oh, but I have,' I said without thinking first.

His look of surprise made me flush again.

'I happened to come across one of your poems in *The Literary Review*.'

'You read the *Review*?' He took my hand, thankfully it was steadier now, and kissed it. 'I'm tremendously grateful for your help.'

'Anna, there you are.' Karl's voice made me jump. 'Our guests are hungry,' he said briskly. 'We must go to dinner.'

He scrutinised Antoine. 'I don't believe we've met?'

'This is Antoine Clérmont, Karl. He's a friend of Edouard's.'

Karl nodded dismissively. In an instant, the temperature of the room plummeted. I only had time for a brief goodbye before Karl hurried me away.

At the restaurant, a private room awaited our party.

'I've made an alteration to the seating plan,' Karl murmured as we walked in. 'I've sat you next to the banker, Barbizon. Be nice to him.'

My heart sank for I disliked Barbizon, a fat, self-important bore, whose conversation consisted of boasting about his dubious business deals. I sometimes wondered why Karl had anything to do with him and I felt sure he knew I didn't care for the man.

'Must I?' I murmured back. Karl ignored me.

As dinner progressed, Barbizon ate copiously and drank a prodigious amount of fine burgundy. I hated the way he took every opportunity to look down the front of my dress. When he leant close, the smell of garlic and wine on his breath made me queasy.

'A pretty necklace you have on, Madame,' he said, leering at the diamonds around my neck. 'When Karl pulls off his latest venture, he can buy you many more of those.'

Glancing at a man nearby whom I recognised as a high-ranking official, Barbizon tapped a finger against his nose. 'Karl's as lucky in business as he is in love. He has friends in all the right places, if you know what I mean.'

I willed Karl to rescue me but to no avail. He was punishing me, I was convinced of it. He wanted to remind me that without his protection, I would be fair game for men like Barbizon.

After what seemed an eternity, Karl rose and sauntered down the table, pausing to exchange a few words with each guest on the way. 'Barbizon, my dear friend,' he said when he reached us. 'I really can't allow you to monopolise Anna a moment longer.'

He held out his hand and gave me a silky smile.

'Come Anna, there are other guests who wish to greet you.'

The clock in the hall struck two as we arrived home and I felt exhausted. I hoped that Karl wouldn't come to me, but soon after Rose had helped me get ready for bed and left, he appeared from his own room.

He came to the dressing table where I was still sitting. The mirror threw his reflection back at me. 'I fear you did not enjoy our little dinner party, Anna.'

Tiredness made me incautious. 'You know I didn't. I wish you hadn't sat me next to Barbizon.'

Karl shrugged. 'He's useful.'

I stood up to go to bed.

'What, no pretty smiles left for me? Did Monsieur Clérmont have them all?'

I tensed as he twitched a fold of my nightgown. 'Take it off.'

I hesitated. What might he do if I refused? His expression made me fearful of finding out.

My nerves jangled as I lifted the nightgown over my head. The silk felt cold against my bare skin. Uneasily, I covered my breasts with my hands, but Karl grabbed my wrists and pulled them away.

'Get on the bed.'

He forced me down so that I sat with my legs dangling over the side, then he pushed my thighs apart and moved to stand between them. He unbuttoned himself and hoisted me onto him. At the first thrust, I let out a cry of pain, but he ignored it and continued. The splayed fingers of his right hand weighed heavily on my breastbone, ramming my spine into the bed and his nails gouged the skin at the base of my neck. It was hard to breathe and my head thrummed as the blood rushed to it.

When he had finished, he pulled himself out and closed my legs. The gesture felt like a final humiliation. 'I'll sleep alone tonight,' he said coldly. 'I trust you won't forget this.'

And with that, he was gone.

Wretched and sore, I crept to the bathroom and douched with one of Mariette's potions. The white enamel fittings and brass taps winked maliciously at me. What a hideous end to the evening. I had paid dearly for my lapse.

I closed my eyes and rested my forehead on one hand. My thoughts went back to Antoine. Our conversation had been innocent. All I had wanted to do was to help a talented young man. Didn't I have the right to make such a small choice?

The palm of my hand stung and I realised that my fist had been clenched so tightly that my nails had made red wheals in the skin. I pressed the place against my cold cheek to soothe it. In reality, I knew the bitter truth. In Karl's eyes, I had no rights. I belonged to him, and if I displeased him, his charm splintered easily.

Chapter 15

Karl behaved as if that night had never happened and a few days later, he left for Berlin on one of his business trips. I had known about it for a while and had planned to join Péri and Mariette for an evening out but, still shaken, I wasn't sure I could face company - even theirs.

I should have known Mariette would respond to my excuses by visiting me. 'You don't seem ill,' she said suspiciously. 'What's happened? Is something the matter between you and Karl?'

What had happened after the Summer Salon was still too raw in my memory to speak of, but eventually, for the sake of peace, I let her persuade me and we went to join Péri.

It was a balmy evening and on the drive up to Montmartre, aromas of tobacco and coffee drifted from the crowded terraces of the cafés.

Our destination was the Moulin de la Galette, one of Mariette's favourite nightspots. It was crowded and noisy. Behind the long, wine-stained bar, harassed girls struggled to serve their jostling customers.

'Phew,' Péri shouted above the din. 'It's busy tonight. Fine weather always brings out the crowds.

Let's go into the garden, maybe there's a table free there.'

The air was fresher outside and thousands of tiny white lights sparkled in the trees. At one end of the garden, a small orchestra played a polka under the direction of a stout conductor with thickly pomaded hair and an extravagant moustache. In vain we scanned the tables around the dance floor for an empty one.

'We'll have to go elsewhere,' Péri said.

Mariette pouted.

A burly, jovial young man with sandy hair and a full beard stood up from one of the tables and came over to us. He greeted Péri warmly.

Péri clapped him on the back. 'Henri! What a pleasant surprise. Mariette, Anna, this is Henri Bertin. He painted the scenery for *Orfeo* for me.'

'I hope you and your friends will do us the honour of joining us?' the young man asked. I glanced at the table he indicated and, to my dismay, saw that Antoine Clérmont was among the party. Jules Fauchon had found a publisher for his book and Antoine had sent me a long letter of grateful thanks, but I simply returned a polite message of congratulation. I knew it was best not to see him again.

Mariette beamed. 'We'd be delighted.'

Unable to think of an excuse, I followed them to the table. I recognised Antoine's friend, Paul Vallon - he didn't look in the best of tempers. His eyes, just visible under his panama hat, were faintly bloodshot. Two young women sat there as well. One of them smiled at us. She was plump and pretty with blonde hair piled up under a cornflower blue hat that matched her dress. The other merely nodded. Her mousey hair and faded complexion gave her a dejected air.

Henri made the introductions. The blonde young woman was his wife, Virginie, and her mousey companion was Paul's wife, Camille, who was also Antoine's sister.

Antoine stood up to greet us, smiling at me, but I quickly looked away and took the seat Henri held out for me at the other end of the table.

The general conversation absolved me of the need to say much. Only Paul Vallon didn't join in, staring moodily into his glass which he refilled frequently. When the bottle close to him was empty, he reached clumsily across the table for another. It rocked and would have fallen if Henri hadn't caught it.

'I think you've had enough tonight, Paul,' Henri said firmly.

Paul scowled. 'Don't tell me what to do.'

His voice rose above the hum of conversation and an awkward silence ensued. A wary look flashed between Henri and Antoine. Camille stared at her lap.

Just then, the orchestra struck up a popular tune and Mariette grabbed Péri's hand. 'Oh, this is my favourite. Let's dance.'

'Of course, my love.'

'Come on, Paul,' Henri said in a mollifying tone. 'I see Camille's foot tapping.'

Paul had the grace to look a little embarrassed after his outburst. He stood up and offered Camille his hand. Henri and Virginie followed, leaving Antoine and me alone.

He came to sit beside me. 'Would you like to dance?' His voice travelled up my spine; it would be madness to give in to my longing to feel his arms around me. I shook my head.

'Madame Daubigny … Anna.' He stopped. 'I hope I may call you Anna?'

I didn't reply, my heart hammering.

He frowned. 'I'm afraid I've angered you in some way.'

'Angered me? We hardly know each other, Monsieur.'

'I thought perhaps…'

His expression drained the blood from my heart. I couldn't bear to hurt him. 'Forgive me,' I said. 'I'm tired and too hot. I didn't mean to be rude.'

'Would you like to take a walk? It will be cooler away from the dance floor and all these people.'

We strolled along, at first in silence, but soon talking of all kinds of things. Being with him seemed so natural and easy, what harm could there be in enjoying one evening in his company?

'It's too hot to dance any more,' Mariette gasped, coming to join us with Péri in tow.

We chatted for a while then returned to the table to say our farewells to Henri and the others. Antoine's eyes held mine as we said goodbye, 'May I see you again?' he asked quietly.

I felt a tug at my heart. If only I were free to follow it. I murmured something non-committal and his uncomprehending, disappointed expression cut me to the core.

Péri went to find a fiacre to take us home.

'You're a dark horse, Anna,' Mariette smiled while we waited. 'He seems very nice, that Antoine. Lovely eyes – very romantic. But you will be careful, won't you?'

The ache inside me grew. 'Don't be silly, Mariette. We were only talking, it didn't mean anything.'

She shrugged. 'Have it your own way.'

Péri came back to us. 'No luck yet, I'm afraid. I just wanted to make sure you were all right, then I'll go and try again.'

'We're fine, but don't be too long, it's getting chilly,' Mariette said.

She put her hand to her throat. 'Damn, I left my shawl inside. Go back for it for me, would you, my love?'

A few moments after he'd gone, a group of men lurched out, tipsy and laughing noisily. One of them saw us and stopped. 'Looking for someone to go home with, ladies?' he leered.

Mariette scowled at him but he persisted, grabbing her by the waist. With a well-aimed kick, she sent him hopping away on one leg, howling.

She seized my hand. 'Come on, we'd better go and find Péri before they get nasty.' A volley of imprecations followed us.

Péri had found the shawl and was weaving his way back through the tables. It was then that I saw Antoine. He wasn't with his friends any longer; he stood with a tall, dark-haired woman who wore a crimson dress. They didn't notice me and as I watched them, the woman tilted her face up to Antoine's and gave him a lingering kiss.

A wave of nausea swept over me and a void opened beneath my feet. How dared he speak to me as he had done tonight? The only reason he was courting me was that I might be useful to him. What a joke he and his lover must be enjoying at my expense. I wished I had never helped him.

'Anna? Whatever's the matter?' Mariette tugged at my arm. 'You look as if you've seen a ghost.'

I whirled round, thankful she hadn't noticed Antoine.

'Nothing's the matter. Let's go home.'

Chapter 16

Karl travelled frequently to Berlin that winter and the following spring and even when he was in Paris, I saw little of him. The stream of invitations we usually receive slowed. It was not hard to guess why - anti-Prussian sentiment was on the rise.

Relations were strained between the two countries, made worse by the situation in Spain. Some time ago, the Spanish queen, Isabella, had fled to France after a revolution in her country. Since then, the Spanish throne had been vacant and the question of who should succeed to it was the subject of a great deal of speculation and rivalry.

King William of Prussia and his chief adviser, Prince Bismarck, fanned the flames when they proposed that a Prussian prince should take Isabella's place. The idea of a Prussian puppet state on France's southern border enraged the Emperor. In his view, he should be the one to dictate the succession in France's interests.

Summer came, and one morning I was reading an article about all the diplomatic wrangling that was taking place, when Edouard was announced. He had forsaken his favourite crumpled tweeds, but the dark trousers and jacket he wore still looked baggy and comfortable rather than stylish.

'I'm worn out,' he announced. 'Those Council meetings at the Académie will be the death of me: a lot of old men droning on for hours.' He sighed. 'And your stairs don't get any easier, especially in the heat. Karl should install one of those new-fangled elevators they have in America.'

My lips twitched. 'I'll tell him.' I reached for the bell. 'Do sit down. Shall I order us some iced tea or would you prefer a brandy?'

'Brandy please, my dear.'

He glanced at the newspaper I was reading. 'You mustn't worry yourself with such stuff,' he said. 'Bismarck and William are sure to back down. When it comes to it, they won't want to take on France. It's all sabre-rattling.'

I frowned. 'I hope so.'

'What does Karl say?'

'We don't talk of it. I hardly see him, he's away so much.'

Edouard squeezed my hand. 'Unrest is bad for business. He's bound to be preoccupied. I'm sure when everything returns to normal he will be his old self.'

I nodded, but inwardly I shuddered. It was a relief that Karl took so little notice of me; I was not at all sure I wanted that to change.

We talked for an hour then Edouard heaved himself out of his chair.

'I must leave you, my dear. I promised to visit Jules Fauchon this afternoon. By the way, he's impressed with that young man, Clérmont, you introduced him to. Apparently his novel is selling well.'

My chest tightened. Edouard looked at me.

'Is something the matter?'

'Nothing at all,' I said recovering my composure. 'I'm glad for him, of course, but I really had nothing to do with it.'

Edouard shrugged. 'I must have misunderstood.'

He pulled a handkerchief from his pocket and mopped his brow. 'My goodness, even standing up is too much effort.' He patted his ample middle. 'Perhaps I should lose some of this.' He stuffed the handkerchief back in his pocket. 'Well, give my regards to Karl.'

He put his hand under my chin and tilted my face up to his. 'And don't worry, everything will be fine. Life will go on as it always has. Do you know what I think?'

I shook my head.

'A change of scene would do you good. I'll call for you tomorrow morning and take you for a drive in the Bois de Boulogne. It will be pleasant out there.'

'That would be lovely.'

'Very well - until tomorrow.'

*

Edouard was right. It was pleasant to leave the hot, dusty streets behind and drive through the Bois de Boulogne. The sky was a deep, cloudless blue and the dappled shade under the trees refreshed my spirits.

We turned down a broad carriageway and I saw a magnificent landau approaching us, flanked by outriders in maroon and cream livery. Edouard's driver abruptly slowed our horses and swerved to one side as the equipage flew past. In it, I caught a glimpse of a corpulent man whom I recognised. He was Barbizon - the banker Karl had sat me next to at dinner on that dreadful night. But it was the dark-haired woman beside him who sent a shock through me. She was the same one I had seen with Antoine at the Moulin de la Galette.

Edouard grimaced. 'No manners.'

Our driver brought the horses back to the path and we moved on but my pleasure in the drive had been snuffed out. Was the woman with Barbizon playing a double game, deceiving Antoine just as he had duped me? Or did they both know exactly what was going on? Were they as cold and calculating as each other? I suspected the latter. I had seen them together, kissing as lovers do. They deserved each other.

I remembered my first meeting with Antoine and the subsequent one at the Summer Salon. He had seemed so genuine. What a naïve fool I was to trust in appearances. Had life taught me nothing?

Edouard's carriage slowed again and I looked up to see that it was to let a troop of cavalry overtake us. Harnesses and accoutrements jangling, they trotted by, each man ramrod straight in the midnight-blue and white uniform of the Imperial

Guard, their sabres and plumed helmets gleaming in the sunshine.

Edouard gave an approving nod. 'Magnificent, aren't they? Paris has nothing to fear with such men to protect her.'

*

The next morning, faced with the prospect of another long day alone in the house, I decided to visit Mariette in the afternoon but, forestalling me, she arrived soon after the maids had cleared away breakfast. We greeted each other warmly then, with a glance at the clock on the mantelpiece, I asked if it wasn't rather early for her to be out and about.

She laughed. 'I don't *always* stay in bed half the day, Anna. Anyway, I have plans. Péri and I happened to see Henri and Virginie last night. They're going out to the river at Argenteuil today to make the most of this lovely weather. They asked if we'd like join them. We said we would. They're such a charming couple. I would be nice to know them better. Why don't you come too?'

'Oh Mariette, I'm not sure I should.'

'Karl's still away, isn't he?'

'Yes, but—'

'Then what harm can there be in it? Tell the servants you're going shopping. Rose will be discreet.'

I felt uncomfortable. It wasn't fair to grow into the habit of expecting Rose to help explain away my absences. It might get her into trouble. In Karl's household, I was never certain who could be trusted. Even though Karl knew Péri and Mariette, I wasn't sure he would think it appropriate for me to spend a great deal of time in their company these days. There was another consideration too: I didn't want to meet Antoine again. Still, as long as he was not in the party, an afternoon by the river would be a welcome distraction.

'Who else will be there?' I asked.

Only us three, Henri and Virginie – oh, and perhaps the Vallons.

I hesitated, but then decided that if Mariette was wrong and Antoine joined us, I would simply stay close to her and Péri. If Antoine had the gall to single me out, I'd have no compunction in snubbing him, in fact it would give me considerable satisfaction. Why should I stay here on my own and be miserable, just because of such a scoundrel?

I smiled. 'Very well, I'll come.'

'Excellent. So hurry up and get ready.'

*

We made the short journey out to Argenteuil by train from the Gare St Lazare. Henri, Virginie and the Vallons were already there, comfortably established in a picturesque spot along the towpath in the shade of some poplar trees. A picnic of bread, cheese and fruit was laid out on a blue and white checked cloth.

Henri and Paul stood up. 'Here you are!' Henri beamed. 'We're so glad you came.'

Virginie kissed Mariette on both cheeks and welcomed me warmly. Even Camille and Paul seemed in a sunnier mood than they had done at the Moulin de la Galette.

Dotted with the rust-red hulls of sailing boats and skiffs, the Seine glided lazily along between its wide banks. Mats of waterweed floated on the water, creating a mosaic of emerald and marine blue. In contrast the sky was azure, dabbed with powder-puff clouds.

Péri inhaled deeply. 'What a beautiful day. It calls for a glass of wine, don't you think?' He held out the basket we had carried down with us.

Henri chuckled. 'A man after my own heart: I already have one cooling.' He went to the riverbank where a string tied to a bush at the water margin disappeared into the water. He hauled on it and up came a dripping bottle, swathed in weed from the depths. He sloughed off the weed and touched his hand to the green glass.

'Just right.'

Péri passed him the basket. 'Take these to replace it.'

The wine poured, we sat chatting for a while then Henri, who had been lounging back on his elbows, sat up and stretched his legs.

'Well, if you will excuse us, it's time Paul and I did some work.'

'Even on such a beautiful day?' Mariette asked.

'Especially on such a beautiful day, the light is too good to miss. Look at the water, how it shimmers in the sunshine.'

He went over to a tree and fetched back the easels, small canvases and bulky satchels stacked there.

'Mon Dieu,' said Mariette, 'did you really carry all that on the train?'

'It's not so difficult. We do it all the time. Paint comes in tubes these days which is a great help. We tie the canvases tightly to our easels if the wind's blowing - et voilà! Mind you,' he chuckled, 'we've had a few disasters. Once Paul went to the seaside to paint and mistook the time of the tides. A wave washed him into the sea with all his equipment. He was flailing around like a madman - paints, canvases, brushes, floating off in all directions.'

'And I'll never be allowed to forget it,' Paul said, but he laughed too.

'So you sell the paintings in Paris?' asked Péri.

'Anywhere I can. Sometimes there are tourists here who like a memento of their visit. Usually they refuse to give much, but it all helps pay the bills.'

After they had gone to find the view they wanted to paint, Péri yawned. 'If you ladies will excuse me, I think I'll have a snooze for a few minutes.'

Mariette snorted. 'A few minutes? An hour more like. And you'll snore, as you always do.' She stood up. 'Would anyone else like a walk?'

Virginie got to her feet and shook out her skirt. 'I'll come.'

'And so will I,' Camille said.

I chided myself for it, but I half wanted to draw her out on the subject of her brother, so I agreed to go as well.

The four of us strolled along the towpath chatting. As usual, Mariette took the lead in the conversation but Virginie seemed friendly and took the trouble to address some of her remarks to me. Camille was a different matter. She showed no interest at all in talking to me. I wondered if Antoine had even told her of how I had helped him. If he had, her behaviour was unpardonably rude, but I tried to give her credit for being in ignorance.

We returned to Paris before sunset. At home, the porter let me in but none of the other servants were about. The lamps had not been lit in the hallway and it seemed dark after the brightness of the day. Still preoccupied, I went upstairs to take off my outdoor clothes but when I rang the bell for Rose, she didn't come. It was a little strange she hadn't returned yet. Even though I had given her the afternoon off, it was unlike her to stay away so long. I rang the bell once more. Again the sound faded into an uncanny silence.

I sat down at my dressing table and unpinned my hat. A few coils of hair slipped down over my shoulders as I removed it. All at once, tears of frustration filled my eyes. I dashed them away with the back of my hand and snatched up a powder puff, dabbing furiously at my face to hide the flush on my cheeks. Footsteps outside the door broke the silence. They were not light and bustling like Rose's.

The door opened and I jumped. Silhouetted against the light from the passage, Karl stood watching me.

My pulse raced. 'Karl! I didn't expect you home so soon.'

'Evidently.' He stood behind me, his hands a heavy pressure on my shoulders. 'I was worried about you,' he said. 'Your maid told me you had gone to boulevard Haussmann to do some shopping, but none of the coachmen recalled driving you there.'

Ice entered my veins. 'I had planned to do that,' I stammered, 'but it was such a fine day. Mariette and Péri from the theatre invited me to go out to Argenteuil with them instead. I've been alone here so much recently. I thought you would have no objection.'

He didn't answer and my mouth went dry. 'I hope you don't mind,' I added lamely.

The pressure on my shoulders increased. I fought down the urge to try and shake him off.

'I'm surprised your maid wasn't aware of your change of plan,' he said curtly. 'Why didn't you tell her?'

'I thought I had… she must have misunderstood me.'

I winced as his fingers dug into my flesh. He bent over me and with a swift movement twined one hand in my loose hair and wrenched my head back. His face was a few inches from mine, his eyes scorched me. 'You're lying,' he hissed.

My heart kicked against my ribs. I was terrified that he would take me by force again.

'No, I swear it.'

'Why should I believe you?'

'It's true,' I gasped. The room filled with grey mist as I fought to breathe.

Abruptly, he released me and my head jerked forward, striking the mirror at the back of the dressing table. For a moment, dizziness dimmed my vision then I saw Karl's implacable expression.

'This time, I'll accept your explanation,' he said sourly, 'but don't test my patience again. I shall dismiss your maid. I'll select a more trustworthy one myself.'

'Please, Karl, let Rose stay. None of this is her fault.'

'Then your punishment will be the knowledge you have put her on the street.'

I gnawed my lower lip. Clearly, there was to be no discussion.

'In any case, we may not be in Paris much longer. My business in Berlin is more important.' He smiled. 'It is a much finer city than Paris. I'm sure you will be happy there and I shall be with you far more often too. There will be no need for you to be lonely.'

Chapter 17

The next few days were wretched. I disliked the maid Karl hired, a ghastly woman called Agathe. Her face was habitually set in an expression that would curdle milk. My guilt over Rose's dismissal ran deep too. She had wept when she said goodbye and even that had to be done in Agathe's stony presence. All I had been able to do was whisper to Rose that she should go to Mariette and tell her what had happened. I hoped Mariette would help her find her feet again.

Karl and I went the opera that week, and to the races at Longchamps to watch his horses run. Wherever we were, though, it was impossible to ignore the way people whispered behind their hands as we passed. If they couldn't avoid us, they greeted us with coldness.

Even Edouard was less confident than he had been that there would be no war. 'You must prepare yourself, Anna,' he said, his demeanour more grave than I had ever seen it. 'If war comes, Karl will have to leave France, or be imprisoned as an enemy alien.'

'He's already talked of going back to Prussia,' I said unhappily.

Edouard sighed. 'With your Russian nationality, you should have no difficulties in Prussia, but you'll be missed here. I'm an old man, Anna; I shall be seventy soon and I have no family. You've become like a daughter to me.'

I kissed his cheek. 'Oh Edouard, I would miss you so much too.'

*

A few days later, on the way to my dressmaker in the boulevard Haussmann, the carriage jolted to a halt.

'Shall I get out and see what is the matter, Madame?' Agathe asked. Karl insisted she accompanied me everywhere. He said it was for my safety.

'There's no need. I'm sure we'll move on again soon.'

The coachman's face appeared at the open window. 'I'm sorry, Madame Daubigny, we may have to go another way. There are gendarmes turning carriages back.'

I leant out and saw two men in the familiar blue uniform of the gendarmerie running by.

'What a nuisance, I'll be late for my appointment. See if you can find out if it's really necessary for them to stop us.'

I sat in the stuffy carriage fanning myself. Whatever was happening, it was causing a great deal of noise. Perhaps there had been an accident of some kind.

After a few minutes, a gendarme appeared at the window. 'I'm sorry you are inconvenienced, Madame, but this is for your own safety. There's a mob up ahead.'

The word sent a shudder through me. I remembered what Emile had said about the mob. I had thought his opinion cruel then, but as the carriage wheeled round and I saw hordes of people blocking the road, punching the air with their fists and baying for blood, I felt very vulnerable. Karl had recently purchased a coat of arms and had it emblazoned on the doors of all his carriages. Unlikely as it was that these people would recognise it, I was very glad when the yells of *Down with Bismarck! Down with Prussia!* faded into the distance.

Agathe remained silent, her hands folded in her lap and her expression grim.

*

The July heat did nothing to cool Paris' volcanic mood, but after a few days, there was good news: the Prussians had withdrawn their candidate for the Spanish throne. Surely that would be the end of the matter and Karl would stay in Paris? I felt greatly relieved. It seemed the crisis was over.

But events took an unexpected turn. The Prussians' change of heart was not enough to satisfy the Emperor. He demanded a personal letter of apology from King William and a guarantee that Prussia would never again meddle in the affairs of

Spain. If it was not forthcoming, he made it clear that France would declare war.

Karl was furious, certain that Bismarck would never advise his king to bow down to such insulting treatment. Within a day, workmen filled the house. Paintings, silver, porcelain and glass vanished into tea chests and wrappings. The statue of Daphne and Apollo was padded with straw, swathed in cloth and removed. The smaller, more precious pieces of furniture, including the Marie Antoinette desk, went with it. I wondered if it wasn't already too late to get them out of Paris but decided it was wisest not to ask questions.

Our departure for Berlin approached and once more I faced the prospect of a new life in Prussia. My dismay increased with every passing hour. I was leaving dear friends behind, and my future happiness with Karl was by no means assured.

The house looked bleak, devoid as it was of all its beautiful treasures. Karl had also dismissed most of the servants, leaving a few trusted ones whose job it would be to stand guard in our absence.

'I'm in no hurry to return,' he said grimly, 'but I won't sell the place yet. The market is always bad in wartime and I've a considerable investment at stake.' I didn't dare say that the French might have other ideas about what should happen to the house.

The day before we were due to travel, Karl announced we would dine at our favourite restaurant in the rue de Rivoli. I tried to persuade him it would be best to stay at home but he refused to listen. When he came to my room that evening, he frowned at the dress I had decided to wear – a simple grey crêpe-de-chine trimmed with Brussels lace. Around my neck I wore a single strand of pearls. I had thought the ensemble elegant, yet understated. I had chosen it because I didn't want to draw attention to myself that evening.

Karl shook his head and ordered Agathe to bring out a selection of gowns. He studied them intently.

'The crimson taffeta.'

'It's such a hot evening,' I pleaded. 'I shall be far too warm in taffeta.'

He scowled. 'Help Madame to change, Agathe, and bring her the diamond and ruby necklace, it will add the perfect finishing touch.'

Inwardly, I groaned. My hopes of going unnoticed were dashed.

When I came downstairs, Karl stood in the hallway pulling on his gloves. With a glance at the gilt-framed mirror above one of the side tables, he flicked an infinitesimal speck of dust from the satin lapel of his jacket then brushed his lips coolly across my cheek.

'Much better.'

Outside, our carriage waited under the porte cochère. Karl held out his hand to help me in. As my foot touched the first step, one of the horses jibbed. The whites of its eyes flashing, it backed into the carriage, setting it rocking violently.

Karl caught me as I stumbled then he turned on the groom who held the horse's head.

'You stupid fool,' he spat. 'What do I pay you for? Can't you control the animal? I'll show the pair of you who is master.' He grabbed the whip from the man's hand.

The groom turned pale and the horse reared up on its hind legs, froth spewing from its nostrils. I clutched Karl's arm. 'Karl, I beg you, it was an accident. I'm unharmed. Let the groom calm the poor creature in his own way. It will be quicker.'

I held my breath, my heart knocking. Karl's face was pale with rage. It seemed that an hour rather than a moment had passed when he shrugged.

'Very well, if you wish it.'

He nodded to the groom. 'Be thankful that Madame spoke up for you.'

The groom mumbled his thanks; beads of sweat glistened on his forehead. When he had calmed the horse, he shot me a grateful glance.

At the rue de Rivoli, the maître d' hurried to greet us with an abject expression on his face. 'Monsieur Buhler, a thousand apologies - we have no tables free tonight.'

I looked over his shoulder to the dining room, gleaming with brass and mahogany and crystal chandeliers. I could see several empty tables.

Karl snorted. 'Rubbish.'

The maître wrung his hands. 'I am sorry...'

Another party arrived and swept past us in a gust of expensive perfume and disapproving stares. 'What insolence,' one of the women said to her partner, in a voice she clearly intended us to hear.

Karl's brow darkened. 'Come, Anna, we'll go elsewhere.'

But it was the same story at the next restaurant and the one after that. Eventually, Karl's coachman found a place where we were not known and we sat down to our meal. No longer hungry, I struggled to eat. The food tasted like sawdust and the wine vinegar. I was very glad to leave and return to the Champs Elysées.

At the lodge there was no sign of the porter. Instead, a large crowd of men and a few women and children were huddled outside the wrought-iron gates. They were shabbily dressed and, in the waning light, I saw hostile, sullen expressions on the faces of those nearest to us. When they noticed the carriage, they got to their feet.

'This is intolerable,' Karl snarled. He rapped on the carriage wall to summon the coachman. The carriage swayed as the man clambered down from his box. His perturbed face appeared at the window.

'I don't think they'll move, Monsieur Buhler.'

'Where's the porter?'

'There's no sign of him.'

'Get some of the footmen then. Use force if you have to.'

The coachman looked doubtful. 'There are more than a hundred of them, Monsieur. Perhaps we should go to the rear entrance.'

Karl didn't speak and for a moment I was afraid he would refuse. Then he exhaled sharply. 'Oh, very well, I suppose it will mean less delay.'

The carriage was just moving off when a boy ran forward and snatched at the sill of the open window. Karl brought his cane down hard on the boy's hand. He cried out and let go, then disappeared from view. A violent jolt startled me. It was followed by a high-pitched scream.

I clutched Karl's arm. 'He might be hurt. Shouldn't we try to help?'

The line between Karl's brows deepened. 'Don't be foolish, Anna. One urchin less is of no importance.' I would have persisted but his grim expression frightened me.

I had always entered the house by the front entrance; it was a shock to see that the approach to the rear was completely different from the grand frontage and immaculate gardens on the Champs Elysées. The coach wended its way through narrow alleys lined with ramshackle dwellings. Late as it was, many people were still about. Pinched women, cradling their rag-swaddled babies, threw us resentful looks. Nameless filth sullied the ground and the air smelt sour.

Karl pulled up the window. 'Disgusting! How can they live like this?'

I didn't dare say that they probably had no choice.

We reached the rear entrance to the house and the carriage slowed to pass the guards stationed there, but as we drove into the courtyard, a shiver went down my spine. The noise from the alleyways we had left behind had been fading, but suddenly it increased. Shouts and running feet echoed all around us, insistent, menacing, growing louder by the second. Before the guards had time to close the gates, shots rang out. With a deafening roar, the mob surged through and overtook us.

I shrank into the corner of my seat as grimy hands wrenched open the door on Karl's side of the carriage. He lashed out at the first of his assailants, punching him squarely in the face. The man reeled, blood spurting from his nose. The men behind him, faces contorted with hatred, pulled him aside and jostled to climb into the carriage. Karl tried to strike again but the confined space hampered him. The blood roared in my ears and I screamed. Karl had no chance of beating off so many. We were trapped.

I felt a breath of air on my cheek and I froze. The door on my side had opened and a face loomed out of the darkness. I closed my eyes and waited for the blow to fall, but instead, someone jerked me out of the carriage. I landed on the ground on all fours; my hands and knees burned. The voluminous skirts of my evening gown tangled around my legs as I struggled to stand up. I fell once more and cried out in pain.

A swift slap knocked me sideways. I tasted the metallic tang of blood and knew my lip had split. The groom I had saved from a beating was standing over me. 'Quickly,' he hissed. 'Before they finish with your fancy man and turn on us.'

'I can't get up.'

'You have to.'

He half dragged, half carried me towards the outbuildings that ran along one side of the courtyard.

'What do we do now?' I gasped when we were safely inside one of them.

'We? I'm getting out of this place. You can wait here until things quieten down. Pray they don't think of looking for you.'

'You'd leave me?'

'Haven't I done enough for you? Unless…' His eyes ranged greedily over my necklace.

My hand went to my throat and I felt the hard, cold stones against my palm. 'It's yours, but only after you get me out of here.'

My heartbeat raced. I'd be no match for him if he decided to take the necklace anyway. My only hope was that whatever goodwill I had gained by helping him earlier in the evening would carry me through.

He chewed his lip.

'Take me to my friends,' I pleaded. 'There'll be more money for you.'

'All right,' he said at last, 'but you'd better not be planning to cheat me.'

We were in a large storeroom where sacks of dry goods were stacked around the walls. Crates of vegetables and fruit stood on shelves and strings of onions and garlic hung from the beams. It was a homely, well-ordered sight, but my nerves were already strung to breaking point. The pungent smell of the garlic and onions administered the final twist to my churning stomach. I doubled over and vomited.

When I had finished, a violent bout of shivering overtook me.

'I'll find you some different clothes,' the groom said. 'If you go out in that dress, you won't last a minute.'

He upended a crate of cabbages and they bumped across the floor as he tore a stout piece of wood off the crate. The exposed nails glinted.

'Here,' he said, handing it to me. 'It'll be better than nothing if anyone comes in. If that happens, you're on your own.'

'That boy—' I said wretchedly.

'What of him?'

'We should have stopped to help.'

The groom gave an ugly laugh. 'And be slaughtered there? You don't know the mob like I do. Word probably got round that Buhler's Prussian - why else would they be waiting for him – but if they'd planned to stop at a few insults, the boy changed all that.'

I crouched on the stone flags, waiting for the groom's return. Outside, there were running feet, shouts and whistles. I heard gunshots too. Karl's guards must be trying to beat off the mob.

By the time the groom came back, the noise sounded further away. He dumped a bundle of clothes on the floor. 'They didn't spot me,' he said. 'Most of them are in the main part of the house. I found these in the laundry. I'll turn away while you get into them.'

I struggled out of my gown and put on the maid's dress, making sure its high collar hid my necklace. There were serviceable boots to replace my ruined satin pumps and I tucked my hair under the maid's cap.

'Are you done?'

'Yes.'

He surveyed me briefly. 'You'll pass.'

'I don't know your name.'

'Jacques.'

'Thank you, Jacques. You're very brave to do this for me.'

He shrugged. 'I'm doing it for myself too. Plenty of people hereabouts know I work for

Buhler. I'll get short shrift if they catch me. Now come on.'

A rind of moon cast its light over the courtyard. Our overturned carriage looked like the carcass of a huge beast. The coachman's body lay spreadeagled close by it. I hesitated, but Jacques grabbed my arm and pulled me on. Lights shone in the house's windows and figures moved across them. The mob was inside. Ahead of us, a gang of men pelted into the courtyard, brandishing flaming torches. 'Hey! You're going in the wrong direction!' one of them shouted.

Jacques squeezed my waist and grinned. 'Smash a few windows for me, friends. Just now I've better things to do.'

The man sniggered. 'Come back when you're done. No point letting the Prussian bastard's stuff go to waste.'

Nearer to the gate, we passed more bodies. Jacques put a foot under one of them and rolled it onto its back.

'The captain of the guard,' he said. He bent down and ripped off the captain's epaulettes. 'Nice bit of gold thread in these.' He patted down the captain's trousers and scooped a few coins from his pockets.

Lanterns hung from brackets attached to the tall gateposts. To my horror, a body dangled at the end of the rope thrown over one of them. It swung slowly round and bile rushed into my mouth. 'Don't come over faint on me,' Jacques growled. 'Look somewhere else.'

But it was too late for that: I had already seen Karl's battered and bloodied face. His clothes were half torn away, showing terrible wounds on his body.

I swayed and Jacques caught me. 'No use crying over him now,' he muttered.

The maze of alleys we entered echoed eerily with our footsteps. A throbbing head and a buzz in my ears was the only legacy of the uproar of the mob.

'I expect they've all gone off to drink the cellars dry,' Jacques said wryly. 'I could do with a drink myself.'

We walked north and reached an area where there were more people about. The smell of stale cooking and cheap tobacco in the café we went into made me clutch the doorjamb to steady myself.

Jacques sat me down at a table and went up to the counter.

'Courtesy of our deceased friend, the captain,' he said when he came back with a carafe of wine and two glasses.

I shivered and he raised an eyebrow. 'It's no use to him, is it?'

The wine was rough, stripping my throat as I swallowed it. It must have been strong too, for after one glass, I felt light-headed.

'Should we go to the police?' I asked Jacques.

He laughed. 'And spoil the fun? Oh, don't worry. Someone's probably called them by now. There'll be a grand fight when they get there.'

He slopped some more wine into his glass and knocked it back. 'So, where do you want me to take you?'

'Do you know the Lorette quarter?'

'Of course, but I'm surprised you have friends there.'

He nodded at the carafe. 'More of this before we go?'

I shook my head.

'Then I'll finish it.'

In the street, Jacques pointed to the smoke drifting from the direction of the house. 'The fools must have torched it,' he frowned. 'It'll go badly with them when they're rounded up. Property counts with the authorities, even if it was a Prussian who owned it.'

The wine seemed to have no effect on Jacques but my head was muzzy. We were nearly at Mariette and Péri's apartment when the bells of Notre Dame de Lorette struck four. Each stroke was like a hammer blow. At the street door, Jacques stopped, grabbed my arm and held out his hand.

'Give it to me then.'

For a moment, fear had driven our bargain out of my mind and I stared at him. He spun me round and twisted my arm up my back. 'You heard me. The necklace.'

My hands trembled as I reached up and unclasped it. Rubies would always remind me of that night. I never wanted to wear them again.

'Here, it's yours.'

Jacques stuffed the necklace in his pocket, but rather than releasing me, he pulled me close. 'How about a little extra reward,' he said thickly. His teeth bruised my lips and he forced his tongue into my mouth. I jabbed my knee into his groin. With a howl, he let me go and doubled over. 'You little whore,' he wheezed.

I didn't wait for him to recover. The street door wasn't locked and I ran in. Upstairs, I banged on the door. 'Mariette! Péri! It's me, Anna! Let me in.'

I slumped against the wall. The reviving effect of the wine had all gone and exhaustion had taken its place. I was ready to slide to the floor when the door opened and Péri peered out, dressed in his nightclothes. His jaw dropped. 'Anna! What in the name of Heaven—'

Mariette pushed him aside. 'Don't stand in the way,' she snapped. 'Can't you see something's wrong?' She held out her arms to me and the last vestige of my composure crumbled.

She helped me inside and made me sit down. 'Get your breath back, then you can tell us what's happened.'

I tried to explain but soon floundered.

'Fetch her some brandy, Péri,' Mariette said.

'I don't want any,' I sobbed.

'It'll help calm you,' Mariette said firmly.

After I'd drunk the brandy and managed to tell them everything, Péri stood up. 'I'll get dressed and go and see what's happening now,' he said.

'Be careful,' Mariette warned.

'Don't worry, I will be.'

When he returned, he had a grim tale to tell. A large number of firemen and water trucks had arrived at the house but not in time to prevent a great deal of damage. Most of the main building had already collapsed and the blackened walls that remained looked as if they would need to be demolished too.

'I couldn't get close,' Péri said. 'It was too hot for one thing and anyway, the police have set up a cordon to keep looters at bay.' He put a hand on my shoulder. 'I'm sorry to bring you such bad news, Anna.'

Mariette helped me to my feet. 'There's nothing more we can do for now. Come, you need to sleep.'

*

Mariette insisted she and Péri give up their bed for me and I slept until late afternoon. When I woke, Péri had gone to the theatre but Mariette took me out to find something to eat. The café she chose was more pleasant than the one Jacques had picked the previous night, but still very shabby compared with the places I had grown accustomed to. We sat down and Mariette studied me anxiously. 'You're very pale, Anna.'

'I'm just tired.'

The owner bustled over and wiped our table. She smiled at Mariette. 'What can I get you?'

'Bring us a carafe of wine please, and your plat du jour.'

'Certainly.'

The plat du jour was a stew of beans with onions, garlic and a few pieces of stringy meat. I wasn't used to plain food any longer but I was hungry enough to eat almost anything.

'I know this place doesn't look much,' remarked Mariette as we ate, 'but the food's all right and it's cheap. Business isn't very good at the theatre at the moment, and now Péri and I are on our own and I don't have a rich man around, we have to watch what we spend.'

To my shame, her words precipitated a bout of tears and they splashed into the stew making it even more watery than before. Mariette took the spoon from my shaky hand and pushed the plate away.

'I'm so sorry,' I wept.

'Don't be silly. I'm the one who should be sorry. It was a thoughtless thing to say. You've had a terrible experience. Cry as much as you need.'

I wiped my eyes. 'Karl wasn't always kind to me, but to be murdered so horribly – he didn't deserve that.'

'I know.'

'What do you think will happen? I hate to think of his body being treated with no respect. I should at least try to see he has a decent burial.'

'Did he have any family?'

'I don't think so. If he did, he never spoke of them.'

'Friends?'

'We were invited to a lot of occasions but he never seemed close to anyone.'

Suddenly, I thought of Edouard. He was always kind and would care about giving Karl a respectful end. I must make sure he knew what had happened.

'I think I know one man who'll help,' I said.

'Then we'll go and find him.'

*

As I had hoped, Edouard took charge immediately. He made the arrangements to recover Karl's body from the morgue and had it taken to the cemetery of Père Lachaise. The funeral was a very quiet affair: the mourners consisted of Edouard, Mariette, Péri and me. To my dismay, I realised I didn't even know what religion Karl followed, if he followed one at all. What if no one would agree to conduct a burial service?

'We won't worry about that,' Edouard had said dryly. 'I expect that when it comes down to it, money will talk.'

My head bowed, I stood by the grave and listened to the priest Edouard had found intoning the prayers for the dead. I added my own that Karl would find peace. It saddened me to think of the distance that had remained between us, in spite of what we had shared. His family, his early life, his loves, his friendships, were all a mystery.

On the way back to the place Vendôme, we drove past the Hôtel de Ville. A large crowd had gathered outside. When we drew near, I saw a statuesque, dark-haired woman on the steps. She had draped the Tricolor over her dress and, in a powerful contralto voice, she sang the *Marseillaise*.

'Mon Dieu,' Edouard murmured. 'If I were to paint *Marianne,* that singer would be the model I would choose. How can France fail with women like that to inspire her armies?'

Mariette frowned. 'Do you think there really will be a war?'

'I believe it is inevitable now.' He studied Mariette's troubled expression. 'But don't be afraid. We'll teach the Prussians a lesson they won't forget in a hurry. It'll be all over in the blink of an eye.'

Chapter 18

Mariette and Péri's apartment was small and I didn't want to impose on them for more than a few days, even though they both assured me I was welcome to stay for as long as I liked. In the end, however, Edouard insisted I stay with him.

I confess it was a great relief. I was still shaken by my narrow escape and Karl's death. I wasn't ready to make a sensible decision about what to do with my life. One thing I did want, though, was to find Rose, for I needed a maid and I certainly didn't want Agathe back.

'I had no luck getting her a place as a lady's maid,' Mariette said. 'Without a character reference, no one would consider her.'

'That was my fault,' I said unhappily.

'Oh, stop blaming yourself, Anna. Péri had the answer. She helps to look after the costumes at the theatre and does a bit of cleaning. She's a good girl and she works hard but if you want her back, I'm sure he'll let her go. I expect she'll be happier with you.'

The arrangements were soon made and I settled down to life in Edouard's house. Yet it was hard to feel tranquil, not just because of what I had been through, but because Paris was in ferment: all everyone talked of was war.

'Thank God Péri is too old to fight,' Mariette said. 'I saw poor Virginie Bertin yesterday. She was in a terrible state. Henri has been conscripted and they have no money to pay for a substitute.'

'What do you mean?' I asked.

'Someone to fight in his place in exchange for money. Don't you have that in Russia?'

I had to admit I didn't know.

*

As Edouard had predicted, the Emperor had lost patience with waiting for the apology he demanded and declared war on Prussia.

A surge of anxiety went through me. If Henri had been conscripted, Antoine might have been called up too. Then I felt angry with myself. I had sworn not to think of him again. Why was I so foolish? Hadn't I had enough of men who made me wretched? Antoine didn't care a jot for me.

The first stage of the conflict bore out Edouard's confidence in France's military superiority. The Emperor himself left Paris to take command of one part of our forces, the newly titled Army of the Rhine, comprising more than two hundred thousand men. Everyone in Paris was convinced that, in a few weeks, they would be home again victorious.

The newspapers were full of cartoons of loutish, bemused Prussian soldiers facing spruce, confident French ones. One particularly popular cartoon showed a French soldier with a mitrailleuse, a new type of gun that was being hailed in Paris as France's secret weapon. It had several barrels that could fire shots in quick succession. The cartoon showed the soldier, still with bullets to fire, looking around in vain for another Prussian target.

I learnt from Mariette that Henri and Antoine had been sent to a camp somewhere near Mulhouse, close to the Swiss border. 'Poor Virginie is very anxious,' she said. 'Although I'm sure there's no need for it. Péri says we're sure to win.'

Jules Fauchon, who came to visit Edouard one day, was equally confident. 'Austria-Hungary will join in on our side. It's in their interest to liberate the South German states from Prussian control. Once Bismarck and King William realise they're isolated, they'll capitulate. This war will be over in a few weeks.'

*

A few mornings later, I was posing for Edouard in his studio. The painting he was working on was a historical one, its subject the story of Dante and Beatrice. The dress I wore was styled in the Renaissance fashion with a high waist and flowing skirts. A white lawn chemise billowed from the low, embroidered neckline. Edouard was too absorbed in his work to want to talk and I was bored. It was hard not to fidget for my muscles ached with the effort of staying still.

Edouard put down his brush. 'I suppose you deserve a few minutes rest,' he said. Relieved, I stood up and wandered around the room as he busied himself with mixing more colours. Propped against one wall was a painting I hadn't noticed before.

A draped sheet half hid the subject so I moved it carefully aside. The painting was a portrait of a man in evening dress, the likeness so lifelike that it gave me a jolt. It wasn't Edouard's skill that shocked me, however; it was the identity of the sitter. He was Count Marly, the man who had ruined Emile.

Edouard came to stand beside me, wiping his hands on a rag. 'What do you think?' he asked.

My head had emptied.

'No good, eh?'

'It's not that,' I stammered.

Edouard frowned. 'Then what is it that displeases you?'

I'd told him Emile had left Paris because he was in debt, but never mentioned Marly's role in his fall.

'It's Count Marly, isn't it?'

'Yes, do you know him?'

'It was because of him that Emile left Paris. He was the one Emile owed money to.'

'Ah.'

'I hope I never have to meet him again.'

'There's little likelihood of that. I finished the work months ago but Marly ignored all my messages and hasn't come to see the picture. It's strange because he was in a great hurry for it when he gave me the commission. When I made enquiries, I discovered he'd left Paris. From what I could find out, he was no more a count than I am, just another of the crooks and swindlers the Imperial court attracts.'

He pointed to the eight-pointed gold star on the royal blue sash across Marly's chest. 'That decoration was bogus too. Ah well, I wasn't the only person he duped. He left debts all over Paris.' He reached for the sheet. 'I'll cover the wretched thing up before the memory makes me angry. I suppose I'll paint over the canvas one day and use it for something else. I'm sorry the sight of the rogue distressed you, Anna.'

'There's no need to apologise, you weren't to know.'

'Are you ready to begin again?'

'Yes.'

I returned to my chair and Edouard arranged my costume to his satisfaction then began to paint again. How ironic, I thought. Marly was a fraud: no more honest than Emile.

*

In spite of Jules Fauchon's prediction, the Austro-Hungarian forces did not rush to France's aid, but all the same, in early August, the telegraph wires hummed with the news the whole of Paris longed to hear. The troops under the Emperor's command had won a resounding victory at a place called Saarbrücken on the border with Southern Germany. They had routed the Prussians and there were reports that the Prussian Crown Prince had been killed in the fighting. Surely after such a blow his father would surrender? In the streets and cafés people rejoiced and raised their glasses to toast the Emperor.

But Paris' mood turned to anger when news of a second battle came. It had taken place near a town called Wissembourg and allowed the Prussians to carry the war into France.

Chilling tales of the destruction and house-to-house fighting filled the newspapers. 'I went through Wissembourg when I was a young man,' Edouard said sadly. 'It was a lovely place – a medieval town with many beautiful old half-timbered houses.'

He patted his capacious stomach. 'Believe it or not, in those days, I could walk all day without getting tired. I covered hundreds of miles exploring France, paying my way painting portraits of local dignitaries. I walked all through the Vosges and down into the Rhine Valley. I recall Wissembourg had a fine church. Before the Great Revolution, it belonged to a Benedictine abbey. There were fields of ripe corn stretching for miles from the town walls. The church looked like a ship sailing on a golden sea.' He shook his head. 'I hope it was spared.'

When Mariette came later in the day, she was far less interested in the fate of houses and churches than the fact that the fighting had taken place well to the north of Mulhouse. 'So Henri and his friend Antoine will be safe,' she said. She gave me a curious glance. 'Aren't you glad?'

'Of course, I'm happy for Virginie that Henri's still safe.'

'And his friend?'

I shrugged. 'I wouldn't wish harm to come to anyone, but he's nothing to me.'

Two days later, Wissembourg surrendered and soon afterwards, France sustained another crushing blow. The Crown Prince, very much alive in spite of the reports, led the Prussian army into battle with a force far larger than our own. Faced with the prospect of a massacre, the Emperor retreated.

The Paris newspapers screamed their derision and the Republican factions seized on the chance to berate the establishment and urge rebellion. Rumours abounded that the French army was in chaos, the men short of ammunition and even food.

The famous mitrailleuse had not been a success either. According to Péri, the word in the cafés was that it had turned out to be as unwieldy as a small cannon but lacking in a cannon's range. 'And it was so secret,' Péri grimaced, 'that it was only issued to the men a couple of days before they left Paris, so they had no time to train to use it.'

'France will be a laughing stock if this goes on,' Edouard growled, his paintbrush stabbing the canvas as if it were the Prussian enemy.

Poor Virginie. It looked as if her days of anxiety wouldn't be over for some time. How lucky I was that no one I loved had gone to war. How fortunate that Antoine had unmasked himself before I lost my heart to him.

*

'Paul Vallon has asked for my help,' Edouard remarked during one of our sittings. 'He's avoided conscription so far, but if he stays in France much longer, he'll be obliged to enlist. The army needs all the men it can get now the war's not going well.'

He sighed. 'I suppose I shouldn't condone a Frenchman avoiding his duty, but on the other hand, it would be a tragedy if such a talented young man was lost. He went to see his father in Le Havre, hoping he would pay for a substitute to enlist in his place, but the old man refused, so Paul intends to leave the country. He's still in Le Havre trying to find a passage on a ship to England. He wants me to bring Camille to him there. Will you come with us, Anna?'

I felt the heat rise in my cheeks.

Edouard looked puzzled. 'Is there a problem? She's a nervous little creature. It would be a great kindness if you'd try to bolster her spirits. I'm sure she'd find it comforting to have another woman to talk to, and she seems to have no close friends.'

Unable to think of a graceful way of refusing his request, I agreed.

Camille lodged in a shabby house in the Latin Quarter. I followed Edouard up a bleak stairway to the attic floor. He stopped for breath by a window on the topmost landing and looked out across the rooftops.

'These stairs would be the death of me,' he wheezed, 'but there's no denying the view's magnificent.'

We knocked and after a few moments, Camille opened the door. Her small sitting room contained a few pieces of cheap furniture. Its white walls were scuffed and dingy and there were no rugs on the wooden floor.

'I've brought Anna with me, Camille,' Edouard said cheerfully. 'I thought she would be company for you on the way to Le Havre.'

Camille inclined her head a fraction in my direction. 'It's very good of you to spare the time,' she said stiffly.

Edouard didn't seem to notice her coolness. 'I'll leave the two of you now and be back in an hour or two,' he said. 'Can you be ready by then?'

'Yes, I think so.' Camille gestured to the small room. 'As you see there's very little to take.' She flushed. 'I'm afraid it's been hard to make the money Paul left last out.'

Edouard patted her hand. 'Don't give it another thought. I'll speak to the concierge on my way out and settle what is owing.'

A smile lit Camille's pale, careworn face. 'Thank you, Monsieur Blanchard. I don't know what I would have done without you.'

He squeezed her hand. 'Edouard, please – no need to be formal, my dear. Don't worry, we'll soon have you safely back with Paul.'

The door closed behind him and Camille returned to packing the clothes laid out on the bed. Her small, white hands smoothed the already neat folds of a green dress. I recognised it from one of Paul's paintings that Edouard had bought.

'What can I do to help, Camille?'

'Nothing, thank you.'

'There must be something, surely?'

She hesitated. 'Well, the floor is very dusty. I haven't had time to sweep it, or clean the windows, but they're not jobs for a lady.'

'Nonsense,' I said briskly. 'If it will help you, I'm happy to do them. Just give me a broom.'

Camille fetched the broom and I started work. It didn't take me long. 'Do you have any newspaper?' I asked when I had finished.

'There may be some under the sink. I don't read much but Paul liked to see who was exhibiting at the galleries and what the critics had to say.'

I rummaged under the sink and, finding a few yellowing sheets, scrunched them up and rubbed away at the windows. Camille continued to wrap her few possessions and put them with her clothes in a battered old trunk.

'You must be looking forward to seeing Paul,' I remarked.

'Yes.'

'Has he been away for long?'

'A fortnight.'

She fell silent again and my stomach knotted with irritation. I hadn't wanted to come in the first place.

She looked up with a wan smile. 'I'm sorry, I'm poor company today. It will be wonderful to be reunited with Paul, but I'm worried about my brother. I had a letter from him. He and Henri Bertin were together, but of course he couldn't say exactly where.' She banged the lid of the trunk shut.

'Oh, this horrible war! Everything had started to go well for Antoine – the people who matter were taking him up at last.' She shook her head. 'The success he deserves was within his grasp, but now…' Her eyes brimmed.

Selfish anger quickened my pulse. It seemed Antoine had not even given me any credit for helping him. Camille's lower lip trembled and I felt sorry for her. Her frosty manner might just be due to shyness, and she was clearly deluded about her brother.

'Poor Jeanette,' she went on. 'It broke my heart to see how unhappy she was when he left.'

I stiffened. She must be the woman I'd seen at the Moulin de la Galette.

Camille wiped away her tears. 'She and Antoine planned to marry and I couldn't wish for a better sister-in-law. I pray for both our sakes he comes back unharmed.'

My heart was cold as stone. I didn't want to hear another word about Antoine Clérmont. He wasn't worth a moment of my time.

*

At Le Havre, the port hummed with activity as people besieged the offices trying to buy tickets to board ships leaving for England. The smell of the fish market pervaded the air and flocks of screeching gulls fought on the quays for the pickings left behind by traders and fishermen.

Edouard's coachman drove us to the small hotel where we were to meet Paul. It was a pretty little place close to the seafront with sky blue shutters and pots of crimson geraniums on the windowsills. The hotel's gay appearance was at odds with the agitated demeanour of the hotel keeper's wife. When she heard we came from Paris, she fastened anxiously on Edouard. 'Is it true, what people are saying, Monsieur? That the Prussians might win?'

He gave her a benevolent smile. 'I think you may sleep easily, Madame. France has suffered a few minor setbacks, nothing more.'

'Do you really think so, Monsieur?'

'Most certainly. Now, we've had a long journey. I for one would like to wash off the dust of the road. Please have plenty of hot water and towels sent up to our rooms. After we've rested, we'll need dinner. What do you have?'

The woman brightened, no doubt scenting deep pockets. 'Crab and lobster, and good Normandy beef too, Monsieur.'

'That sounds excellent. Another gentleman will be joining us.'

He suggested we meet for dinner in two hours then looked sternly at Camille. 'And I want to see you with a proper appetite, my dear. I refuse to send you off to those English with their execrable cooking without plenty of good French food for your last meal.'

Camille gave a shy laugh. 'I'll try my best, Edouard.'

We were ready to sit down to dinner when Paul arrived. Camille flung her arms around his neck. 'Now, now,' he smiled, disentangling her. 'I've only been gone a few days.'

He kissed my hand and greeted Edouard warmly. 'I'm so grateful to you, Monsieur.'

'So, is everything ready?' asked Edouard.

'I have a passage booked for us tomorrow morning.'

We sat down to the excellent dinner the hotel keeper's wife served us. It would have been a pleasant evening but in spite of my resolve to forget everything to do with Antoine Clérmont, my earlier conversation with Camille kept repeating in my head. She spent most of the meal in silence while Paul talked and ate heartily. He didn't seem to notice how quiet she was.

I watched him curiously. The intensity in his dark eyes and his rapt expression were almost messianic. I couldn't help thinking what a strange man he was. While he cracked open the shiny, coral-coloured lobster claws on his plate and sucked out the snowy meat, he talked excitedly of the light in Le Havre, the sea and the skies and the colour in the markets. I wondered if the thought of Camille, anxiously waiting for news in Paris, had entered his mind very often. Perhaps the same question had occurred to her.

In the morning, we went to the port and helped the two of them to board the ship. I clung to Edouard's arm for fear of being knocked over in the surging mass of people waiting to embark. 'So many people leaving, Edouard,' I shouted over the din. 'It frightens me. Do you really think everything will turn out all right?'

He patted my hand. 'Of course it will.'

Chapter 19

I was spending the morning with Mariette when Virginie rushed in. I had always thought of her as a rather indolent person who took life at her own pace so I was surprised to see her in such a hurry.

'Henri's here in Paris,' she said when she had recovered her breath.

Mariette frowned. 'Are you sure? Why isn't he with the army?'

'He is: his regiment's at the Gare Pantin.' She tugged at Mariette's sleeve. 'Please, come with me. I'm desperate to see him but I'm afraid of going alone. I'll need your help to find him. There's bound to be thousands of people there.'

It was quite a distance to the Gare Pantin which was situated at the eastern edge of Paris and we had some difficulty finding a fiacre to take us. Several drivers refused, saying only a fool would go near the chaos, but Mariette was hard to resist when she was determined to get her own way and eventually one agreed.

Virginie babbled nervously all the way, veering from anxiety to elation at the prospect of finding Henri. For my part, indecision tormented me. What would I do if Antoine was there with Henri? Even more alarming was the thought we might see Jeanette on a similar mission.

When we reached the station, I realised straight away that there was a far greater danger we would never find Henri. The station concourse was a sea of uniforms. Amid the hiss and belch of steam from the locomotives, soldiers stood about or sat on their kitbags; some played cards or dice, some smoked and chatted. Others dozed or just stared into space. The atmosphere contrasted sharply with the cheerful optimism with which men like these had marched through the streets of Paris only a few weeks earlier on their way to war.

Someone tapped my shoulder and I swung round, the colour already rising to my cheeks. A wiry, dark-haired soldier grinned at us. 'If you can't find your sweethearts, ladies, my friends and I'll stand in for them.'

'Cheeky devil,' Mariette sniffed but she let him have a peck on the cheek. 'Now you have to help us,' she said. 'Do you know Henri Bertin? This is his wife. We need to find him for her.'

The soldier gave a wry smile. 'You may as well look for a needle in a haystack, my darling. I don't know anyone of that name, but I wish you luck.'

Two hours later, we were exhausted and on the point of leaving when we saw him. 'Henri!' Virginie screamed. She picked up her skirts and ran towards him. The soldiers in her path goggled at her. Some tried to catch her as she flew past them but she took no notice and blundered on through the crowd. 'Henri!' she screamed again, and this time, he looked up. He leapt to his feet and started to run too, stumbling over his comrades and their outstretched legs, kicking aside their kitbags and mess tins and winning himself volleys of curses and a good few blows that almost knocked him flying.

Yet as he and Virginie drew closer to each other, people understood. The curses turned to roars of encouragement and suddenly, strong arms lifted Virginie up and passed her over the heads of the last few groups of men separating her from Henri. A few moments later, they were in each other's arms.

'Thank heaven, we found him,' Mariette shouted in my ear. 'We should leave them alone for a while. Look! There's Antoine Clérmont. Let's try and get to him. Poor fellow, he looks so miserable.'

I grabbed her arm. 'We won't manage it,' I shouted back, thankful that with the din going on, she would never hear how loudly my heart pounded.

She shot me a look. 'Why are you so unfriendly? I like Antoine, don't you? And I'm sure he needs cheering up.'

Not stopping to wait for my reply, she started off in his direction, gaily clearing a path through the soldiers, for a brief moment turning the glum expressions on their weary faces to smiles.

I didn't want to be left on my own, so I followed. Antoine's face brightened when he saw Mariette and they embraced. Then he saw me and a startled look came into his eyes.

'Madame Daubigny! I'm so happy to see you.'

He took a step towards me, his lips brushed my cheek and a shockwave went through me. I stepped back quickly, trying to hide my confusion. To my relief, Mariette chattered away to Antoine, giving me time to compose myself.

At last, Henri and Virginie made their way to us. His bear hug enfolded Mariette and then me. 'Forgive me,' he laughed when he let me go. 'My heart's so full, I couldn't stop myself.'

'There's no need to apologise,' I smiled. 'I'm very glad you're safe. Virginie has been so worried. We all have.'

Henri sighed. 'I must be honest, it's been no Sunday picnic. They marched us all the way to Mulhouse then, just as we thought we might see some action, they told us we were off back to Belfort and onto the troop trains for Paris. That last night at Mulhouse, we'd only set up camp a couple of hours earlier. The stew was bubbling, but not ready to eat, and we had to throw it all away.'

Virginie hung onto his arm as if she was afraid he'd vanish in a puff of smoke at any moment. 'Can you come home tonight, Henri?' she asked.

He kissed the top of her head. 'No, my love, not tonight, we've orders to stay here and wait to be told where we're going next.'

She made a face. 'Why can't you stay in Paris? I need you to protect me. Tell your officers you can't go.'

Henri tilted her chin and looked into her eyes. 'And be shot as a deserter? Not a good plan, I think.' He glanced over his shoulder. 'I'm afraid we'll have to leave you soon anyway, my love – we're due on parade.'

Reluctant as she was to say goodbye to Henri, after a few more minutes, he persuaded her to go with us, but first, we left them to one last embrace. Mariette was talking to a soldier who had claimed her attention when I realised Antoine stood close beside me. I tried not to meet his eyes but it was impossible.

A muscle twitched in his cheek. 'There's so much I want…'

I frowned. How dare he think I would be duped again?

He stayed silent and a shadow crossed his face, then he asked quietly if I would wish him luck.

'I wish that for every man here, Monsieur.'

His expression was so wretched, if I had not known better, I would have believed he truly felt something for me. There was an awkward silence until Mariette tugged my sleeve.

'We should go now, Anna. Virginie's getting very upset. It will make it harder for Henri to leave her.' She hugged Antoine. 'I'll pray for you, chéri. Come back safely.'

With Virginie between us, we struggled back through the crowds of soldiers. When we were almost clear, the same wiry, dark-haired fellow we had spoken to at the beginning stopped us. 'Did you find him?' he asked.

Mariette nodded. The soldier peered at Virginie's red-rimmed eyes and patted her shoulder with a leathery hand. 'He's a lucky fellow, your husband. Don't worry, he'll be back.'

'If he's not worn-out with hunger and marching before that,' his comrade snorted contemptuously. 'The way this army's run, we'll probably keel over from starvation before we see so much as a glint of a Prussian helmet.'

The wiry man elbowed him. 'Shut your trap, Maille. Don't mind him, ladies. Always moaning about something, he is. Just let us get at those Prussians, we'll make them sorry they tangled with France. Then we'll all dine like emperors.'

Virginie wanted to go back to see Henri again the next day, but it was not to be. Late that same night, just as they must have been hoping for some rest, the troops at the Gare Pantin were ordered to pack up their kit and set out for Rheims. Virginie was beside herself with grief and anxiety. Mariette and I took turns to be with her and the need to console her provided a welcome distraction from the turmoil of my own feelings. When I was alone, Antoine's sad face was often in my mind's eye. Knowing what fate might await him, I felt guilty for the cold way I had treated him. But then I remembered Jeanette.

*

The great events going on fascinated Edouard and Péri, who had become good friends. They spent hours poring over maps and discussing what the commanders' tactics should be. Reports of the fighting continued to flood in. Now it was concentrated around Metz where the French troops confronted the Prussians in a great battle. This time, the French forces had been augmented and outnumbered the Prussians but in spite of that, Prussia won the day.

Edouard and Péri greeted the news that France's proudly titled Army of the Rhine was now trapped in Metz with grave faces. The only glimmer of good news was that the Emperor was safe, spirited away to join Marshal MacMahon's forces at Chalôns-sur-Marne before the Prussians closed on Metz.

'Apparently the regiment Henri Bertin and Antoine Clérmont serve in is with them,' Péri remarked. 'And the report is they didn't lose many men, so there's a real chance our friends are safe. Anna? That's welcome news, isn't it?'

I looked up and saw his surprised expression. 'I'm sorry,' I said quickly. 'I was thinking of something else. Of course it is.'

*

In the days that followed, I watched Edouard and Péri move inkwells and brandy glasses to and fro across the map of the Ardennes as they chewed over the tactics of the Emperor and his commander-in-chief, Marshal MacMahon. From reports, it seemed they were marching away from Metz rather than going to its relief.

'The papers say MacMahon makes all the decisions now,' Edouard frowned. 'The Emperor's sick, with a gall stone the size of an ostrich egg in his belly. His doctors can't help him and he's not up to taking charge any longer. Some days he's too weak even to leave his quarters.'

'It's all over for him whatever happens,' Péri shrugged.

'What do you mean – whatever happens?' Mariette asked. 'Surely you don't think we'll lose the war?'

'Of course not,' Péri said quickly. 'I just meant however long it takes to beat the Prussians.'

The blanket of gloom and anger that had settled over Paris lifted briefly when news came that MacMahon had, after all, changed his course to face the Prussians.

'Now we'll show them,' said Péri, rubbing his hands. 'We'll make those swine scamper all the way back to Berlin with their tails between their legs.'

The battle took place near Sedan, a quiet little town where the River Meuse marked the border of France with Belgium. The first dispatches to reach Paris lifted the city's spirits. France had won the day. Joyful crowds thronged the streets and flags billowed from the windows of the houses. Cannon boomed and bugles blew in celebration. Prussia was humbled; the natural order of things was restored.

However the celebrations came to an abrupt halt a few days later when very different news came from the front. This time, we heard that the battle at Sedan had actually ended in a massive defeat for France. Humiliated, the Emperor had been forced to surrender. Even now, he was on his way to imprisonment in Prussia.

In Paris, many people were too shocked to believe that Prussia had overwhelmed the mighty armies of France.

'Six weeks. Defeated in a mere six weeks.' Péri shook his head sadly. 'It's incredible. How could

248

such a disaster come about?' His shoulders slumped and Mariette put her arms around him. 'Perhaps it's not as bad as they say,' she said soothingly.

He stroked her cheek. 'Perhaps.'

I saw the look in his eyes and knew it wasn't true.

He picked up his hat and went to the door.

'Where are you going?' Mariette asked

'Out. I want to know what's going on.'

'Then I'll come with you. Give me a minute to get ready.'

He shook his head. 'No, my dear, it might be dangerous in the streets. People don't like defeat. There could be trouble.'

Mariette pouted but he remained adamant.

Hours later, long after darkness had fallen, he returned badly shaken, one eye blackened and his hat lost. He downed a glass of brandy before telling us what he had seen.

'Extraordinary sights - crowds all down the rue de Rivoli, from the Tuileries Palace up as far as the Hôtel de Ville. Everyone was chanting "Down with the Emperor and the Empress" and "Long Live the Republic". I was knocked over once and lucky not to have been crushed.'

'Oh, Péri,' Mariette cried, 'what does it all mean?'

'It means, my love that the Emperor is finished and the Republicans have seized power.'

'But what about the Empress?'

'Already gone. They say she sneaked out of the Tuileries Palace by the back door. Who knows where she'll go? One thing's for sure, she'll stay out of France if she has any sense.'

I thought back to the beautiful Eugénie whom I had seen at so many operas and balls, always the glittering centre of attention - beautiful, remote and regal. How would she bear such a terrible reversal of fate?

*

The next morning, a mob broke into the Tuileries Palace. They stormed through the magnificent rooms, smashing and looting, taking vengeance for every long-held grievance and deprivation they had suffered. The attack went on all day. At nightfall, when they wearied of their rampage, hardly anything remained in the palace's cavernous rooms.

The newspapers later reported that it was the Empress' dentist, an American, who had saved her from the mob's wrath. If it had not been for him, she would have been defenceless when they attacked. Instead, she was on her way to the coast. At Calais, she and her children crossed the Channel to England and begged the English Queen, Victoria, for sanctuary.

*

The day after the riots dawned clear and sunny. Tired of being cooped up, Mariette and I persuaded Edouard and Péri to take us out into the streets and there we saw extraordinary sights. Paris had shaken off the gloom of the terrible defeat and abandoned herself to a wild spirit of carnival. The National Guard seemed more inclined to join in the fun than help the police keep order. Their muskets sprouted bunches of flowers and red ribbons fluttered on all the lampposts. Near the Tuileries Palace, we saw a young man shin up to the top of one and swing there, singing the Marseillaise at the top of his voice.

We walked to the Hôtel de Ville and as we came close, the roar of voices grew louder. A great crowd had gathered in front of the building, leaping up and down like lunatics and snatching at some kind of confetti that floated from the windows. Péri buttonholed a man on the edge of the crowd. 'What's going on?' he asked.

'Voting. Now the Emperor's been kicked out, the new deputies are being voted in. The papers have the names of the candidates on them. We catch them and, if we approve, we shout as loud as we can for that man to be elected.'

He raised a fist in salute. 'Democracy is come again! Vive la République!' And with that, he turned and barged on into the crowd.

Péri frowned. 'Poor Paris, the mob rules her once more. I dread to think how this will end.' He caught the arm of another man pushing past. 'Who's been elected so far?'

The man rattled off a few names before he shook Péri off and hurried on into the fray.

'What's the matter?' asked Mariette, her eyes sparking with all the excitement.

'This is bad. The men appointed so far are no better than cynical cads, interested only in their own advancement. Politics is a game to them. I very much doubt they have any real feeling for the nation and the sacrifices it's made.'

Mariette tweaked his arm crossly. 'Oh Péri, don't be so gloomy. Everything will be all right now we have the Republic, of course it will. It's only the Emperor and the Empress the Prussians hated. They haven't any quarrel with ordinary people like us.'

A man standing nearby grinned and blew her a kiss. 'Quite right, my love. They won't come now.'

Slowly the last of the pieces of paper fluttered to the ground and the excitement died down. The crowd grew bored and started to disperse. We walked away from the Hôtel de Ville. By the Tuileries Palace, the young man still clung to his lamppost, singing lustily. An insistent tapping, like the noise of a thrush breaking a snail upon a stone made us look up. Balanced precariously on wooden ladders propped against the palace's façade, two workmen were hard at work chipping away at the Imperial eagles and the initials 'N' and 'E' carved in the stone window frames.

'Madness,' Edouard sighed. 'Complete madness.'

Chapter 20

The new Government soon installed itself in the Tuileries Palace and for a few days euphoria swept Paris. It didn't last long. Not content with their victory at Sedan, the Prussian armies advanced on Paris. Fear gripped the city as roads and railway stations were overwhelmed.

Many Parisians closed up their houses and fled, only to be replaced by legions of curious foreigners, possessed of a strange, ghoulish desire to see Paris' plight for themselves. Péri even found an advertisement in one of the newspapers for rooms to let to "gentlemen wishing to attend the Siege of Paris", as if it were some kind of party. The prospective landlord had added helpfully that if the Prussians did come, his house possessed a shell-proof basement for those of a nervous disposition. Thousands of people from the areas beyond the city walls added to the confusion, struggling through the barriers with their possessions heaped onto carts, all terrified of being left outside at the mercy of the Prussians.

Paris' ancient city walls were thirty feet high and beyond them was a moat. Further out again, a ring of sixteen great defensive forts guarded the approaches. The fortifications instilled a welcome sense of safety and, as the days of waiting went by, it was soon a popular amusement to drive out to inspect them and watch the workmen dig earthworks to strengthen them even further.

The weather that autumn was glorious, with crisp mornings and mild, bright days. Edouard took to going out to the walls to sketch, saying he wanted to record the scenes for posterity.

On one of the afternoons when I joined him, I sat in the sunshine, a book open but unread in my lap, watching the trains flash by on the narrow-gauge railway inside the wall. It transported men and munitions between the bastions and smartly uniformed soldiers packed the open carriages. Some wore brown, some sky blue, some a vibrant green. The air resounded with the rumble of cannonballs being unloaded from wagons; the sound of orders barked at full volume; the rattle of passing trains and the scrape of innumerable spades on stony ground.

A tall young officer jumped down from a nearby wagon and strode across the parade ground in our direction. The book in my lap slid to the ground with a thud. To my annoyance, I realised that what had startled me was that he bore a resemblance to Antoine. He stopped and bent down to pick up my book, returning it to me with a smile.

I went back to my reading until raised voices disturbed me again. Two soldiers had stopped beside Edouard, interrupting him in his work. One of them snatched his sketchbook and began to rip out the pages. The other seized his chalks and pencils and threw them into the crowd that had gathered to watch. A chant of 'spy, spy,' swelled.

My heartbeat quickened then I saw the tall officer again. I ran to him.

'Please, Monsieur,' I begged. 'Help us. My friend isn't a spy; he's Edouard Blanchard, the distinguished artist. He means no harm.'

The officer thought for a moment and I feared he would refuse to help then he nodded. 'Of course, Madame.'

He barked an order to a group of soldiers nearby. They waded into the crowd setting about them with the butts of their muskets. The crowd melted away and the soldiers who had tormented Edouard with it. He was safe but he looked a lonely, sad figure, staring bewildered at the broken pencils and crumpled pieces of paper on the ground. Blood oozed from a cut above one of his eyebrows.

I rushed to him and tried to staunch the flow with my handkerchief but he shook me off irritably. 'Don't make a fuss, Anna. I'm all right.'

The officer frowned. 'You have this lady's quick thinking to thank for your life, Monsieur. I've seen men beaten to death before now.'

Edouard dragged the back of his hand across his eyes, smearing the blood. 'Forgive me, Anna. I shouldn't have snapped at you.' He accepted my proffered handkerchief and held it against the cut. 'And you, Captain, I thank you for your assistance.'

'I merely did my duty, Monsieur. Do you have a carriage here? May I escort you to it?'

Edouard nodded. 'Thank you.'

With the captain leading the way, we were soon installed and on our way home but the incident left an unpleasant taste in my mouth. Paris had enough to face without her own people turning on each other.

Edouard was uncharacteristically subdued for several days; the incident had deeply distressed him. 'Perhaps it's good for me to be reminded of my age sometimes, Anna,' he remarked ruefully late one afternoon. We had spent most of the day in the studio while he put the finishing touches to a painting of Dido, Queen of Carthage I modelled for. I had to admit, I found the subject rather disturbing. I knew the story of poor Dido's tragic fate in the blazing ruins of Carthage.

I smiled at him. 'You're not old, Edouard.'

'You're kind to say so, my dear, but that incident the other day told me a different story. Once I would have given those soldiers a good kicking but I couldn't save myself, let alone you. I put you in danger - if anything had happened—'

'I wasn't in danger. You have nothing to blame yourself for.'

He took my hand and kissed it. 'Thank you, my dear, but you're too generous. I'm an old fool who should have known better. I was there in 'forty-eight when we threw King Louis Philippe out.' He shook his head sadly. 'I should have remembered how the mob behaves.'

*

Paris turned into a huge war factory. The Tuileries Gardens acted as a vast artillery park. Factories that had previously manufactured the luxuries of peace cast cannons and churned bullets and cannonballs off their production lines. The authorities rounded up the girls in the brothels and on the boulevards and put them to work sewing uniforms in workshops that only a few weeks before had made fashionable clothes for society women.

The Bois de Boulogne rang with the sound of axes felling its beautiful trees to make barricades. Huge herds of oxen and flocks of sheep, driven in from the countryside to feed the city, tore up the grass and trampled the ground to mud. Even gardens and squares were filled with animals.

From morning to night, carts rumbled into the city from miles around, loaded with sacks of flour and grain, cabbages, pumpkins, leeks, onions and fruit. Everything that could possibly be transported was brought into Paris to keep it out of the enemy's hands. Even the game in the surrounding forests was hunted down mercilessly.

Edouard worked long days, supervising the selection and crating-up of treasures at the Louvre. In the evenings, he was exhausted and often dejected. 'Three trainloads packed off to Brest today,' he said gloomily one night. 'I pray they will be safe there. I hated to see them go. I felt as if I was nailing the statues in their coffins. Who knows when they will return?'

Mariette, who visited us that evening, looked dismayed. 'Surely it won't be long? Soon we shall have peace?'

Edouard roused himself. 'Of course, of course.'

In the days that followed, however, the news of the enemy's advance was increasingly grim. The Prussians scythed through France's lines of defence, swallowing villages, farms and fields, even some of the forts the Parisians had looked on as indomitable. The soldiers who abandoned them crept back into the city with the guilty, haunted look of beaten men in their eyes. Many were arrested as deserters and paraded through the streets with their coats turned inside out.

September came and we heard the news that Versailles had fallen. The Prussians had also overrun the Châtillon Plateau, a major vantage point from where, as we later discovered, the range of their huge guns could reach right into the heart of Paris. The twin disasters shook the city. Finally it was impossible to ignore the danger we were in. Before the month was out, the Prussians were encamped around the walls.

Paris was under siege.

*

In a strange way, the disaster spurred the city into action. With renewed vigour, Parisians threw themselves into the war effort, organising parties and rallies to raise subscriptions to build more guns. The prevailing mood of nervous excitability magnified fear and hope, in particular the fear of spies intensified. In the rue des Martyrs, a furious mob invaded a house where a too-bright light burnt in a window and beat the owner half to death. The next day, a man sitting reading a map in the Tuileries Gardens was dragged to a pond and nearly drowned. With a shudder, I remembered Edouard's narrow escape.

By a stroke of good fortune, Henri Bertin had been among the soldiers who managed to flee the battlefield at Sedan. He had kept ahead of the Prussian army, arriving in Paris just a few days before they cut the city off from the rest of the world. He was weak with exhaustion and wounded in one leg but miraculously, gangrene hadn't set in and with time and good nursing, he was likely to recover. On Virginie's behalf, Péri enlisted Edouard's help in removing him from the military hospital he had been sent to and bringing him home to care for him there.

'She's very wise,' Edouard remarked, squinting at an area of his painting where he was applying delicate highlights to Dido's intricate gold necklace. 'Most of the hospitals are filthy and completely lacking in fresh air. Men are in almost as much danger there as they were in the field. I've told Virginie she mustn't hesitate to ask for my help if she needs money.'

Henri made his first tentative venture from home a few days later and came with Virginie to thank Edouard in person for his kindness. The poor man was very thin, his once imposing physique reduced to skin and bone. Virginie fussed around him, anxious he shouldn't talk too much and grow weary but he told us a little about what had happened to him.

His regiment had been ordered to occupy a plateau directly north of Sedan. 'When we reached it,' he said, 'we lay for hours in a field of cabbages, pinned down by enemy fire and waiting for further orders. It was early in the morning and the dew still sparkled on the cabbage leaves. I remember thinking how beautiful the dewdrops looked, but the stink of those cabbages – it will stay with me forever. I've told Virginie that unless she wants me to leave home, she must never cook us cabbage again.'

Virginie smiled and stroked his hand. 'I promise I won't.'

When he continued however, I saw the strain in his eyes and a more serious tone replaced the lightness. I could tell how hard it was for him to speak as he gave a brief account of how the battle went on. He had been wounded shortly before his officers had ordered a retreat. Antoine had dragged him to one of the carts taking some of the wounded back into Sedan before going back to help others. Henri had not seen him again.

His eyes misted and Virginie put a gentle finger to his lips.

Edouard filled the silence. 'It's too soon to give up hope. He may still return. Let's not spoil this happy afternoon. We're all very glad to see that you at least are safely home.'

Henri smiled. 'Thank you, sir. Virginie tells me you offered to help with our expenses while I was gone. I'm more grateful than I can say and of course I will repay you. I hope to be well enough to work again soon, that is if the army doesn't call me back.'

Virginie turned pale and I felt sorry for her.

'If that happens, you must let me intervene on your behalf,' Edouard said. 'I think you've done your duty and more.'

'I hope so,' Henri said sadly. 'Although who knows what will happen now.'

That night, I dreamt of the battlefield Henri had described. In my dream I stumbled over fields ploughed up with deep ruts, but the crop that sprouted from the earth was not cabbage, it was human heads. A feeling of dread seized me yet still I walked on, unable to stop myself from searching for the face I wanted to find.

I woke with my stomach roiling and a throbbing in my head. I knew the man I had been looking for was Antoine. Even if he had survived the war, it might be years before he returned, if at all. The lives of prisoners of war were cheap to their captors. I relived those few moments of our last meeting. If only I had let him speak. Now I would never know what he wanted to say to me.

Then the bitterness returned. What could he have wanted to say except more lies? If he did return to Paris, it would not be to my arms. It would be to Jeanette's.

Chapter 21

The trickle of news from the outside world dried up and isolation sapped the city's spirit. Poor Paris! She thrived on novelty and entertainment, always one step of her fashionably shod feet ahead of the rest. Now the days dragged and the city of night owls was in bed by ten o'clock.

Before long, boredom and inactivity bred dissent. Clubs frequented by agitators, soon nicknamed Red Clubs, sprang up to provide a new form of entertainment. Péri started to frequent one of them. Clearly he found the mixture of fiery speeches and cheap wine exciting, but rumours that the clubs promoted free love as well as revolution alarmed Mariette. When she tried to persuade him to take her with him, he steadfastly refused, inflaming her suspicions even more. After several weeks when he seemed to spend almost every night at the Club de Montmartre, she determined something must be done.

'I have to follow him and find out what he's getting up to,' she frowned. 'Anna, you will come with me, won't you?'

'But suppose he sees us?'

'He won't know it's us.'

'What do you mean?'

'I still have some of the clothes my little duke left behind. If we dress up in them, Péri will never recognise us.'

I didn't think it was a very good plan but in the end, she talked me into it. In the bedroom, she produced dark suits, beautifully stitched white shirts, silk cravats and patent leather shoes.

'Lucky, he was small,' she remarked, then giggled, 'though not in every department.'

Her eyes darted round the room then she snatched up a shawl and tore it into strips.

'Mariette! Whatever are you doing?'

'We'll bind these round us. Here, take off your dress and corset, I'll do you first.'

With some trepidation, I complied.

'Now, take a deep breath.' She wrapped the first strip around my breasts, pulling it so tight it squeezed most of the breath out of me. 'Mariette,' I gasped. 'Looser, or I shall faint.'

'Oh, very well,' she slackened the binding a little.

To my surprise, when the operation was over and I stood in front of the mirror dressed in the duke's shirt and suit with a royal blue cravat tied at my throat I might have passed quite convincingly for a young man had it not been for my hair. Mariette fetched a net and hairpins and fastened it securely to the top of my head then she delved into a drawer and produced a top hat. She rammed it firmly on my head and stood back to survey me. 'Excellent, no one will suspect a thing. Now it's my turn.'

It was not so easy to disguise her curves. She thought for a moment then pulled a black opera cloak from the wardrobe. 'This should do the trick,' she smiled.

*

At the Club de Montmartre, tobacco smoke thickened the air. My eyes smarted and my ears rang with the cheers and raucous laughter of the patrons. We stood at the back until our eyes adjusted to the dim light then Mariette dug me in the ribs and pointed to a table near the front where Péri sat with a large group of men. We found seats at a table close enough for us to watch them, but not so close that they would see us clearly. I glanced around, hoping no one would be suspicious of us. I was worried that our clothes were too smart for the company but luckily, the club's patrons were too busy ogling the scantily clad dancers on the stage to notice us.

'I knew it,' Mariette hissed in my ear. 'I'll make him pay for this, see if I don't. Political speeches my eye.'

She signalled to a waiter who brought us a carafe of wine and two glasses. The wine was rough and oaky and it made my tongue prickle.

Mariette carried on muttering in between gulps from her own glass. 'I know those kinds of girl,' she scowled. 'They'd do anything for a good time and a slap-up dinner.'

I couldn't help my lips twitching. After all the stories Mariette had told me of her youthful antics, this burst of respectable outrage was most amusing.

'What are you laughing at?' she asked crossly.

'You. You're turning into a bourgeois matron.'

She sighed. 'I can't bear the thought he'll leave me for someone else, Anna.'

I reached for her hand. 'That won't happen, Mariette. Anyone can see he adores you.'

Her expression brightened. 'You really think so?'

'Yes, I do. Now, this wine is vile and the smoke in here makes my eyes water. Can we go soon?'

'Just a little longer – please? I want to be sure he isn't getting up to anything.'

'Oh, very well.'

I pushed the rest of my wine away and sat waiting for her to be satisfied. My reassurances were genuine. It was perfectly natural for Péri to want a night out with his friends sometimes, I was sure he would always be loyal to Mariette. The sorrow that so often overcame me welled up inside. She was so lucky to have found him.

The girls danced off into the wings to whoops of merriment and all of a sudden, the room erupted with renewed applause as a tall man swaggered onto the stage. With his patrician nose, coppery hair and extravagant moustache he had an aristocratic air about him. Tight, snowy britches encased his long legs, his high cavalry boots gleamed and gold braid loaded his scarlet tunic.

Shouts of 'Flourens! Hurrah for Flourens!' went up.

The man strode around the stage for a few moments, stroking his moustache, before raising his hand. Immediately, silence fell on the room.

'My friends!' he began. 'Why have you come here tonight?' - He didn't wait for an answer – 'I'll tell you why.' He lowered his voice and the audience strained forward in their seats to catch his words. 'You've come here because you know it's time for change. The men who govern us are a pack of fools. Tenth-rate lawyers and pen-pushers that helped the Empire oppress the people for eighteen years. They aren't fit for the task of defending Paris. Why aren't they harassing the enemy day and night? Why is there no plan, no call to arms for the masses?'

Shouts of assent boomed out. Flourens smiled and waited for the noise to reach its crescendo then he raised his hand again. Once more the room hushed. It was impossible not to admire the way he controlled the crowd, just like a circus ringmaster.

'Our patience is exhausted,' he said. His voice was soft but held a menacing quality that sent a shiver down my spine. Suddenly, his fist punched the air. 'The time has come!' he shouted. 'The time has come to rise up!'

He lowered his hand and laid it over his heart. 'The time has come,' he repeated. 'Let us go forward and crush these little men.'

His speech unleashed a tumult; boots hammered the wooden floor, men leapt onto tables or drained their glasses and tossed them over their shoulders.

A man stumbled against our table, the alcohol on his breath kicked like a donkey. 'Great man,

Flourens,' he slurred. 'I seen him lead his men from the front on Capitaine. Know Capitaine, d' you? Finest horse in that old bugger Napoleon's stable.' He tapped his nose. 'Flourens'll see us right. I'd follow him to the gates of Hell. Great man—'

He slumped into Mariette's lap and she pushed him off with a moue of distaste. 'He won't be much use to anyone tonight,' she remarked loudly. A man at the table next to us swung round and peered through the smoky haze.

'Mariette, hush,' I whispered. 'Your voice…'

'Sorry.'

'Very fine,' the man leered, leaning across to finger Mariette's cloak. 'A very handsome piece of cloth. Must've cost a packet.'

Mariette shrugged and turned away but he persisted. 'Not going to talk to me, eh? Too high and mighty are we?' He lunged for her throat and she screamed. The rest of the table watched now, sniggering and nudging each other.

Fear gave me strength I didn't know I had. I jumped up and pulled the man off Mariette. He wasn't ready for my onslaught and fell heavily. Wine bottles toppled and his companions forgot us in their haste to stop them rolling on the floor and smashing.

Mariette clutched her throat. 'Come on,' she said hoarsely. 'We'd better get out while we can.'

She seized my hand and we pushed our way towards the door. In the street, rain poured from the gutters and glistened on the cobbles. Gas lamps threw feeble rays into the darkness. We dashed along the wet pavement, our leather-soled shoes slipping and sliding but suddenly cramp shot through my left leg, forcing me to stop. I leant against the wall of a house. Ahead, Mariette hurried on. 'Mariette,' I gasped, 'I can't go on, let me rest for a moment.'

She turned and walked back, her face flushed and her hair slipping from its pins. She grimaced. 'I'm soaked to the skin.'

'Me too,' I panted, doubling over and rubbing my leg as I waited for the cramp to subside.

'I hope you're satisfied,' I said as the pain ebbed, 'Heaven knows what would have happened if that man hadn't fallen over.'

For a moment, we glowered at each other then she started to laugh. Unable to help myself, I joined in.

'Thank you,' she said at last. 'I'm sorry I dragged you into it, but you do understand, don't you? I had to know. Now I've seen it's just a lot of men's nonsense, I'm happy.'

*

October came and cold, damp days and nights descended on Paris. France suffered a fresh blow when Metz fell to the Prussians. With General Bazaine and his army taken prisoner, there was no one left to come to Paris' aid. Rumours that the Government planned to sue for a peace at any price buzzed around the city like angry bees. Simmering discontent soon turned to fury and the city erupted.

'Now we'll see if I'm right,' Jules Fauchon remarked grimly. 'I mistrusted the National Guard from the first. Most of them are the riff-raff from the Belleville slums. A rifle and a few francs don't buy much loyalty when the bullets fly.'

'Don't judge them too harshly,' Edouard frowned. 'What do they have to thank our leaders for, or the bourgeoisie for that matter?'

Jules shook his head. 'You've always been a liberal, Edouard.'

'And so have you.'

'Granted, but liberal is one thing, crazy is another. What happens when peace comes and the Government tries to disband them? Do you really think they'll give up their pay meekly? Or their rifles? The Government will be sorry it armed them. We'll all be.'

*

The rift between the Government and its opponents widened. By the end of October, open warfare broke out. Trapped in the Hôtel de Ville, its disgraced Chief Minister, Trochu, was powerless to act.

Edouard went to see if he could find out anything but he failed to get through. 'They're letting no one in or out,' he said when he returned. 'I met Jules on my way back. I told him not to waste his time but he never listens.'

In fact, Jules Fauchon did somehow manage to gain admittance and he returned with the story of the events inside the Hôtel de Ville.

'It's Gustave Flourens who's taken charge,' he said, mopping his brow with his handkerchief. I remembered the flamboyant orator at the Club de Montmartre.

'Shouting orders and striding up and down the long table in the council chamber in that cavalry rig he likes so much,' Jules went on. 'His boots were on the same level as old Trochu's nose. Trochu didn't care for that, I can tell you. The Prefect of Police tried to restore order and didn't get very far but at last he managed to smuggle Trochu down the stairs and out through the cellars. After that the mob swarmed in. Some of them tried to join Flourens on the table and it collapsed under their weight.'

He mopped his forehead again. 'It's dangerous madness. Trochu needs to restore order as soon as possible. He must make a show of strength and punish the perpetrators.'

But several days passed before Trochu regained control and when he did, very few arrests were made. Edouard shook his head at the news. 'Now the rebels know Trochu is weak and Paris will suffer for it.'

Chapter 22

A few mornings after the attack on the Hôtel de Ville, Mariette and Péri sat with me in the salon on the first floor of Edouard's house. All of a sudden, we heard a commotion in the street below. Péri hurried to the window and gave a low whistle. 'Come and see this.'

We went to join him and a remarkable sight met our eyes. High above the rooftops, a huge red and yellow striped balloon drifted slowly across the sky. As it passed over the place Vendôme, the wind caught it and it twisted and turned like a weathervane before it resumed its stately course.

Mariette clapped her hands with excitement. 'Oh, isn't it beautiful!' she cried. 'I've never seen one fly before. The one the photographer Nadar showed at the Great Exhibition just stayed in one place.'

'Let's hope it makes it,' Péri said. 'Some poor brave bastard – sorry Anna – is risking his life up there.'

I watched the balloon drift further and further into the distance until it was a mere speck in the pale sky, then nothing.

The men who flew the balloons were indeed brave. Steering them was an uncertain business. Once airborne, they were at the mercy of the wind, to say nothing of the perilous crossing over the Prussian lines before the balloonists could risk a landing in friendly territory. Paris was lucky to have pilots prepared to face the dangers involved; hot air balloons were one of the few things that connected us to the world outside. They carried out letters and dispatches as well as leaflets to drop on the Prussian army carrying messages like "Death to the invaders!" or "Paris defies her enemies!" There was however no means of bringing any responses back - landing the balloons back in the city was impossible

'You saw the balloon? Magnificent, wasn't it,' said Edouard, coming down from his studio. 'I hear Nadar's set up a factory at the Gare d'Orléans to refurbish the ones that were already in the city and construct more.'

Mariette was eager to see the balloons close to, and Edouard – who had met Nadar on many occasions - offered to take us to visit his factory the following day.

At the great station, an extraordinary sight greeted us. Above rail tracks already overgrown with grass, balloons billowed and swayed like gigantic whales. Hundreds of volunteers scurried between them, repairing rents in the cloth, applying varnish to strengthen it and mending broken struts and baskets. Sailors toiled in the former station waiting rooms braiding hemp into ropes.

'A tremendous achievement,' Edouard said, looking around him approvingly. 'Ah, there's Nadar. Come with me to congratulate him.'

Nadar smiled as we approached. 'Monsieur Blanchard! What a pleasure to see you. What do you think of my factory? I have another at the Gare du Nord where more balloons are being built.'

Edouard clapped him on the back. 'Magnificent! Paris is forever in your debt.'

Nadar shrugged. 'One does what one can. The steering of course is a problem.' He laughed. 'I already have several sacks of letters and drawings suggesting ways of solving the difficulty: steam engines, propellers, sails, oars, rockets, even an idea for harnessing eagles to the baskets. No doubt before this is all over, I shall have many more.'

Edouard laughed. 'All of them sound alarming.'

'Now that you've seen the balloons, would you like to see our pigeons?'

'Very much,' Edouard replied.

We followed Nadar out of the station hall, across a yard and up several flights of stairs to a large room. It smelt of bird lime and was dimly lit. One long side had been fitted out with rows and rows of cages which contained the birds. Several men were working there but in the low light, it was hard to make out what they were doing. One of them came over to us.

'Good morning, Monsieur Nadar.'

'Good morning, Pierre. I've brought more visitors to see our little beauties. Fetch one out, would you?'

Pierre went to the cages and brought back a pigeon. We followed him to a table and Nadar turned up the lamp there so we could see well.

Apart from the little jerking movements it made with its head, the pigeon lay still in Pierre's hand, its bright, beady eyes watching him. Close to, I saw how pretty its plumage was, the soft grey shot through with pink and green tints.

Nadar held up a small cylinder no bigger than my little finger.

'Well, ladies, what do you think this is?'

'It looks like a roll of paper,' Mariette said.

'Very good. It is, but of a special kind. See, it's as thin as a butterfly's wing. We can shrink photographs of documents so that just one of these can hold as much information as might be contained in a whole book. We roll the paper up tightly and fix it to the pigeon's leg – like so. When the bird reaches its destination, a magic lantern enlarges the documents so they can be transcribed by hand and read. After that, the bird's homing instinct brings it back with messages for Paris.

'Most ingenious,' Péri said.

'The only problem is that some of them are shot down by Prussian sharpshooters for the pot.'

Mariette frowned. 'But then won't they be able to read what the pigeons carry?'

Nadar shook his head. 'They don't have the skill.'

We talked for a little while longer then said our farewells. On the way home, I felt heartened that men like Nadar were there to help Paris. Each time I looked up at the sky and saw a homing pigeon, I felt we were not entirely alone.

Yet in spite of all these efforts, Paris suffered from her isolation. Frustration mounted and the Red Clubs' activities spilled out onto the streets. Péri was eager to be in the thick of the action and joined a march of many thousands of men to the Hôtel de Ville. At their head was Gustave Flourens, the flamboyant orator we had seen at the Club de Montmartre.

'Chief Minister Trochu himself met with us,' Péri said jubilantly on his return. 'He listened to our demands that he mobilise the National Guard to break out of Paris, and to our call for an election. At last we shall see some action.'

I looked at Edouard's face and noticed he was not so sanguine.

Sure enough, a few days later, there was bad news. Tired of waiting for action, the Reds had marched to the Hôtel de Ville once more. This time, they received no hearing; instead Trochu and his ministers were ready for them with snipers stationed at every window. It was lucky for Péri he hadn't been among the marchers, for there were many casualties.

'What do you think will happen now?' I asked Edouard.

He shrugged. 'Trochu may still order an attack on the Prussian lines, if only to pacify the mob, although I very much doubt it will do anything but spill more French blood.'

He was right. The National Guard's attempt to break out of the city failed, leaving many dead or wounded. Enraged, the mob stormed the Hôtel de Ville once more and for an interminable day, we had no idea whether Trochu or the Reds were in control.

In spite of Mariette's protests, Péri went out to see what was happening. He returned angry and depressed.

'The inside of the Hôtel de Ville is in an appalling state,' he said, running his hand through his hair. I saw the streaks of grey in it. 'Windows broken, furniture smashed. Even the banisters have been ripped from stairways. Looters were carrying away everything they could lay their hands on. Flourens and his men have taken over the Council Chamber but I made very little sense of what was going on. It seemed everyone talked and no one listened.'

The chaos went on for several days then just as it seemed power would slip from Trochu's grasp, he showed his hand. A little-known secret passage beneath the Hôtel de Ville connected the building to the outside world. It gave the loyal troops a perfect opportunity to surprise the Reds who were swiftly disarmed. Although Trochu gave his word there would be no reprisals, it was not a promise that he kept for long. The following day, twenty-two Red leaders were arrested and thrown into prison.

'This show of strength comes too late,' Edouard said scornfully when we heard the news. 'The Reds have many supporters now, and they'll neither forgive nor forget.'

*

For the time being at least, the threat of rebellion was crushed but it left Paris with a different enemy: hunger. As the siege went on, the cattle and sheep penned up in the gardens and squares vanished.

'All eaten,' Edouard said grimly. 'Cook comes to me grumbling there's nothing worth having in the shops. She calls the butchers names even I hesitate to use.'

He sighed. 'I've told her to spend whatever's necessary. She claims she needs more kitchen maids as well. Apparently the ones we already employ haven't time to stand in the food queues as well as doing their other duties.' He turned to me with a despairing gesture. 'Anna, you must deal with her. I have no aptitude for these domestic matters.'

In the wealthier areas, butchers still had meat to sell but it was more likely to be cat or dog than beef or mutton. The fashionable Boucherie Anglaise had bought the animals from the zoo and crowds besieged the shop on the day the butcher displayed the carcasses. Those of the elephants, Castor and Pollux, caused the greatest stir. I really believe the poor creatures aroused more excitement dead than they had alive.

In spite of all the difficulties though, the best restaurants still had a miraculous knack of producing good meals for favoured customers. Generous as ever, Edouard often treated Mariette, Péri and me to expensive dinners. It became one of our games to try and guess what meat we would be offered.

'Elephant tonight, I think,' Mariette speculated one evening.

Péri shook his head. 'Even Castor and Pollux's carcasses must be exhausted by now. No, I think it will be kangaroo.'

We arrived at the restaurant Edouard had selected and the head waiter greeted us warmly before showing us to our table. 'I'm glad to see you keep your standards up,' Edouard remarked, indicating the crisp, white damask cloth and gleaming silver.

The man smiled deferentially. 'Thank you, Monsieur Blanchard. I fear that all the same, what we have to offer is more limited than I should like. I only hope it will be to your taste.'

Edouard picked up the menu, written as it had always been on thick, creamy parchment, bound at the spine with crimson cord. He studied the dishes and we all followed suit.

Mariette wrinkled her nose. 'Ragout du rat. Ugh, I couldn't possibly.'

I had to admit, the idea did not appeal to me either but Edouard and Péri scoffed at our timidity.

Edouard summoned the head waiter. 'The ragout du rat, do you recommend it?'

'It is not to everyone's taste, Monsieur, but our chef prides himself he has created an excellent sauce that makes the meat very palatable.'

'Then I shall try it,' Edouard declared. 'Will you join me, Péri?'

'With pleasure.'

The ragout arrived sizzling hot in a silver dish; slivers of pale meat poked up through a blanket of glistening white sauce that smelt of wine and tarragon. Mariette and I watched in horrified fascination as Péri put the first forkful into his mouth. He chewed and swallowed thoughtfully. 'Delicious.'

Edouard laughed and began to eat as well.

'Now we are all together,' he said between mouthfuls, 'I have a proposition.'

I knew what he was going to say for we had already talked of it. I hoped Mariette and Péri would agree.

'I hope that you will forgive me if I suggest that you may be finding life a little difficult these days?' Edouard continued.

'Well,' said Péri, 'I won't pretend it's easy to manage. We've no money coming in since the theatres had to close. The Government passed that new law suspending rents, but there's food and fuel—'

Edouard raised a hand to interrupt him. 'My house is much larger than Anna and I need. Most of the rooms are unused. I should be honoured if you would come and live with us until better times.'

Mariette looked at Péri.

'Please say yes,' I begged.

Péri flushed. 'We can't impose on your generosity in such a way.'

'Nonsense, you would be doing a kindness. An old fellow like me makes poor company for Anna.'

'Are you sure?'

Edouard chuckled. 'You should know me well enough by now to understand that I never make an offer I don't wish to keep.'

'Then we accept gratefully.'

Edouard beamed. 'Good, that's settled.'

Chapter 23

Even though Cook continued to grumble, life at the place Vendôme was much more comfortable than it was for many Parisians and we were never seriously short of food. Apart from having sufficient money to buy whatever was available, no matter how high the price, Edouard had for some time owned two Black Leghorn hens and a Jersey cow.

The hens, Sheba and Cleopatra, were gorgeous creatures with glossy blue-black plumage and they laid delicious brown eggs. They lived in the small courtyard at the back of the house, where they strutted about regally, their piercing, jet eyes always on the lookout for food. Watching as they pecked up the grain and scraps the servants threw down for them, I could not help reflecting, with a guilty pang, that they probably ate better than many of the poor of Paris.

Aphrodite, the Jersey cow was kept out to graze on a small patch of ground near one of the windmills at Montmartre where a local man was well paid to guard her. Edouard took me to see her on numerous occasions for he was endearingly proud of her. With her russet hide and melting brown eyes fringed with ginger lashes, she was a beautiful, placid creature. Twice a day, one of the servants went out to milk her then brought a tin pail of her rich milk down to the house. Cook saved what she needed for her recipes and the rest was churned to butter and cream.

But as winter closed in, the grass ceased to grow and it became impossible to find fodder. Reluctantly, Edouard decided Aphrodite must be slaughtered. On my next visit to the kitchens to discuss the week's menu with Cook, I found her trimming a fine rib of beef, well marbled with glistening white fat. Poor Aphrodite, I thought sadly. That evening, Cook surpassed herself, but Edouard did not eat with his usual gusto.

*

Péri joined the National Guard, but before long his patriotic enthusiasm waned. 'The Government called for us to enlist,' he grumbled, 'but oh no, we aren't good enough for the regulars. They turn up their noses and boast about their rifles being so much more modern than ours. Then they say it doesn't really matter because we don't know one end of them from the other anyway.' He scowled. 'It's not our fault if we aren't given proper training.'

He came back early one morning after a night on guard duty looking weary and morose. Mariette poured his coffee and he wrapped his hands around the cup to warm them. 'What's the point of it all?' he muttered. 'All we do is march, march, march. Back and forward along those accursed walls. Or we're sent to sort out a few fellows who've had a skinful of liquor and are making a nuisance of themselves in the streets.' He raised an imaginary rifle to his eye. 'Bam! Let me kill at least one Prussian before I die.'

Mariette grimaced. 'Don't talk like that, Péri, you know it frightens me.'

'A soldier fights, my love, it's what he's for. We can't stay holed up here forever. The Government must act and show they are true patriots who want to save France. If not, the people will rise and find leaders who do.'

The National Guard, dressed in a motley collection of uniforms, continued to drill every day. Time seemed to stand still, then at last Péri's wish was granted. The Government announced a fresh attempt to break through the Prussian lines.

On the day of what became known as "The Great Sortie", thousands of people cheered the troops as they marched out to fight, but Mariette and I were not among them. Poor Mariette was more distressed than I had ever seen her. She sat all day hardly speaking, twisting one of Péri's handkerchiefs in her lap. Even Edouard's jokes and anecdotes didn't coax a smile from her.

Inevitably, after the euphoria, a more sombre mood descended on Paris. Huddled in their winter overcoats and scarves, Parisians scurried through the streets under the grey November skies, throwing furtive glances at every distant boom of the guns. When the wind blew towards the city, it brought a pall of sulphurous smoke that darkened the streets.

On the third day, the first of the bedraggled survivors limped home, but twelve thousand men would never return. The Great Sortie had failed.

Mariette was distraught for there was no news of Péri. Edouard sent some of the menservants to scour the makeshift hospitals that had been set up to treat the wounded but they returned with no news. Eventually Edouard went himself to his own doctor and asked for his help to find him.

That night neither Mariette nor I slept. The housemaid looked at me doubtfully when I told her to make up the fire in the small salon. I knew she worried about using precious firewood without Edouard's instructions, but I was in no mood to be disobeyed. When the fire was lit, Mariette and I sat beside it. In spite of the cheerful blaze, the room still felt cold and I wrapped my shawl around me. Perhaps it was foreboding that made me shiver. We talked for a while then Mariette fell into a doze. I found a blanket and tucked it round her, glad she would have some respite from this agonising wait.

Only the crackle of the fire and the slow tick of the mantle clock disturbed the silence. Mariette murmured in her sleep and sank deeper into her chair. I felt such pity for her. To lose Péri would break her heart.

I must have slept awhile. I woke to find a wan, grey light creeping into the room. The footsteps that had roused me grew louder. The door opened and Edouard stood there, smiling.

Mariette woke with a start, jumped from her chair and ran to him. 'Have you found him?'

'Yes, my dear.'

'Where is he? Why isn't he with you? Is he wounded?'

Edouard took her hands. 'I won't lie to you, he is, but his life isn't in danger. I've had him moved to Dr Barbet's clinic. You mustn't be afraid - Barbet says there's every chance he'll be able to come home in a few days.'

'I must go to him straight away.'

Edouard laid a hand on her arm. 'Not yet.'

Mariette looked at him in astonishment. 'Why ever not?'

'He needs to rest, Mariette.'

She burst into tears and rushed from the room.

'Anna, go and calm her,' Edouard said quickly. 'I'll explain later.'

I found her already donning her cloak. 'Mariette, wait: you must trust Edouard. I beg you, don't go like this.'

Her face crumpled and I put my arms around her. 'Please, Mariette, do as he asks. I'm sure it's for the best. Try to rest awhile.'

She gulped and nodded. 'You'll wake me if there's any more news?'

'I promise.'

In the salon, Edouard jabbed a poker into the fire. 'I'd almost given up hope when I found him,' he said wearily. 'Lying on a blood-stained stretcher, wounded in the arm and suffering great pain. I only hope Barbet can do something for him.'

The fire blazed up and spat out a shower of crimson sparks. 'He wasn't the only one suffering,' Edouard went on. 'Most of the men around him were badly injured and suffering from shock. I spoke with an orderly who'd been on the battlefield helping to bring in the wounded. He said there were so many of them it was virtually an impossible task. Madness, he called the whole campaign. Ill-prepared and ill-judged. Apparently many of our soldiers had only been issued with a handful of bullets.'

He threw the poker down in the grate. 'It made me angry to hear a common fellow criticise our generals, but I fear he may be right. Paris is as good as lost.'

*

The next day, we went to the clinic to see Péri. In former times it had occupied only a few rooms on the ground floor of Doctor Barbet's fine, spacious house on the boulevard Haussmann but now it had grown to take over the whole building. Karl and I had attended several receptions at the house in the past. I remembered the scent of the great bowls of perfumed lilies and roses in the hallway, but there were no flowers now. Instead the air had a sickly smell overlaid with the sharp odour of disinfectant.

There was no sign of Doctor Barbet but a young man with an American accent came out to the hall to greet us. His thick, dark-brown hair stuck out in little wings just above his ears. He was clean-shaven, and steel-framed spectacles accentuated the roundness of his face. He apologised for Doctor Barbet's absence and introduced himself as his assistant.

'Your friend's still very weak, you must be prepared for that,' he said. 'I'm afraid we had no choice but to amputate his arm.'

Her face as white as the marble floor, Mariette swayed. The young American caught her and called out to a passing nurse to bring a glass of water. He helped Mariette to a chair and held the glass to her lips. 'Sip it slowly,' he said gently. 'There's no hurry to get up. If you'd rather, you could stay here while your friends go upstairs.'

She shook her head. 'I'm sorry to be so foolish.'

'I'm the one who ought to apologise. It was crass of me to break the news so bluntly, I should have tried to spare you the shock.'

She gave him a shaky smile. 'You're very kind, Doctor—'

'Silver, Ethan Silver.'

She drew a deep breath. 'I'm all right now, Doctor Silver. Shall we go?'

He frowned. 'Are you sure you want to?'

'Of course. If Péri must bear it then so must I.'

The young American took her arm and led the way up the wide staircase to the grand salon. The magnificent Aubusson rugs I remembered lay rolled up under dust covers at one end of the room and dozens of beds had been set up on the bare boards. The gilt-framed mirrors on the walls threw back images of the harassed nurses tending to the patients. Some of the men dozed, their pain-lined faces relaxed a little in sleep. Others called out for water or groaned softly.

Even though the American had tried to prepare us, shock sliced through me at the sight of Péri.

Where his left arm had been, nothing remained but a bandaged stump. His eyes were dull but at the sight of Mariette, he managed a feeble smile. She bent over to kiss him and he lifted his good arm and stroked her hair. 'There, there,' he murmured. 'It's not so bad. At least I still have this one. If anyone will have me, there's somewhere to put the wedding ring.'

I saw how Mariette's brave effort at cheerfulness nearly foundered. She nodded, unable to speak.

'I expect you and Mariette would like to be alone for a while,' Edouard said gently. 'Doctor Silver, will you take us downstairs again?'

I averted my eyes from many of the patients as we left the ballroom, and felt ashamed of my squeamishness. Doctor Silver glanced at me sideways and gave me an encouraging smile. In the hall, he and Edouard talked briefly then he made his excuses and went to attend to his other patients, leaving us to wait for Mariette.

*

The failure of the Great Sortie plunged Paris into gloom once more. Queues for food lengthened as supplies ran perilously low, not just stocks of fresh food, but of flour, rice, sugar and even salt, that precious ingredient without which every dish was bland and tasteless. The Government began to promote strange, unappetising foodstuffs, including a sort of bread made from wheat, rice and straw that

Edouard said tasted like an old Panama hat picked out of the gutter.

Soon the ugly spectre of disease raised its head. Before the siege, most drinking water had been drawn from the clean wells and unpolluted springs outside the city, but with the Prussian troops encamped around the walls, these could no longer be tapped and the Seine had to provide for Paris' daily needs.

I often thought of Monsieur and Madame Roche, but when I talked of visiting them, Edouard frowned. 'There are rumours of cholera in that part of the city. I'd rather you stayed away.'

'Edouard, please let me go. I can't bear to think they might be suffering. At least let me take them some food.'

He shook his head. 'I'll send one of the servants.'

I pleaded, but he was adamant and I had to be satisfied.

The servant brought back Madame Roche's thanks but none of the news of my kind friends for which I longed.

'You can't blame the poor man, Anna,' Mariette said. 'He probably wanted to get away from there as soon as he could, and it's no wonder.' She saw my downcast expression and hugged me. 'Try not to worry. I'm sure they'll be safe. The rumours are probably much worse than the truth. You'll see, soon the danger will be over and you can visit them in safety.'

But several weeks passed before Edouard agreed to my going. Then he insisted on coming too.

Away from the centre of the city, our carriage attracted bitter, envious looks and I was glad of his protection. In the poor districts, ragged children watched with listless eyes as we passed by. Once, when the carriage slowed to turn a sharp corner, a boy who was probably no more than seven or eight years old lifted up a tiny girl in his scrawny arms and called out to us to stop. The girl raised her hand to her grubby face and stuffed her fingers into her mouth in a pantomime of eating.

Edouard fished in his pockets for some coins and tossed them out of the carriage window. As we drove on, I looked back and saw the children scrabble for them in the dirty slush. Outside the bakeries, long queues of grim-faced women waited with empty baskets over their arms. Most of the other shops had their shutters down.

A lump came into my throat. It was one thing to hear of the sufferings of the poor, another to see them. 'These people - what will happen to them? Can't something be done?'

Edouard sighed. 'It saddens me too, but I doubt it. When I was young, I thought the world could be made a better place. Now that I am old, I fear it never will be.'

When we reached the house, Edouard stayed in the carriage and let me go up alone. I knocked but no one answered. Tentatively, I tried the latch; it lifted and the door opened.

Even through the warm velvet of my cloak, I shivered at the damp cold that met me. There were no baskets of laundry on the floor and the stove was out. The scrubbed pine table where we had shared so many meals had gone and there was only one chair drawn up beside the narrow trestle where Madame Roche used to work.

I heard her call out from the other room. 'Who's there? Don't you touch any of my things, you rascal, or I'll beat you black and blue.'

With a swish of skirts, she marched into the room and stopped dead when she saw me. 'Anna! Where did you spring from? You gave me a fright and no mistake.'

'Forgive me, I didn't mean to alarm you. I knocked but—'

'Oh, never mind. I'm glad to see you.'

There was an awkward silence.

'You look well, Anna,' she said at last.

'I'm sorry I haven't come before.'

She smiled dryly. 'Thank you for sending the food, I was very grateful. There's no need to apologise. If I'd been in your shoes, I wouldn't have come either.'

'Have things been very hard here?'

She shrugged. 'It's not been easy, I won't pretend it has.' She gestured to the bare room. 'As you see, I've not much work. The way prices have gone most people have enough trouble buying food to keep body and soul together. They just have to go dirty.'

Suddenly, I noticed something else missing. The old clay pipe that Monsieur Roche smoked in the evenings was not on the shelf by the stove and the room lacked the acrid smell of the strong tobacco he favoured. The comfortable, shabby jacket he had liked to put on when he came in from work was gone from the nail on the back of the door.

Madame Roche followed my eyes. 'Poor old Roche,' she said quietly. 'I wanted to keep his things but I needed every bit of money I could get.'

My heart ached for her. 'I'm so sorry.'

'None of that,' she said brusquely. 'I don't want anyone's pity.'

I held out the purse Edouard had given me. 'I'd be so pleased if you'd accept this.'

'I don't want charity either.'

'It's not charity. You helped me when I needed it.'

'I won't deny it'd be welcome,' she said gruffly.

'There then - take it - please.'

I pressed the purse into her hand and closed her work-worn fingers around it. 'I have to go now. A friend's waiting for me downstairs.'

I moved towards her, but she stepped back. 'Best not come too close, it might not be safe. You take care.'

'May I come and see you again?'

'If you like, now you'd better get along. Goodbye, Anna.' She turned away and as she did so, I thought I saw a tear glisten on her cheek.

*

In December, the freezing streets shone like glass. Icicles, brittle as mermaids' bones, hung from the eaves of the houses. The cold seemed to squeeze the life out of everything and my breath turned to steam when I walked out of doors. Paris grew used to the sight of men and women dressed in threadbare clothes using axes, knives, even their bare hands to hack down for firewood what remained of the city's trees.

Just before Christmas, Edouard went to fetch Péri home. We had visited him often but even so, it was a great relief – for Mariette most of all – to have him back.

'I saw that American doctor, Silver, again,' Edouard remarked. 'He's a likeable fellow and Barbet speaks well of him. I told him to visit us if he wants to. He doesn't seem to know many people in Paris so I thought it might go some way to repaying his kindness. He's cared for Péri with great compassion.'

We had Péri's return to celebrate that Christmas, but otherwise, the situation was far from good. The Prussian guns were well on the way to pounding the remaining forts around the city into submission. Once they fell, the bombardment started in earnest.

The first shells ploughed up the earth in the Montparnasse Cemetery where the occupants were beyond harm, but then the terrible destruction began. The vast domes of Les Invalides and the Panthéon made easy targets for the Prussian gunners and the areas around them suffered more than most. Even some of the hospitals were shelled, in spite of the red crosses marking their roofs. People left their doors unlocked, in case passers-by needed to take shelter.

In spite of everything though, with their irrepressible spirit, Parisians still managed to derive some amusement from their predicament. The bombardments became a kind of macabre entertainment. On moonlit nights, hundreds, sometimes thousands of people would gather in the place de la Concorde to watch the explosions light up the sky. In the mornings, ragged children scrabbled in the dust of shell craters to find anything they could sell for souvenirs.

They were strange days. We were like mice playing behind the wainscoting. Waiting with patient menace outside, the Prussians were the cat.

Chapter 24

'This house must be the only place in Paris where a man can get warm,' Jules Fauchon remarked, spreading his hands out to the fire.

'Any news?' Edouard asked.

'There's talk that the Government plans another attempt to break through the Prussians lines.'

I read Edouard's scepticism in his face and sadly it soon proved justified. The sortie took place but many men died, especially among the battalions of the National Guard that had been recruited from the slum districts where the Reds held sway. Bitter attacks on the Government followed. The Reds accused it of deliberately sacrificing the poor. Once again, a mob marched on the Hôtel de Ville. There, the loyalist Guards panicked and opened fire, killing and wounding many of the demonstrators as they tried to scramble to safety.

'Mark my words,' Edouard said, 'those shots will cost the Government dear. The Reds want revenge and the Government can't fight on two fronts. Jules is convinced that if they are faced with the prospect of civil war as well as famine, they'll decide to make peace with Prussia, and I agree with him.'

Soon, their prediction came true. The Government sued for peace and talks began, but not before Chancellor Bismarck had forced it to agree to the victorious Prussian troops marching in triumph through Paris and occupying the city for two days. In exchange, he opened the lines to allow food to pass. It was a joy to see the shops and markets full once more. After a few mutterings about waste when some early deliveries of food from Britain and America to Les Halles were trampled underfoot by excited crowds, Cook returned to her old cheerful self, content that once again she could obtain the ingredients she wanted.

For the moment, Parisians were content to fill their bellies, but each day, the prospect of the Prussians' victory march loomed larger. People said they wanted no part in it, yet when the morning came, curiosity triumphed and thousands lined the Champs Elysées.

In sharp contrast to the fun and fizz that usually attended great Parisian events, the mood was sombre. A group of Prussian cavalrymen, mounted on perfectly matched horses whose coats gleamed like molten pitch, appeared at the top of the avenue. Straight-backed and broad-shouldered in their white and gold dress uniforms, the riders urged their mounts forward and one by one, sailed effortlessly over the chains that guarded the hallowed space beneath the Arc de Triomphe. The scarlet plumes cresting their gold helmets tossed like a lash to Paris' pride.

The riders wheeled their horses abreast, slowed, and set off at a trot down the avenue. Behind them came the main procession. The elderly King William of Prussia, now Emperor of Germany, rode at its head, flanked by the Crown Prince and the gigantic figure of Chancellor Bismarck. After them came more cavalry with the gun carriages behind them. The monstrous cannons that had crushed Paris raised gasps from the crowd.

The Prussian infantry brought up the rear: row upon row of immaculately uniformed soldiers marching in perfect time, their heads held high and their backs as upright as the iron spikes on their pickelhauben. On the faces of the crowd around me, grudging admiration mingled with anger and sadness. Bismarck wished to humiliate Paris and he had succeeded.

For the next two days, the Prussians strutted about the city, glorying in their victory. Most of the shops and cafés in the occupied area remained closed and many of the proprietors had draped black cloth over their windows. Those that did open had their windows smashed and if they were found to have served any Prussians, their walls were daubed with red paint and their furniture and fittings were looted.

On the third day, the Prussians left the city as they had promised and Paris' relief was tangible. Huge bonfires crackled on the boulevards, tended by men and women with wild eyes and flushed, streaming faces. It was as if they needed to perform a kind of pagan ritual to cleanse and purify the city of every trace of the departed enemy. Some even got down on their hands and knees and scrubbed the tainted ground.

Edouard, Péri, Mariette and I walked through the streets, observing these desperate measures. Ahead of us in the rue de Rivoli, three National Guards staggered down the road until one of them stumbled and fell, pulling one of his companions down with him. The third upended the bottle of wine he carried over their heads and a fight began.

Edouard looked at them with distaste. 'I hear Bismarck backed down from his demand that they should all be disarmed. Adolphe Thiers will regret he negotiated that concession. How many battalions will be loyal if it comes to a fight with the Reds? People won't forgive the Government for making peace on such humiliating terms.'

Adolphe Thiers was the new leader of the Government, an elderly lawyer turned politician for whom Edouard had little time. Apart from winning the concession Edouard deemed unwise, he had fought unsuccessfully over the terms of peace. France had to give Prussia a vast sum in war damages and cede to her the wealthy cities of Metz and Strasbourg together with the whole of Alsace. Some insults can be forgotten, but to a proud city like Paris, the very heart and head of France, no amount of scrubbing and burning could eradicate this atrocious stain on her honour. Someone must pay.

The man singled out for the greatest hatred was Thiers. Day by day, his hold on Paris weakened. The Paris mob, angry that the better life their grandfathers had fought for in the Great Revolution seemed further from their grasp than ever, took to the barricades. Disaffected National Guardsmen, anti-government intellectuals and anarchists swelled their ranks and gave them hope that their grievances would be listened to if Thiers and his ministers could only be sent packing. Eventually, he gave up the struggle and fled to Versailles. Later, his magnificent mansion in the place Saint-George was razed to the ground and its treasures distributed among Paris' museums and libraries.

In a matter of days, new leaders emerged from the rebels. To general rejoicing, they proclaimed they would rule in the name of the people. A Commune was declared and a rush of exhilaration swept through Paris.

A vast platform was built in front of the Hôtel de Ville. The crimson cloth that swathed it and the gay scarves and sashes of the Commune's leaders made a defiant splash against the building's sombre, Gothic façade. The new leaders took the salute as tens of thousands of National Guardsmen marched past, the sunlight glinting off their swords and bayonets. The cheers of the crowd competed with the boom of gun salvoes and the music of the military bands. The noise drowned the speeches of the leaders who gave up trying to speak and simply beamed like tailors' dummies.

Among the new men, I recognised the fiery orator from the Club de Montmartre. He wore sky-blue pantaloons and a tunic of the same cloth. His ferocious appearance was magnified by the enormous curved scimitar slung at his side and a great belt stuffed with pistols.

'That's Gustave Flourens,' Péri shouted over the din. 'He's wearing the uniform from the years when he fought in Crete.'

Mariette smiled at me. 'I wonder what Péri would say if he knew where we first saw Flourens,' she whispered.

I hushed her but I need not have worried. Already Péri was distracted by one of the other leaders' magnificent regalia. 'What a day,' he exclaimed. 'Now Paris can begin again.'

*

Edouard worried about Jules Fauchon. He was well known to be no friend of the extremists among the Commune's ruling body. When the offices of several newspapers that criticised the new regime, some of which Jules wrote for, were ransacked and closed, Edouard persuaded him to leave Paris for a while and go to Edouard's house in the country.

A small exodus of public functionaries had by then already taken place. Numerous judges and senior police officials had left with Thiers, but contrary to expectation, the number of crimes went down rather than up. For most citizens, there was nothing to make them fear that a new terror might be unleashed on Paris. Anti-Communards who kept their views to themselves had no need to lie awake at night dreading the knock at the door.

Many changes appeared to be for the better. Paris was certainly cleaner than she had been for a long time, probably because the street sweepers were given an increase in their pay. New laws and edicts presaging reform and social justice poured from the Hôtel de Ville and, to the poor and oppressed workers of Paris, it must have seemed that the tide had at last turned in their favour.

In his letters from the country, Jules Fauchon wrote of coming back but Edouard continued to counsel him to stay away. I felt sorry for Jules. Paris was his lifeblood and he must be suffering, but Edouard was right: it was too soon for him to return.

The Commune allowed theatres to open again and Péri threw himself into making plans. 'Paris will be hungry for entertainment,' he said. 'I must speak with Henri Bertin. I wonder if he's well enough to take on any work yet - I'll need new scenery painting.'

Mariette and I had visited Henri and Virginie often during the siege and each time we went, my admiration for Virginie increased. I felt ashamed that I had originally judged her rather frivolous, demanding too much of Henri's attention and taking advantage of his easy-going, sunny temperament. Now I saw the steel in her and the strong love she had for Henri. She guarded him like a lioness and did everything in her power to speed his recovery from the injury he had sustained in the war. As times had grown harder in the besieged city, she had accepted help, but only if it benefited him, not for herself.

I discovered she was an accomplished needlewoman and she took in any work she was offered. I did my best to help and found customers for her from among my well-off acquaintances although at times I wondered if it was really doing her a kindness. Frequently, her eyes were red-rimmed with tiredness and she would admit she had sat up half the night sewing while Henri slept.

Henri gladly accepted Péri's commission and soon the theatre's first production opened to sell-out audiences. It was the same story all over Paris: pavement cafés strained at the seams with patrons enjoying the spring sunshine. Eager customers flocked to the shops to buy the little luxuries that had been denied them during the Siege. In the parks, families picnicked on the grass and stalls selling cakes, bonbons and syrupy drinks – heaven to children deprived of sweet things for so long - did a brisk trade. Laughing crowds watched puppet shows, and soldiers, still in uniform, walked arm in arm with their wives or sweethearts.

Chapter 25

'I'm afraid Edouard's not at home,' I said. 'He's gone to the theatre to give Péri some help with the preparations for the new show. It opens in a few days.'

Ethan Silver smiled. 'Please give them both my regards. I'm glad to hear Monsieur Périchon is getting back to work – it's a good sign. He's a lucky man,' he added. 'Without his friends, he might not be here today. Many of the wounded ended up in hospitals I wouldn't trust to treat my dog.'

'What will you do now the war's over? Do you plan to go home to America?'

He shook his head. 'I came to Paris to train under Doctor Barbet and I intend to finish my studies.'

'It was very brave of you not to leave Paris when you had the chance.'

A slight flush showed above the line of Ethan Silver's stiffly starched white collar. 'It's kind of you to say so, Madame Daubigny, but I only did what any honourable man would do. In any case, my family's a military one. My grandfather fought in the War of Independence and my father served in the army all his working life. My brothers fought too - for the North in the Civil War. I suffered from tuberculosis as a child and it left my lungs weak so the US army wouldn't take me. When I saw there was a way I could help here, I didn't want to turn my back.'

'Even though it wasn't your fight?'

'It made no difference. Soldiers needed help and I knew how to give it.'

'Your family must be glad you're safe.'

'My father died a few years ago and my mother, being an army wife, is used to it. I know that even if anything happens to me, she'll be well cared for. My brothers live close by her in Boston.'

'I've never been to America.'

'It can't compete with Paris in many ways but our cities grow all the time and Boston's one of the finest. The waterfront's beautiful and we have some of the oldest buildings in the States.'

'I'd like to see it some day.'

He gave me an uncertain look. 'Maybe your husband will take you.'

'I doubt it,' I said, more sharply than I had intended.

'Forgive me, I didn't mean to intrude.' He studied the cups and saucers on the tea tray between us, picked up a spoon and put it back down again.

Edouard's arrival broke the awkward silence. 'Ah!' he beamed. 'Doctor Silver, a pleasure to see you.'

'I took you at your word, sir,' Ethan said awkwardly.

'And so you should have. I'm glad to find Anna has company. I've been out all afternoon and neglecting her.'

Apparently impervious to the atmosphere, he looked at the tea tray and raised an eyebrow. 'Tea? A drink fit only for invalids. You'll join me in a cognac I hope, Doctor Silver?'

'I'm afraid I don't drink, sir.'

'Don't drink? Have we taught you nothing in Paris?'

Ethan laughed. 'I've learnt a great deal, but drinking isn't one of those lessons.'

Edouard scratched his head. 'I suppose you know your own mind. So tell me, what do you think of our masters in the Hôtel de Ville? No, on second thoughts, don't tell me. The less one voices one's opinions at the moment, the better. Are you fond of art?'

Ethan looked a little bemused by the sudden turn in the conversation but he smiled. 'I know very little about it, sir. I studied the sciences at school and college, but I'm happy to learn.'

'Then when you've finished that infernal drink, we'll go up to my studio.'

After they had gone, I felt ashamed of my snappish reply to Ethan's question. My predicament was no fault of his.

I sighed. Time had worn away my love for Emile, but it had not resolved the problem of my marriage. Even though I no longer wanted to be Emile's wife, I had no choice. My thoughts strayed to Mariette and Virginie. Both of them had the men they loved and a purpose to their lives. What did I have? Edouard was kindness itself and I tried to repay him by modelling for his paintings, and doing whatever I could to make the house run smoothly, but was it enough? Most people probably considered me very lucky, and I knew I should be grateful for my good fortune, but I wished my life didn't feel so aimless. I was a wife, yet not a wife, and I didn't want to be a mistress again. What else could life hold for me?

Chapter 26

Those halcyon days of early April lulled Paris into a sense of tranquillity. We were probably naïve to expect it to last, but its abrupt destruction was still shocking. One night, Adolphe Thiers launched a surprise attack from Versailles. His troops seized the bridge at Neuilly and threatened to advance into Paris. Enraged, the Communards hastily assembled their forces to retaliate.

What followed was a disaster for the Communards. The motley crew of National Guardsmen who marched out on that glorious, sunny, Sunday morning were half drunk from celebrating what had seemed to be a return to Paris' carefree life before the war. At the first sight of the enemy, most of them fled, not to be seen again. Only a few remained to swell the small private armies mustered by the Communard elite.

'They still have Flourens,' Péri said. 'If anyone can save the Commune, it will be Flourens.'

I had to admit, I cared very little about who governed Paris; I just wanted the brief spell of peace the city had enjoyed to continue. Mariette agreed with me, although, for Péri's sake, she wanted Flourens' army to win.

'Péri admires him so much,' she said. 'And Péri really believes in the Commune too. He'll be devastated if Versailles takes back power.'

Her fears were realised when news reached Paris that Flourens' attempt to drive the Versailles troops back had failed. The inhabitants of a small village where he had stopped to rest his men for the night had betrayed him. He and his men were seized by the Versailles troops and brutally executed.

The news of this disaster introduced a dark and sinister turn into the Commune's rule. They proclaimed that anyone who opposed them would be arrested on a charge of treason. Those found guilty would be held as hostages, and for every Communard killed by Versailles troops, three hostages would be shot. Unsurprisingly, the remaining newspapers still published hailed the measure as a master stroke in a just cause. I wondered what Péri thought of the Commune's brutal response. He didn't comment on it, and later Mariette told me in confidence that she had forbidden him to talk politics in the house. 'Edouard has been so good to us,' she said. 'I won't have Péri arguing with him.'

For his part, Edouard had been angered by the news. 'It's tyranny. We might be better off if Thiers does come back, but for now, we must get on with our lives quietly. At times like these, the less one stands out, the better.'

*

The Versailles troops dug in on the outskirts of the city and from their position, the city was in range of their powerful guns. If I had to leave the house for any reason, I did not stay away for long. I avoided sending Rose on errands as much as possible too. It was unfair to expect her to run risks I did not want to take myself. At the end of each day, I felt a deep sense of relief that all of us were safely home, but my relief was soon dispelled by the knowledge that, the next day, we would have to face danger all over again.

Edouard thought of our leaving Paris to join Jules Fauchon in the country but eventually decided against it. A large part of the Prussian army was still encamped in the countryside around Paris, no doubt waiting for the peace terms to be honoured. 'With them as well as the Versailles troops in the way, it's too dangerous to travel,' Edouard said.

The Commune's leaders began to fight among themselves and the faction that prevailed held the extreme beliefs of the Jacobins of the Great Revolution. As Thiers' guns pounded the Pont du Jour area to rubble, decrees and proclamations poured out of Hôtel de Ville. Among them, the Commune appointed a Committee of Public Safety.

'The very name chills me,' Edouard said. 'Self-styled guardians of the public good always have their own interests at heart. Thank God Jules accepted my advice and stayed away.'

Edouard's fears were well grounded: soon a redoubled campaign of persecution and intimidation began. More than three thousand people were arrested, quite a few of them priests suspected of treasonous activity. Masons hacked off church crosses and replaced them with the red flag. There was even talk that Notre Dame would be stripped of its statues and furnishings.

May came, except now we had to call it by the Jacobin name of Floréal, and the struggle to hold back the Versailles invaders went on. One by one, the forts encircling Paris fell and the surviving defenders limped into Paris. The few hospitals still open were overwhelmed with wounded men. Many of those who had escaped injury had nowhere to go and prowled the streets desperate for food and shelter. Edouard insisted that Mariette and I only went out if he or Péri came with us.

The Commune's next act of vandalism was the destruction of the Vendôme column, which was condemned as a royalist symbol. It had stood at the centre of the place Vendôme for more than fifty years, built to commemorate the victories of the Napoleon Bonaparte.

The day after the column had been torn down, the huge arsenal at avenue Rapp exploded. The roar could be heard for miles around and a pall of smoke drifted across Paris. The disaster might have been accidental, but a witch hunt for spies and traitors was soon on foot. Privately, I was afraid on my own account. Would the Commune start to accuse foreigners of working against them? I had heard that women as well as men were being arrested and tried.

In spite of their repressive acts, however, the Commune made an effort to preserve some semblance of normal life and distract the pleasure-loving Parisians. Museums and galleries re-opened with free entrance and there were free public concerts in the parks.

Edouard suggested that an outing to one would do us all good and, one Sunday, we went to the Tuileries Gardens with Péri and Mariette. It was strange but pleasant to be sitting in the shade of the plane trees, listening to the orchestra play popular tunes from the operas, knowing all the while that the reality was that Paris was under threat from within and without. All around us, other people were enjoying themselves too, as if they had forgotten the danger we lived in. Pompeii on the evening before its destruction could not have been more carefree.

When the concert ended, we returned home to the supper Cook had prepared. A plainer one than we had enjoyed the week before but nonetheless probably much better than many people could look forward to. We sat up talking for a while then retired to bed.

Just after midnight a tremendous clamour woke me. All across the district, church bells rang, accompanied by the sound of bugles and drums. I threw a robe over my nightgown and hurried out onto the landing to hear Edouard's voice calling for the servants to light the lamps. As I passed the door to Mariette and Péri's room, it opened and Péri came out, already dressed.

I seized his arm. 'What's going on, Péri?'

'It's the tocsin! The call to arms! The Versailles troops must be attacking the city. Edouard and I are going out to see what's happening.'

I found Mariette looking pale and anxious. 'I wish Péri would stay here,' she said, 'but he won't listen. Oh why are men so stupid?'

After Edouard and Péri left, Mariette and I sat in the salon. I suggested a game of bezique in the hope of distracting her from her anxiety but soon she threw down the cards. I had to admit, I was hardly less anxious.

The two men didn't return until dawn. The clean clothes they had gone out in were unrecognisable they were so torn and filthy. Edouard's hands were black and his fingernails ragged and crusted with blood. Péri's face was bruised.

Mariette flew at him. 'What have you done to yourself? You promised me you wouldn't get into any trouble.'

'Don't nag me, Mariette. We've spent most of the night hauling sandbags and paving stones up onto a barricade.' He grimaced. 'Not that I was much use. The Versailles troops are in the city. They found the gate by the Pont-du-Jour unguarded and just walked in. Whoever was responsible for that ought to swing for it.'

Edouard limped to a chair and flopped down. 'The Commune's officers were grabbing anyone they could find, forcing them to help build defences. They would've left Péri alone but he wouldn't leave me, the fool.'

'Your hands are in a terrible state,' I said. 'Let me wash and bandage them.'

'Get me a brandy first, Anna. I don't care what time of day it is. Fetch one for Péri too.'

It was hard to wait patiently for news, but we had little choice. I think Mariette would have nailed herself to the door rather than let Péri go out again and Edouard was clearly so shaken and exhausted that he had no desire to.

Around midday, there was a commotion in the square and shots rang out. Edouard went to the window. 'National Guardsmen,' he said, 'but whose side they're on it's hard to say.'

Péri joined him. 'Communards, I suspect. Their rifles look like tabatiers, too old to belong to the Versailles troops.'

Suddenly the window exploded and glass rained onto the floor. The force of the blast knocked Péri sideways and if Edouard had not grabbed him, he would have fallen.

Edouard wiped his forehead. 'That was close. We'd better draw all the curtains. I should have thought of it sooner. We were probably mistaken for a sniper.'

I rang for one of the servants to sweep up the glass; it seemed an age before the gunfire stopped and only the distant pulse of heavy guns rumbled on.

In the early evening, the battle came close again. Péri hurried to the window and pulled one curtain aside before Mariette had time to stop him.

'Guardsmen coming from the direction of the rue de la Paix,' he said. 'That's where one of the barricades was. They must be retreating.'

Mariette snatched the curtain from him and pulled it back across the window. 'Didn't you hear what Edouard said?' she asked angrily.

The shouts, running feet and whistle of bullets suddenly gave way to the roar of cannons, and the sound of falling masonry as they found their targets. We heard screams and more shouting then silence. In spite of Mariette's protests, after waiting a few minutes, Péri went to look out again. 'They've gone.'

'The Communards will probably pull back towards the Belleville slums,' Edouard said. 'The Versailles troops will have their work cut out flushing them out of there, but they'll do it in the end. They're better armed. Mark my words, Thiers will soon be back in control.'

Soon, from the level of noise from the guns, it was clear the battle had moved to another part of the city. It left us a subdued party that evening; no doubt only one of many small islands of normality in a sea of confusion and violence. Powerless to do anything but wait.

Chapter 27

A clap of thunder reverberated around the square, shaking the windows. A picture hanging in an alcove crashed to the floor. Mariette shrieked and clung to Péri. 'It's all right, my love,' he soothed. 'We're safe here.'

She raised her tear-stained face. 'You're not to go out again. You must promise me.' It was so unlike her to lose her composure, but not really surprising. After all the hours of waiting and inactivity, I was close to breaking down myself.

Edouard went to pick up the painting. As he did so, we heard a new sound: the clang of alarm bells. He frowned. 'They sound like the ones they use on the water trucks. My guess is they're somewhere near the rue de Rivoli.'

A flustered maid appeared in the doorway. 'Please Monsieur Blanchard, Monsieur Bertin is here. He says may he come up?'

'Of course.'

A moment later, Henri arrived. His usual cheerful manner had deserted him.

'What's going on?' Edouard asked quickly.

'There's been an explosion, the Tuileries is on fire. The flames are spreading towards the Louvre.'

'Mon Dieu, how did it happen?'

The Communards started it. They're boasting they'll destroy the city before they give in. They dragged sacks of gunpowder into the Tuileries, doused everything with tar and petrol then set light to it. Every fire truck in Paris is on the way there but it may already be too late.'

Edouard's fists clenched. 'Vandals! It's monstrous! The Louvre's collections are irreplaceable. I'm going down there to see if there's any way I can help.'

I tried to persuade him not to go but he was already striding towards the hall, shouting for his hat and coat.

'I'll go with him,' Henri said.

Péri frowned. 'So will I. No, Mariette, don't argue with me. You and Anna are to stay here, do you understand me?'

Mariette opened her mouth to protest but for once his stern expression seemed to quell her. The three men's footsteps echoed on the marble staircase and the door to the square banged shut. Mariette ran to the window. 'Come and see, Anna.'

Edouard and the others were hurrying in the direction of the rue de Rivoli. In the gathering dusk, the crimson sky above it roiled like molten lead. This was a fire that it would not be easy to put out.

*

'Something's wrong, I know it,' Mariette fretted. 'I want to go and look for them.'

Several hours had passed with no sign of the men and the sky over the Tuileries still glowed like a furnace.

'Mariette, it's madness. You heard what Péri said.'

Her chin tilted defiantly. 'I don't care. I've had enough of being cooped up in this house. If you won't come with me, I'll go alone.'

It was impossible to dissuade her so we set off. I shuddered as we emerged into the place Vendôme. The moon was up and its light revealed chilling evidence of the battle that had been waged there the previous day. Patches of dried blood stained the paving stones and the stonework on many of the beautiful houses was pitted with bullet holes.

In the rue de Rivoli, the roofs of many of the buildings had collapsed; blown-out windows that had formerly displayed luxury goods gaped like screaming mouths. The walls around them still glowed in spite of the hoses directed on them by the men working the fire trucks. The tarry taste and smell of smoke filled my mouth and nostrils and made my eyes sting. Sooty water soaked my thin shoes and weighed down the hem of my skirt. We were soon caught up in the crowds surging in the direction of the Tuileries. Firemen, trying desperately to damp each new outbreak of flames, cursed and shouted as people got in their way.

At last, we reached the Tuileries and the sight made me gasp. The once-magnificent palace was an inferno and the air seemed on fire. I put up my hand to shield my smarting eyes and looked around. We had no hope of finding Edouard and Péri among the legions of shadowy figures gathered there. Arcs of water from the fire trucks played on the flames, sizzling and sending up clouds of steam but the task of putting out the fire was so enormous it seemed hopeless.

'Get back!'

I stumbled as a line of policemen waded into the part of the crowd where we stood. A moment later, a rain of sparks descended on us. A woman screamed and clutched at her hair. Her companion doused it with wine from the bottle he carried.

'Get back! Don't you understand plain words?' the sergeant in charge yelled. 'The roof's going any minute.'

The flames climbed higher in the sky and with a deafening crash, the domes that had been such a familiar part of Paris' skyline vanished. The blast of hot air that followed would have knocked me off my feet if I had not been so tightly wedged in the crowd.

The police continued to advance, pushing us back as the walls of the palace crumbled into giant heaps of molten rubble. Lit up by the eerie orange glow, the people around me looked like the devils in one of the old Flemish paintings of which Edouard was so fond. Sweat stuck the bodice of my dress to my back and plastered my hair to my forehead. Every breath of air was like swallowing fire.

'I can't stand this any longer, Mariette,' I said hoarsely. 'We'll never find them among all these people. We won't even be able to get past the police line. Let's go home.'

She wiped the sweat from her face. 'Just a little longer, Anna. We can't give up yet.'

I'd had enough. 'No, Mariette, I want to go now.' With that, I turned and started to fight my way through the crowd. When I reached a place where it thinned out a little, I looked back and saw her following me.

*

'They're back! It must be them.' Mariette rushed to the top of the stairs and I followed her. Péri stood in the hall, his shoulders bowed. His face was pale where sweat had made runnels in the soot that caked it. I smelt the reek of smoke from his clothes.

Mariette ran to him and pummelled his chest. 'Where have you been? How could you frighten me like this?'

I knew at once from Péri's face that something was wrong.

'Hush Mariette, I have bad news,' he said wearily.

'Where's Edouard?' I asked dreading the reply.

'He's hurt. We were helping at the pumps in the rue de Lille when a wall collapsed. He didn't manage to jump clear in time and it fell on him. When we pulled him out of the rubble, he was unconscious. I tried to get help from one of the first aid posts but they all turned me away. They couldn't cope with any more wounded. In the end I found a couple of fellows with a cart. They were boasting they'd pulled a load of dead Communards out of a yard and dumped them up in one of the mass graves. They didn't want to help at first, said they had orders to go back for more, but a few francs changed their minds. They're bringing him home now.'

Mariette and I stared at him, speechless.

'He's in a great deal of pain. Make something ready down here so we don't have to carry him upstairs. I'll go back and find them.'

Mariette sent one of the footmen to fetch Doctor Barbet and I organised a bed for Edouard. When it was ready, I glanced out of the window and saw Péri coming back. The two men with him dragged the cart behind them. I winced for Edouard each time it jolted on the cobbles.

'Make a stretcher,' I commanded the servants. 'A trestle or anything like it will serve. Pad it with plenty of blankets.'

Edouard's face was a mask of pain. He cried out when they lifted him from the cart onto the stretcher, and then to the bed. His eyes flickered over our faces but he didn't seem to know where he was.

'Have you sent for Doctor Barbet?' Péri asked anxiously.

'Yes, he should be here soon.'

He nodded. 'Well done.'

The torn remains of Edouard's clothes revealed a mass of gashes and bruises disfiguring his body. His breathing was shallow and his hands felt cold and clammy. Powerless to help him, we waited impatiently for the doctor to arrive.

'Where's that fool of a servant?' Péri muttered as the minutes ticked away. 'He can't have made it clear how urgent this is. I'll go myself.'

While we waited, I tried to moisten Edouard's lips with a little water; to my joy, his tongue moved and caught a few drops. 'You're safely home, Edouard,' I said. 'Doctor Barbet will be here soon.'

Edouard's throat rattled as if he was trying to speak, but the words were inaudible. Soon, he slipped back into unconsciousness.

Half an hour later, Péri returned looking haggard. 'I couldn't find him. They thought he'd gone to the hospital so I went there.' His face twisted in an expression of disgust. 'But some of the Versailles troops had already forced their way in and shot any patients they suspected of being Communard sympathisers. There were no doctors left, only a few nurses trying to help the survivors. I tried to persuade some of them to come with me but they all refused.'

He looked down at Edouard. 'How is he?'

'He drank a little water, but now…' I couldn't finish the sentence.

Mariette put her arm around my shoulders. 'Anna, we mustn't give up.'

Péri's voice thickened with emotion. 'On the way back from the hospital, I watched a line of prisoners being marched away to Versailles. Their hands were tied together and some could hardly walk. There were men and women of all ages among them, even some children; the cavalry riding alongside kept lashing out at the slower ones with their sabres. I saw an old couple knocked to the ground with a rifle butt and shot where they lay. A soldier cut the ropes that held them in line and left their corpses on the ground.' His voice shook. 'I never thought to see such brutality on the streets of Paris.'

'Please don't go out again,' Mariette implored. 'You've done all you can, Edouard will know that.'

'Perhaps,' Péri said wretchedly.

Doctor Barbet arrived at last. 'I'm sorry I didn't come sooner,' he said. 'I was out helping with the wounded all last night. I've only just heard the news.'

He circled Edouard's wrist with his thumb and forefinger. 'His pulse is very faint,' he said gravely. 'You say he was knocked unconscious when the wall fell on him?'

Péri nodded.

Barbet laid Edouard's hand down gently on the covers. 'Perhaps the ladies would be so good as to leave us whilst I carry out a more thorough examination.'

It seemed we waited for an eternity before they emerged. When they did, Barbet's solemn face alarmed me. 'The prognosis is not good, I fear,' he said heavily. 'Monsieur Blanchard has always had a robust constitution but even so, I'm not confident of a happy outcome.'

'But he will live, won't he?' Mariette asked anxiously. 'Please tell us he'll live.'

Barbet patted her hand. 'Yes, I believe he'll live, but he may not be the man he was.'

My heartbeat quickened. 'What do you mean, doctor?'

'The brain is a formidable organ, but a vulnerable one. The other injuries will heal in time, but a blow to the head could have lasting effects – loss of memory, confusion. I have even known patients who undergo a complete change of character.'

He snapped shut his black bag. 'I'm sorry, I must leave you now. I have other patients to attend to, but I'll return tomorrow afternoon. In the meantime, keep him warm. He may take a little food if he wakes but only water to drink. Above all, he needs peace and rest. I've given him something to make him sleep.'

*

Several days passed before heavy rain finally extinguished the fire at the Tuileries. Thankfully before then the wind had changed direction so only the wing of the Louvre that contained the Ministry of Finance was destroyed.

The Tuileries Palace itself was beyond repair, a blackened shell in a wasteland of scorched, shrivelled trees. The heat of the fire had cracked many of the statues in the palace's gardens. Charred flakes drifted from the sky, covering everything like black snow. The stench of burning lingered for days and people went about wearing mufflers to keep it out.

Thiers was swift to take back control of Paris' battered and broken streets. His troops conducted house-to-house searches, executing on the spot anyone suspected of Communard sympathies.

Citizens were ordered to keep their windows closed or be arrested, or worse, for harbouring snipers. The remnants of the Communard forces fought on as they retreated into the Bellville slums but their cause was clearly hopeless. Overwhelmed by superior numbers and armaments, on Whit Sunday, they surrendered.

Thiers was not magnanimous in victory: his reprisals were savage and swift. So many thousands died in the terrible week that followed that it became known as *la semaine sanglante* – the week of blood. The tests applied to rout out Communard suspects were simple. One of them was the wearing of army boots; another was the discolouration of the shoulder of a jacket or a hand. Both suggested that the man had carried a tabatier rifle, the type the Communard troops habitually used. Tabatiers were of poor manufacture and leaked powder that left tell-tale stains.

'Even Madame Guillotine was not so thirsty for blood,' Péri said sadly.

Mariette was afraid that his earlier association with the Red clubs would be discovered and although I tried to reassure her, my efforts were not very successful.

'Suppose there were spies watching the clubs,' she said. Anyway people use these things to settle private quarrels.'

'But Péri has no enemies.'

She shook her head. 'You can never be sure.'

Fortunately, time proved me right. We were spared the night time knock at the door. Those who suffered worse were the slum dwellers, the poor and downtrodden whose crime had been to look to the Commune for a better life. There was no pity for them.

My days busy with nursing Edouard, I was shielded from the full horror of the brutality going on around us but it was impossible to be completely unaware of it. Day and night Paris rang with gunshots. Army barracks, railway stations and even parks where Parisians had been accustomed to take their Sunday strolls turned into killing grounds. Wagons rumbled through the streets, carting the bodies out to the forts around the city or up to the heights of the Buttes Chaumont. There, gigantic funeral pyres consumed them, belching smoke back into the city and polluting the air with the reek of burning flesh.

At the end of June, Thiers held a review of his troops and declared Paris was at peace. The work of clearing ruins and rebuilding began, and as summer wore on, many who had fled abroad returned. Shops re-opened, omnibuses and fiacres re-appeared in the streets and bateaux–mouches hooted up and down the Seine. Jules Fauchon, back in his beloved city at last, even managed to find beauty in the ruins of the Hôtel de Ville where the intense heat had imparted exotic hues of pink and ash-green to the stone.

*

To my relief, in spite of Doctor Barbet's fears, Edouard improved steadily and was almost his old self again although he was still too weak to paint for long. Inactivity made him cantankerous so it was fortunate that, now patients were less numerous at the clinic, Ethan often visited us. Edouard clearly enjoyed his company, even if he pretended to despair of his persistent refusal to accompany their games of cards with a tot of brandy, or wager anything more than toothpicks.

'I never thought it would come to this,' Edouard grumbled when Mariette and I returned from shopping one afternoon.

Mariette planted a kiss on his head. 'Nonsense, you always say to Anna and me that you look forward to your card games.'

'He usually wins,' Ethan smiled ruefully. 'I'm not much good.'

'You're too modest,' Mariette laughed.

'Thank you for a very pleasant afternoon in any case. I fear I must be going now. Doctor Barbet needs me this evening.'

Mariette kissed him on both cheeks. He turned to me with a hesitant smile but then just gave me a formal bow.

Edouard scooped up the cards. 'Come again soon so I can give you another drubbing.'

Mariette shook her head. 'Take no notice of him, Ethan. I suppose we should be grateful he's recovered enough to be tiresome.' She went to the bell pull and rang for one of the footmen to bring Ethan's hat and coat. While we waited for them, she chattered on and I was glad of it. I did not want to meet Ethan's eye.

Chapter 28

By the following spring, Paris was so much her old self it was hard to believe that not quite a year had passed since the Commune's rule had come to an end. Life went well for those I cared about: Edouard was fully recovered and Péri's theatre was even more of a success than it had been before Paris' troubles began. Henri had regained his old verve and energy and Virginie's dressmaking business expanded and prospered.

'Who would have thought Virginie would be such a magician,' Mariette remarked one day. She swivelled to survey the back of her dress in the mirror. It was one she planned to wear for the weekend in Deauville Péri had promised her. The silk was a beautiful marine blue, with scarlet piping on the bodice and sleeves. 'She's even managed to make my fat arse look slimmer.'

I choked on my cup of chocolate. 'Mariette, really!'

She patted my back. 'Dear Anna, always so ladylike.'

I scowled and she pinched my cheek. 'I'm teasing, don't be so touchy. But it's true all the same. You'll always be a lady, Anna. It's in your blood. Now me, I came from the gutter and that's probably where I'll end up.'

'Nonsense, you and Péri have a bright future ahead, and you're more of a lady than most of the women who call themselves one.'

A shadow passed over Mariette's face. 'Do you really think so?'

'Yes. Now do a twirl. I want to see how that silk moves.'

She spun round and the marine blue scintillated. 'It's lovely,' I said. 'Péri will adore it.'

The corners of Mariette's lips twitched in a wicked smile. 'He'd better. I told Virginie to spare no expense.' She tossed her head and the light played over her strong features. 'Anyway, we can afford it. Now where are my gloves?'

I picked them up and handed them to her: they were of softest kid, dyed scarlet to match the dress's piping, with four mother-of-pearl buttons at each wrist.

Mariette pulled them on and inspected the effect with satisfaction. 'Virginie's trimming me a parasol to match too,' she said.

'You'll be the most elegant woman in Deauville.'

'And what about Ethan? Why don't you drop a few hints you'd like him to take you to Deauville?'

I frowned. 'Mariette, please—'

She laughed. 'Of course, you're much too proper for that kind of thing. You'll just have to wait for him to propose.'

'Mariette!'

'Goodness Anna, he worships you, don't you realise it? When you're around, he behaves like a lovesick puppy.'

I looked away. 'I wish I knew what to do,' I muttered.

'Marry him.'

'Marry him? Have you forgotten? I'm married to Emile.'

'Oh, there must be a way out of that,' Mariette said airily. 'He might be dead by now, in fact he probably is. There, that's the end of your problem.'

'I don't think the law would be as easily satisfied as you, Mariette.'

She shrugged. 'It should be. It's ridiculous to spend the rest of your life shackled to an invisible man.'

'I'm not sure I want to encourage Ethan,' I said quietly.

'Why ever not? He's a good man, very kind, and he's wealthy too. You'd be a fool not to say yes if he asks you. If I know anything about men, he's just itching for you to give him a little bit of encouragement.'

My jaw tightened. 'Stop it, Mariette.'

'Sorry, I didn't mean to distress you.' She put her hand over mine. 'Wait and see, Anna. When the time comes, you'll know what to do.'

*

France paid the last of the war reparations she owed to Prussia. In return, the Prussians released the French soldiers who had remained prisoners of war and allowed them to return home. I wondered if Antoine Clérmont was among them, but months went by and there was no news of him.

On a foolish impulse, I went to Notre Dame on my saint's day to light a candle for him. Afterwards, I lingered in the nave listening to the organist practising in the loft. The smooth, sonorous chords echoed around the ancient walls as I watched other women – mothers, sisters, wives or lovers perhaps – engaged on the same errand as I was. The flickering, yellow light of the candles they lit revealed so many expressions, some rapt with gratitude, some transfused with hope but others dulled by despair. If any of their glances chanced to fall on my face, I wondered how they judged me.

*

In late July, to escape the heat of Paris I went with Edouard to the house in the country. Les Colombes was a lovely old stone manor with green shutters; its low-ceilinged, airy rooms were simply furnished with rustic oak. Outside, the rambling, half-tamed garden stretched down to a river where Edouard kept an old rowing boat. Sometimes he liked to go out on the water to paint – a perilous adventure as often his enthusiasm over a particularly beautiful effect of light and shade or the pattern of a cloud led him to forget that he *was* on water, not dry land.

I soon grew to love Les Colombes. The scent of the garden herbs and old-fashioned roses perfuming the hot, drowsy afternoons and the cooing of the doves that gave the house its name had a soothing effect on my troubled heart. Even so, at night I often found it impossible to sleep and I would get up and go to the window. My elbows rested on the sill, I would stare into the dark sky – so much darker here than it was in Paris. If Antoine was still alive, I wondered if he too was awake, watching the stars glitter and the moon wax and wane.

I remembered our last meeting in every detail. Should I have encouraged him? Perhaps I had been mistaken not to. But then I remembered the day I had helped Camille prepare for her journey. She had been so sure that Antoine and Jeanette loved each other. Camille was Antoine's sister; she must know the truth. Antoine had taken me for a fool.

Edouard didn't comment on my frequent silences and distracted moods but he offered to teach me to paint. He looked gravely at my amateurish first efforts then patiently helped me to improve. Soon I found myself totally absorbed by the act of looking – really looking – at the scenes in front of me. As I became more skilful at translating what I saw into paint, the tranquil pleasure I derived surprised and delighted me. I had never thought I would be happy to be away from Paris, but I realised that this quiet country existence was what I needed.

When I wasn't painting, I borrowed books from Edouard's library. For the most part it contained classics but there were a few modern novels and I spent hours curled up in the depths of the sitting room's faded burgundy velvet sofa, losing myself in other worlds.

In the early evenings when the air had cooled, Edouard and I often strolled in the garden. Deep-hued, velvety clematis scrambled through the gnarled apple and pear trees in the orchard. Vines clothed the wall of the glasshouse and in the kitchen garden, the rich, red earth sprouted pyramids of bamboo canes clothed with the thick greenery of haricots verts or skeins of tomatoes.

Péri was busy in Paris with alterations to the theatre but Mariette often came to visit us. With her usual directness, it wasn't long before the subject of Ethan Silver came up.

'He asks about you every time I see him, you know,' she remarked. 'Why don't you ask Edouard if you may invite him down here for a few days? I'm sure Edouard would be happy to. He likes Ethan.'

'Please, Mariette—'

'Oh I don't mean to nag, you know I don't, but I've said it before, he's a very good match and if you don't snap him up, some other girl will. Surely you don't want to be alone all your life?'

A wave of sorrow I didn't fully understand washed over me. Mariette looked at me with contrition.

'Dear Anna, forgive me, but if it's Emile you're waiting for, you'll wait for the rest of your life. His kind doesn't come back.'

How could I tell her Emile was the last man I ever wanted to see again?

She squeezed my hand and smiled at me sympathetically. 'I know it's not easy, but I think it's time you to came to a decision. Ethan would only need the merest scrap of encouragement.'

Chapter 29

Three months later.

Late for my fitting, I hurried up the stairs to Virginie's atelier. She and Henri had recently moved to a much nicer building than they had lived in before. They had a spacious, airy apartment there, as well as plenty of space for Virginie to work and receive her clients.

In the entrance hall I paused to unpin my hat, then gave it to Eloise, Virginie's maid, who greeted me.

'Madame Bertin won't be long, Madame Daubigny. May I bring you some wine while you wait?'

'Thank you, Eloise, but there's no need.'

I went to the chaise longue by the window, sat down and started to flick through a pile of fashion journals. A few moments later, in a cloud of expensive perfume, a woman swept out from the fitting rooms.

'My coat and hat,' she snapped at Eloise. 'And hurry up about it. I have another appointment to go to.'

Eloise muttered a meek apology and scuttled off.

The woman rolled her eyes and her elegantly shod foot tapped a brisk tattoo on the parquet floor.

'It's just as well Virginie's such an artist, if this is what her customers have to put up with. Of course I get most of my gowns from Monsieur Worth. The service at his atelier is sans pareil.'

Ordinarily, I would have leapt to the defence of Virginie's establishment but I was too shaken to frame the words. The woman was Jeanette.

Eloise returned, laden down with an armful of sables.

'Ah, my fur,' Jeanette drawled, 'at last.'

Eloise helped her into the magnificent coat, one my father would have been proud of, and received a frown for her pains.

'My hat, girl! Mon Dieu, must I wait forever?'

Once more, Eloise scuttled away and came back with a chic white cloche trimmed with a grey cockerel feather. Jeanette put it on then examined her reflection in the large, gilt-framed mirror on one wall. She smoothed an invisible blemish from her cheek, applied a little more rouge to her already scarlet lips then departed.

Virginie came to meet me with outstretched arms. 'Anna, I'm so sorry you had to wait.' She raised an eyebrow. 'Poor Eloise, I'll have to give her a little something extra for being so patient with that wretched Jeanette de Breuil. I'd be only too happy not to do any more work for her, but she spends a lot of money here and she recommends me to so many of her rich friends.'

Virginie put on a good imitation of Jeanette's haughty expression and bored drawl. 'One likes to help the little people, but of course, one buys most of one's clothes from Worth.' She giggled. 'All I can say is that if she buys as much there as she does from me, she must have cupboards the size of a house. Now, I have both the dresses you ordered ready. Shall we try on the peach silk first?'

She pinned and tucked, talking as she worked, but I took no part in the conversation. I was angry with myself for letting the brief encounter shake me, but powerless to quell my agitation. We were halfway through the fitting when Eloise came with a message.

'From Madame de Breuil, Madame Bertin,' she said.

'Put it on the table, Eloise. I'll answer it when Madame Daubigny's fitting is over.'

'The messenger said it was urgent.'

'Tell him to wait then.'

'Yes, Madame.'

Virginie made a face as Eloise left the room. 'Jeanette is more insufferable than ever since she's been the Duc de Varenne's mistress. It makes me laugh to think that in the old days she used to be one of us. She was plain Jeanette Breuil then. In my opinion, Antoine was well rid of her. She only made him miserable.'

'What!' I couldn't help letting the exclamation escape me and wished it hadn't, but it was too late. I went on more cautiously. 'I thought Camille said something about Antoine and Jeanette planning to marry. Camille was very eager for it to happen.'

'Gracious no, you must have misunderstood. I don't think that could be true. Camille always loathed Jeanette. She was so glad when Antoine broke off with her. Jeanette was furious. She likes to be the one who ends things. She kept trying to get him back but fortunately for him he had too much sense to fall for her tricks. And of course, she'd have been off again with the next rich man to dangle a diamond necklace under her snooty nose.'

My whole frame shook.

'Anna? What's wrong?'

'Just a little dizzy,' I said quickly.

'Oh, I'm so sorry. I've kept you standing too long. This one's done now anyway. You must sit down for a while before we start on the other one.'

I let her remove the dress and lead me to a chair. She called for Eloise to bring a glass of wine and I sipped it slowly.

Virginie squeezed my hand. 'There,' she said, 'that's better. You've some colour in your cheeks now.' She smiled. 'I expect I shall have to get used to feeling faint sometimes myself.'

'What do you mean?'

'I haven't told many people yet but I wanted you and Mariette to be among the first to know. Henri and I are expecting a baby.'

'How lovely,' I said quickly. 'I'm so glad for you.'

I smiled and nodded as Virginie chattered on excitedly but I couldn't help feeling a pang of sorrow. She was so lucky to be with the man she loved. It was a joy I feared I would never know.

I didn't sleep that night; my mind was in turmoil. If Antoine had parted with Jeanette, why would Camille lie about it? What distressed me most deeply was that it seemed I had drawn the wrong conclusion and forfeited a chance of happiness. If only I hadn't been so hasty to condemn Antoine, everything could have been so very different.

*

Troubled by what I had learnt, it wasn't long before I gave in to the temptation to confide in Mariette.

'I knew you liked him!' she said triumphantly, when I had finished.

'So who should I believe?'

'Virginie of course, she has no reason to dislike you.'

I frowned. 'What makes you think Camille does?'

Mariette leant forward in her chair. 'You're right about one thing with Camille: she adores her brother. That gives her two reasons. Didn't Virginie say that Jeanette de Breuil made Antoine miserable?' She patted my hand. 'Please don't be offended, Anna, but to Camille you probably seemed just like Jeanette – a woman who wants a little diversion from being a rich man's mistress.'

I winced and Mariette smiled apologetically. 'I know she'd be wrong.'

'And the second reason?'

'Camille's not happy in her marriage. Virginie told me so. I wasn't surprised. Anyone could see it would have to snow ink before that husband of hers thought of anyone but himself and his precious art.'

I couldn't help smiling at the image of a blackened and splattered Paul.

'While Antoine's unattached,' Mariette went on, 'Camille has him all to herself. Why would she want to change that and share him?'

'Perhaps you're right,' I said sadly.

'I'm sure I am.'

*

Ethan had become a frequent visitor now we were back in Paris. He came mostly to play cards with Edouard but sometimes he joined us for dinner as well. I always took care we shouldn't be alone and kept our conversations on comfortably safe topics like the weather or the latest opera. I must admit though that sometimes, my womanly pride found it a little unflattering that he was not harder to keep at bay. Then I told myself not to be contrary. Perhaps he *was* losing interest, but it was for the best.

So, I was surprised when I received a note asking if I would see him alone. He arrived when Edouard was busy in his studio and, refusing my offer of refreshments, paced about the room. I felt the stirrings of dismay.

'Madame Daubigny… Anna… ' he said at last.

I searched for the words to stop him and found none.

He took a deep breath, 'I believe you understood my feelings for you.'

My voice came back to me. 'Please, don't say any more. I wish I could return them, but—'

'I beg you, don't be alarmed. I have no intention of forcing myself on you.'

I flushed. 'I'm so sorry. You're one of the best and kindest men I've ever met.'

'But you could never love me.'

I looked at him in confusion.

'It's all right,' he went on. 'I hope we'll always be friends but I realise now that we'll never be more than that. The truth is there's a girl in Boston. We've been writing to each other over the last few months. Our families are old friends and if she'll have me, I think we'd be well suited.'

He smiled. 'You're a wonderful woman, Anna. I'll always remember you, but it wouldn't have worked, would it?'

His eyes twinkled and for the first time, I felt I saw his real self. 'Blame it on Paris,' he said. 'In Paris, it's impossible not to fall in love.'

Laughter welled up in my throat.

'What is it? Am I so funny?'

'I'm laughing at myself too. I was so worried about what you had to say to me.'

He took my hand. 'Can we be friends?'

'Of course.'

'So, as a friend, there's something I have to tell you.'

'Yes?'

'I chewed it over and over in my mind whether it was the right thing to do. I didn't even know if you'd have me. If you found out, you might have been angry with me for taking liberties.'

'Ethan, please stop being so mysterious. Just tell me, whatever it is.'

'Very well. It's about your husband.'

I started. 'About Emile? You know where he is?'

'In a manner of speaking.' Ethan cleared his throat. 'I'm sorry. I thought this would be like telling a patient bad news, but it's harder than that.'

'Bad news? Is he ill?'

'Anna, maybe you should sit down.'

My nails dug into my palms. 'No, I don't want to. Tell me.'

His hands closed over mine. 'I'm afraid he's dead.'

The room blurred and I sank onto a sofa.

'I'll call Rose for you.'

Through a haze, I saw Ethan stride to the bell pull.

'No, don't call her. I'll be better in a moment.'

He came back and knelt beside me. 'And I call myself a doctor,' he said ruefully. 'I should have known better than to give you such a shock.'

I managed a weak smile and felt my heartbeat slow a little.

'I forgive you.'

'You're sure you're all right?'

I nodded. 'Emile and I have been apart for years. Your news is sad, but I don't feel the grief a wife should feel. Please, go on. I want to know what happened, and how you found out.'

Ethan looked at me quizzically. 'Certain?'

'Yes.'

'It was like this. An old friend of mine is an attaché at the American Embassy here in Paris. When I thought there might be something between you and me, I asked him if he would make enquiries about your husband through official channels. He agreed to help me and a couple of months ago, he came up with some answers.'

Ethan took a breath. 'Have you heard the term "carpetbaggers"?'

I shook my head.

'After our Civil War, the South was in ruins. The carpetbaggers were men from the North who went south to make a quick buck in the reconstruction. They travelled light, just taking what they could pack in a small handgrip, the type that's often made of pieces of old carpet sewn together - hence the name.'

I frowned. 'And Emile was one of them?'

'Yes. My friend started his enquiries with a guess that Emile would have left the country. He checked with all the port authorities and eventually found out that he'd sailed from Le Havre on a ship bound for New York. He stayed there a few months and then he went south. My friend at the Embassy traced him to Georgia.

'He got a job in a company owned by Jack Anderson. You probably won't have heard of Anderson but he's made a big name for himself back home. He dealt in armaments during the war and then put his money into construction.' He frowned. 'It seems Emile did well at first. He became quite a favourite with Anderson, but then things went wrong. Anderson accused him of stealing from the company.'

I nodded.

'The police got involved but Emile gave them all the slip. He went on the run for a few months. The next time he turned up was in a small hotel in New Orleans. The hotelkeeper got suspicious when Emile didn't come out for days. He checked the room and found his body with a bullet wound in the chest.'

I shivered. 'How horrible.'

'There was a police investigation but Anderson has plenty of friends in high places. It was closed off in a matter of days and the coroner recorded a verdict of suicide.'

I let the revelation sink in. I was free, but at that moment, I could not take any pleasure in my freedom.

'That's the whole story,' Ethan said gently. 'At least as far as my friend could find it out.' He looked at his pocket watch. 'I don't like to leave you like this but I'm afraid I have to go. Dr Barbet needs me back at the clinic to take a surgery. Do you want me to fetch someone to come and keep you company? Mariette perhaps?'

'No, thank you. I'd like to be alone for a little while.'

He nodded. 'I understand.'

'I hope you'll visit us again before you leave Paris.'

'Of course.'

He kissed my hand. 'Goodbye, Anna.'

'Goodbye, Ethan. And thank you.'

The door closed and I buried my head in my hands. The house was very quiet. Most of the servants would be in their quarters, resting before it was time to prepare dinner. Edouard was unlikely to come down from his studio until the light waned. I had time to myself to digest this unexpected turn of events. For so long, I had felt bitter towards Emile for the way he had abandoned me. Now some of that bitterness turned to pity. Perhaps one day it would be gone completely.

After a while, I got up and went to the window. I gazed across the rooftops of Paris, stretching as far as the eye could see, gleaming in the low winter sunshine. What should I do with this new-found freedom? My thoughts turned to Antoine. He might never come back, and even if he did, his feelings might have changed.

I had made so many mistakes, but one thing revived my spirits. I still had Paris - beautiful, irrepressible Paris: my city of dreams. She had been humiliated, bloodied and battered but she was already taking back her rightful place in the world. I could not imagine living anywhere else. I must have faith that, as her fortunes turned for the better, mine would too.

**

Other Books by Harriet Steel

Becoming Lola

The true story of how Eliza Gilbert, the daughter of an obscure Ensign in the British Army and his cold Irish wife, became the nineteenth century's most notorious adventuress, Lola Montez.

"Throughout *Becoming Lola* I had to remind myself that the story was based on historical fact. It is a fascinating journey following a woman's single-minded determination to get the very best for herself at all costs." *Historical Novel Society*

"A fascinating read. Lola was such a gutsy character, and Harriet Steel has captured her times and adventures very vividly. It's a must read if you like wild women and strange adventures." *Beth Webb, Author of the Star Dancer trilogy*

Available in paperback, Kindle and other e-book formats.

Salvation

It is 1586: plagued by religious strife at home and with the Royal Treasury almost exhausted, England holds her breath. When will Philip of Spain launch his Armada?
In this world of suspicion and fear, three people pursue their own struggles for happiness and salvation.

When an enemy threatens to reveal his illicit affair with a married woman, young lawyer's clerk, Tom Goodluck, is forced to leave his old life behind him. An aspiring playwright, for a while his future in the burgeoning world of Elizabethan theatre looks bright but then events take an unexpected turn that threatens his very existence. His mentor and friend, theatre manager Alexandre Lamotte, comes to his rescue but Lamotte's past hides tragedy and a dark secret. In trying to save Tom, he puts everything he has achieved at risk. Meanwhile Tom's lover, Meg, is forced to set out on a path that will test her mettle to the limit.

"The story literally thrives on excitement ... the whisper of danger never seems very far away. I have no hesitation in recommending this book as an exciting romp through the hurly-burly of Elizabethan England, when plots and counter plots were the order of the day, and where hidden danger lurked around every corner." *Historical Novel Society*

Available in paperback, Kindle and other e-book formats.

Dancing and Other Stories

The collection takes a light-hearted look at some of the big issues in life: love, hate, friendship, jealousy, revenge and biscuits. It includes the prize-winning story, *Dryad*, co-authored with Joanne Harris, bestselling author of *Chocolat*, for the BBC's National Competition, *End of Story*.

Profits go to WaterAid, the charity working to bring clean water and sanitation to villages in the Third World.

Available on Kindle.

Made in the USA
Middletown, DE
01 December 2019